PRAISE FOR
CAMILLA T. CRESPI
AND HER
SIMONA GRIFFO MYSTERIES

THE TROUBLE WITH GOING HOME
"The picture Crespi paints of the extended Italian family
is emotionally complex, and her knowledge of and love
for them is worth the visit."
—*Drood Review of Mystery*

"A neatly plotted mystery, and insider's view of Rome,
and a loving evocation of an affectionate—if volatile—
extended family. Bravissima, Sigra. Crespi."
—Margaret Maron

THE TROUBLE WITH THIN ICE
"Simona exercises her adorable ways with a vengeance at
a Connecticut Inn…but it is her keen intelligence not her
bubbly personality that wins."
—*The New York Times Review*

"Rich in atmosphere and buoyed by wry wit, Crespi's
briskly paced narrative calls for an encore."
—*Publishers Weekly* (starred review)

THE TROUBLE WITH TOO MUCH SUN
"Engaging…Lush descriptions of paradise and the who-
dunit plot keep the pages turning."
—*Publishers Weekly*

BOOKS BY CAMILLA T. CRESPI

The Trouble with Thin Ice*
The Trouble with Going Home*

WRITTEN UNDER THE NAME TRELLA CRESPI

The Trouble with a Small Raise
The Trouble with Moonlighting
The Trouble with Too Much Sun

*Published by HarperPaperbacks

THE TROUBLE WITH GOING HOME

CAMILLA T. CRESPI

HarperPaperbacks
A Division of HarperCollinsPublishers

This is a work of fiction. The characters, incidents, and dialogues are products of the author's imagination and are not to be construed as real. Any resemblance to actual events or persons, living or dead, is entirely coincidental.

HarperPaperbacks *A Division of* HarperCollins*Publishers*
10 East 53rd Street, New York, N.Y. 10022

Cover illustration by Oren Sherman

A hardcover edition of this book was published in 1995 by HarperCollins*Publishers.*

First HarperPaperbacks printing: April 1996

Printed in the United States of America

HarperPaperbacks and colophon are trademarks of HarperCollins*Publishers*

❖ 10 9 8 7 6 5 4 3 2 1

To my sister Franca, who keeps me going back

I would like to thank Larry Ashmead for being the legend that he is, Carolyn Marino for being a wonderful editor, Charlotte Abbott for nursing my book, Amy Cohen for sending me out there in the big world, Ellen Geiger for watching out for me, Donatella Giannini for her generosity, Guglielmina Clarici, Barbara Lane, and Dr. Jan Mashman for their knowledge, and Judith Keller, Maria Nella Masullo, and Sharon Villines for their sharp pencils.

I thank John Varriano for his book *Rome: A Literary Companion*—John Murray (Publishers) Ltd.—and William L. Vance for his two volumes of *America's Rome*—Yale University Press—which provided some of the quotes I used. I am grateful to Rutgers University Press for kindly giving permission to quote from *Corinne, or Italy* by Germaine de Staël, translated by Avriel H. Goldberger, copyright 1987 by Rutgers, the State University, and to Oxford University Press for *Selections from the Notebooks of Leonardo da Vinci*, edited by Irma H. Richter, copyright 1952.

I thank Stuart most of all.

Cast of Characters

IN ORDER OF APPEARANCE

Simona Griffo   A New York immigrant is being pulled back home by family and past.

Tamar Deaton   A needy American art student ends her search on a Roman sidewalk.

Carlo Linetti   Simona's ex-husband waffles between women.

Olga Griffo   Simona's mother is reluctant to share the weight of what she knows.

Mirella Monti   Olga's good friend scatters love, learning, and confusion.

Nonna Monti   Mirella's ninety-two-year-old mother keeps a firm grip on past and future.

Luca Monti   Mirella's only son, a leftist romantic.

Commissario Perillo   The Italian Judiciary Police commissioner looks like a painting and acts as a friend.

Principe Maffeo   Last in the Brandeschi line, his nobility may be crumbling.

Arthur Hensen   The American businessman thinks his wealth gives him the upper hand.

Oreste Pagano   The ex-Resistance fighter willing to fight another war for Nonna Monti.

Lea Serini   As a drug counselor, she has to believe in second chances.

Stan Greenhouse   Simona's New York lover wants her back.

Willy Greenhouse   Stan's fourteen-year-old son misses more than Simona's cooking.

Gabriele Griffo   Simona's father feels left out.

Plus

An assortment of dogs, cats, international art students, teachers, daughters, mothers, sisters, and the never-dull natives of Rome, the eternal city.

1

Go thou to Rome, at once the Paradise.
—Percy Bysshe Shelley, Adonais

It was the girl who held my attention.

The scooter had whizzed in front of me—two heads and a blur of dark, long hair—but the girl on the sidewalk looked straight at me, her expression thoughtful, not the stunned surprise I expected.

She had just been robbed. I had seen a denim-covered arm swing the large satchel away from her.

With hands still reaching for the stolen bag, the girl floated to the sidewalk. Looking back, I realize my memory isn't right. She fell quickly, witnesses told the police. Five, ten seconds.

A sleepless night and jet lag had blurred my senses. My ex-husband Carlo didn't help. He had surprised me at the airport and was getting my suitcase from the trunk of his car. A man who had given me enormous joy, then overpowering pain, added to my confusion.

"Tamar!" I heard him yell. Carlo dropped my suitcase

and rushed to the fallen girl. The curb cushioned her head; the rest of her long, scraggly body was splayed on the street in the spot where Carlo had wanted to park.

A woman shouted, "My God, call someone!" Her cry shocked me into the urgency of the moment.

Carlo bent over the girl, and the woman ran to the bar across the street.

I spun around to catch the scooter's license number, or at least to get a better look at the purse snatchers. My eyes searched down the long tree-lined boulevard that led to the Vatican, the unusually hot April sun in my eyes. It was much too warm. The swoosh of traffic and the smell of exhaust fumes wrapped around my head.

The thieves were gone.

I turned back. A crowd had gathered, nodding heads, clucking tongues, exchanging opinions, standing close enough to shade the girl.

Carlo waved his arms, shooing them away as if they were chickens.

The delivery boy from the bar ran toward us, bringing a full shot glass. The amber liquid spilled over his hand.

A cat looked up from a pile of spaghetti half-wrapped in newspaper.

The woman who had shouted retrieved two bulging grocery bags from under a young linden tree on the corner.

"I called the ambulance." She looked at me as she passed in front of Carlo's car double-parked on the street. She was a small, gray-haired woman with cheerfully puffy cheeks and a Sicilian accent. "I have to go." Behind her a Fiat 500 honked too loudly for its size. "My son is waiting at home for his lunch."

I nodded in understanding. She was leaving me in charge. The impatient Fiat spurted past her as she walked away. I took the glass, now only half-full, from the bar boy.

"Tamar, Tamar," Carlo repeated, his voice anguished. I knelt next to him and offered brandy to the girl. She did not respond. I took her hand, wondering why my ex-husband knew this girl. Carlo swiped the shot glass and gulped down its contents. I was too distracted by the cold-ness of Tamar's hand to comment.

"Help is coming," I told her, taking off my jacket and blanketing her chest, a useless gesture in the heat. Tamar turned her heavily lidded eyes to me. She had to be in a lot of pain, I thought, not guessing the truth. Her skin had turned yellow, her lips white. Her unfocused blue eyes flickered as she tried to raise her chin.

"Don't move!" I said, deciding she must have hit her head on the curb. Helplessly, I stroked her soft oval face, noticing the three empty holes in each of her earlobes, the hole in one of her nostrils, the henna-red hair, the two-inch black roots. She looked no older than nineteen.

Tamar licked her lips. Carlo moaned and leaned in closer. Emergencies always overwhelm him.

"*Doni!*" Tamar's voice was surprisingly strong, the word spoken with an obvious American accent.

"Gifts?" Carlo asked, translating the Italian word into his accented English. "Did they steal some gifts? Is that it?" He put his hand under her armpit. The gesture was inti-mate and natural. I remember thinking, "Lovers!" and feel-ing a quick, misplaced pang of jealousy.

Tamar closed her eyes.

"Did you recognize the thieves?" I whispered close to her ear. She smelled of turpentine. "Is one of them called Doni?" Her cold hand, smudged with green paint, relaxed in mine.

"She's fainted," I said, looking up at Carlo.

He fell back on his rear end, landing on an oily pizza wrapper, and looked at his hand. The same hand that had snuggled under Tamar's armpit. It was covered with blood.

"Gesù Maria!" My mother's voice distracted me from the meaning of that red wetness. Hearing the words she used to label both minor and major disasters, my heart twitched as if I were still little and didn't know whether I or spilled wine had provoked her cry.

My mother, tall and thick, strode over to us, her eyes only on Tamar.

"She was mugged," I mumbled, somehow feeling guilty. Carlo made a sound I could not decipher. Mamma smacked her lips in disapproval.

"She fainted," I offered again.

Mamma finally noticed me. I had come back to see her, to find out why she had suddenly, two weeks before, left her home and my father. We had not seen each other in fifteen months, and now she was looking at me the way she had four years ago, when I'd announced that I was emigrating to America—with a mixture of disappointment and anger.

"Can't you see the girl is dead?" she said.

I burst into tears.

It was a welcome back to Rome I won't forget.

2

*I chanced to stop in at a midday show,
expecting fun, wit, and some relaxation,
when men's eyes take respite from the
slaughter of their fellow men. It was just
the reverse.*

—LUCIUS ANNAEUS SENECA,
MORAL EPISTLES VII

"She was stabbed," my mother said that evening after dinner, piercing a cotton square with a crotchet hook the width of a toothpick. She was bordering another of her bedcovers. Twin-bed size, I noticed, and I ached at the thought of my parents separating. We had not gotten a chance to talk. Tamar Deaton's death took center stage. A police inspector had come to Mirella Monti's apartment, where my mother was staying while she decided what to do with her life. Mirella was her best friend. Tamar had been killed ten feet from Mirella's building's doorstep. Ispettore Rolfi, sent from the local police station, wanted information to *"chiarire le cose,"* clarify things.

5

Sitting in Mirella's light-filled living room—balcony doors open to budding sycamore trees and the gentle traffic of Viale Angelico—the ispettore repeatedly asked Carlo how he knew Tamar, as if hoping he would trip up on an answer. Carlo explained patiently. Three cups of the inevitable espresso sat on Vasari's *Lives of the Painters*. Only the ispettore drank. I fought the urge to smoke that comes over me when I go home.

Carlo, who has one of those aging boy faces that begs for cuddling, was visibly moved by the girl's death. His full mouth, which I had once found beautifully soft, twitched as he explained. Leaning into the dark green couch covered with white dog hair and hills of files, he combed his curly, graying hair with tense fingers.

"Tamar was a lost soul who needed guidance." He turned to me, the defensive fog clouding his chestnut-sized eyes evoking painful memories. "She was like a sister."

The reason I'd divorced Carlo after six years of a fairly happy marriage was his equal opportunity penis. As I sat stunned one balmy October night, someone kindly told me that he'd been giving out opportunity for six years. The entire length of our marriage.

"Of course, a sister," I said now, suppressing a snort. I didn't feel like baring family resentments in front of the ispettore, who sniffed the air as my mother's cooking odors filtered between the double glass doors of Mirella's living room. Mamma was making *risotto con carciofi*, rice with artichokes, a favorite of mine.

"How did you meet her?" Ispettore Rolfi asked again as the smell of onions sautéing in butter curled around our noses.

Carlo repeated himself. "At a party." He had kept up his relationship with my mother—something I still resented—and had met Tamar through her and Mirella.

"Tamar needed an older man's guidance." Carlo tried to look wise by straightening up and narrowing his eyes. The familiarity of it was making me sick. "She was a foster child. Unhappy, with few friends at school."

Tamar was an American art student studying with Mirella at La Casa dell'Arte, a school funded by an American businessman, which offered American college students a one-year studio art/art history program. In the last week, Tamar had been so nervous that Mirella had invited her to stay at her apartment for a dose of good food and rest, in the hope that she would pass her final exams. The ispettore had found this out from Mirella and was now repeating it to us.

In the hallway, Mirella called the school. I caught her hiccuped crying and my mother's muttered reassurances.

The ispettore glanced at his watch, sniffed the air again, and asked if he could drink my espresso. There were no more questions to be asked. As he had told us earlier, he was from the local police station. He was used to simple purse snatchings, wallets slipping out of breast pockets on the bus, runaway dogs. Homicide was not part of his "menu." He was relieved that he did not have to contact Signorina Deaton's parents.

"I speak no English, which I regret, but on this occasion, perhaps not."

The doorbell rang.

"Perhaps that is *la Polizia Giudiziaria*." The ispettore half stood, gulping Carlo's espresso. Behind the living room door Mirella sounded annoyed. "Oh, *dio*! I'm coming up tomorrow. Why did you bring the oil now?" A boy's voice muttered apologies. The ispettore sat down again. The three cups were empty.

"You'll be summoned," the ispettore told us gravely. I heard the jingle of keys. Despite the welcoming smells, a lunch invitation was not forthcoming. He stood up, a chubby young man with a strong Roman accent. He tugged at his too-tight slacks. They had formed accordion pleats around his crotch. He shook one leg after the other, covering up the gesture by panning the crowded room with narrowed eyes. A thick oak table stood to one side of a battered baby grand, both surfaces heaped with classical sheet music and old copies of *La Repubblica*, the most popular Roman daily. Seashells crowded a shelf above the sofa. The walls were covered with students' drawings of classical figures, self-portraits painted in oil, and Mirella's rustic still lifes. The ispettore nodded his approval at a painting above the piano of a bowl of red and yellow peppers.

"Looks edible," he said, making his way to the door. "But then the hunger is great," he added in a last-ditch effort. Mirella popped open the door, clutching test papers to her chest and pushing her big dalmatian, Gorbi, out of the way. The dog had a dripping black spot on his forehead that mirrored Gorbachev's birthmark.

"Please excuse the mess," she apologized as we walked the ispettore out to the front entrance. She was out of breath.

Sunlight streamed in from the window at the end of the corridor where Mirella kept her desk, piled with books and files. A magnolia branch looked as if it had been painted on the windowsill. I was surprised that my mother, in her two-week stay, hadn't turned Mirella's apartment into a Tomb of Neat.

The ispettore dismissed Mirella's apology with a swirl of his hand, took one last sniff with nose pointed toward the kitchen, and then eyed me and Carlo with a mean, starved eye.

"You could have big problems," he said, one hand on the open door. "Stay in town."

"What problems?" Mirella asked, furrowing gray eyebrows. "It was a *scippo* gone wrong. Tamar must have resisted. Didn't witnesses see her resist? It was her art bag they took." Mirella looked at me, her eyes filling with tears. "She had such talent. You must never resist. I've been mugged three times." The test papers started to slip from her grasp.

Gorbi barked, his mouth as pink as a new eraser. The ispettore jumped at the sound, showing his great courage in the face of no danger. I grabbed the papers.

"Purse snatchers don't kill their victims," the ispettore said gruffly. "At least not here in Rome." He looked at me pointedly. He'd widened his coffee bean eyes when I'd told him I now lived in New York. It had not been an approving look.

Mirella pulled Gorbi back by his collar and cleared the doorway. "He's harmless."

With a sideways glance at the dog, the ispettore left, forced to walk down the four flights of marble stairs because Mirella had not been able to share in the exorbitant cost of the brand-new elevator.

By then it was almost two o'clock and my mother insisted we have lunch. "Death does not stop the body's needs," she stated.

Mirella again tried calling Tamar's foster mother in the States. There was no answer.

"They didn't get along," she said, scratching Gorbi's ear. "She had no father, not even a foster one."

Carlo stayed, assuming he'd been invited, which, on second thought, he might have been. My mother still thinks Carlo is a sensitive, misunderstood man. She was against my divorce.

"What's he mean, we can't go anywhere?" Carlo asked as he embraced a round slab of bread and started to cut thick slices of it with a knife that would have made a grisly murder weapon. "We're not suspects." A bee droned around a sprouting wisteria branch above his head.

The day was so remarkably warm for the beginning of April, Mirella had insisted we eat on her terrace, one flight above her apartment. We had traipsed up the stairs carrying large folding plastic trays I'd brought her from The Pottery Barn. Mirella had been the one to call me in New York a week before to announce that my mother was now living with her, and the sooner I got to Rome the better. It was a secret we shared.

The official story was that since no one answered at my parents' home in Rocca di Papa, a town up in the Alban Hills southeast of Rome where they had gone to live after my father's retirement, I had called Mirella for their whereabouts and *ecco fatto* my mother had answered the phone. Of course, this had all been carefully orchestrated, Mirella telling me exactly when she was going to be out so that my mother would answer.

My father, according to Mamma, had gone to a spa for one of those mineral water cures. She did not tell me which one. Not believing her, I tried their house from New York and again this morning from the Fiumicino Airport. I had no luck.

I didn't listen to the lunch talk. My eyes were burning from lack of sleep. The glow of the Roman sun and the sounds from the street below were painfully renewing lost sensations throughout my body. My bones felt as if they'd traveled cramped in a suitcase. Carlo's presence was an insult. I didn't know this Tamar; I resented her dying at my feet when I hadn't been home for more than an hour, and I was jealous of my mother's obvious affection for her. Not that my mother was crying—my mother never cries, she says she's had enough of water having grown up in

Venice—but she looked pale and shaken and she was ignoring me, her only child, who really wanted to hug her and ask, what's going on? Why did you leave Gigi, my father? I had just turned thirty-eight, but the idea made me shake with childlike anger, surprise, self-pity, and a sense of betrayal. I had no sensitivity left over for anyone else, dead or alive.

"Couldn't we pretend it didn't happen?" I whined. "At least during lunch?" My selfishness still leaves me reeling. I had no thought for what my mother and Mirella must have been going through.

"No, we can't forget her," my mother said, surrounding me with plates of food. "We can eat, which doesn't mean forgetting. Tamara was a fragile soul who didn't deserve to die. And I am furious at the delinquency of this city. Of the world!" She sat down neatly, primly, not at the head of the table where I'd always seen her, but next to me, her tall body casting a shadow over my plate. I wanted to be pleased, but the unaccustomed seating arrangement bothered me. Carlo offered her bread and answered his cellular phone, a toy Italians delight in.

"Tamar had such talent." Mirella rushed around the terrace picking dried leaves from rose plants, geraniums, a trellis full of morning glories, their purple petals beginning to close. "My best student in the studio. She had no money." Her feet kicked twigs and dirt behind two brand-new demijohns of olive oil.

"Mirella, please," Mamma said. "The rice will get cold."

Mirella obeyed, stuffing the gathered leaves in the pocket of her loose blue wool dress and sliding into the closest chair. "*Scusami.*" She gave us her lovely warm smile and clasped Gorbi's head to her lap.

I had in the past sometimes wondered what it would have been like to have soft, gentle Mirella as my mother.

Both of us being messy, distracted women, we might have lost each other in the aisles of a food market. But we would have loved each other in a slobbering physical way I will never know with my mother.

Mirella is a thin, long-necked woman with a mess of shoulder-length wiry gray hair that she tries to tame with bobby pins. The striking features of her face are amber eyes rimmed by green halos that make me think of Venetian glass, an aquiline nose worthy of a Roman emperor's bust, and a smile that conquered everyone except her husband, who walked out on her twenty-eight years ago.

"Tamara was so obviously poor," my mother said, a vigilant eye checking my food intake, which was minimal. "Her clothes were pitiful."

Mamma's homecoming lunch included a hand-sized salami made by Fini in Bologna, a braid of cow's milk mozzarella, a heaping plate of *puntarelle con aglio e acciuga*— a crackling salad that resembles dandelion leaves and is in season for only two months, slathered with the traditional dressing of garlic and anchovy whipped in olive oil—and her renowned artichoke risotto.

I was now flattening the risotto with a fork, ready to eat from the cooler edges as I had done as a child.

"Simona," my mother protested in a pleased voice. I laughed.

"It's delicious," I said, sucking risotto from my fork as if it were mother's milk.

She nodded. When my mother cooks, the word *delicious* is redundant.

"Even the bag they took was worthless," she said. "And why kill Tamara? It doesn't make sense."

I took another bite and gave her elbow a squeeze, wanting to tell her I loved her. She hadn't wanted me to come. She didn't need my meddling at this moment, she said over

the phone, her tired voice echoing. I had come anyway, and
to welcome me she served my favorites. My mother offers
food as her embrace. Food, and aspirin when it's needed.
She has made me a food junkie.

"*Povera Tamar!*" Mirella stooped down to kiss Gorbi's
nose. The dog closed his eyes with pleasure, the white of his
dappled coat as bright as the sheets that hung drying on one
side of the long, wide terrace. "Luca will be devastated." Luca
was her coddled thirty-year-old son who still lived at home.

"Where is he?" I asked. In my self-absorption I'd forgotten about him, and Mirella's mother. "And Nonna Monti?"
Nonna also lived in the apartment, and the last time I'd
seen her, two years ago, we had been celebrating her
ninetieth birthday. "She's all right?" How could I not miss
her the moment I'd walked into Mirella's home? Nonna
had been the one to whisper in my ear, "Go to America,"
when I was miserable and thought I didn't have the
strength to cross the Tiber.

"Nonna is indomitable," my mother said, sounding
envious. "Luca drove her to Poggio delle Rose for her
monthly visit with two old students of hers. You remember, the Tarelli sisters. They came to her birthday party."

Mirella's eyes filled with tears again. "Luca was in love
with Tamar." She fluttered fingers in front of her mouth.

"He's young," Mamma said, distracting herself from too
much emotion by slicing the salami paper-thin.

"I'm forty-five," Carlo announced, slipping his phone
into his pocket. He was sitting at the head of the table,
where he had always sat in our married life, trying to overcome me with sorrowful dark dog eyes that Gorbi would
have found humiliating. He'd also been set against our
divorce.

After lunch, we gathered in the kitchen to clean up.
Carlo said he was in the middle of editing a bad Mafia

movie and had to get back to the moviola. He kissed me on both cheeks so quickly that I couldn't stop him. He smiled, looking much too good.

"*Ci vediamo.*" We'll see each other. He waved his hand.

"No," I answered, closing the door in his face. My mother suggested I nap to recover. I said no again. I wanted to talk to her. She promised we'd have breakfast in the morning, just the two of us.

"My personal problems have little meaning in light of Tamara's death," she said. "She was so young. If I were her mother, I wouldn't survive."

"You're *my* mother."

"I'm well aware of that." I wasn't sure what she meant, but I needed to think that it was a positive awareness.

"I'm going to La Casa with Mirella." La Casa was the school, La Casa dell'Arte. "She needs bolstering." Mamma slipped on gloves. She was dressed in a nutmeg-colored English wool sweater set and a brown tweed skirt. Like most Italians of her generation, my mother carries on a love affair with English fashions. She does, though, have better taste than the queen. I was glad she was wearing the two gold bee pins my father had given her.

"No, no, I'm fine," Mirella protested. "Please, stay here with Simona."

Mamma gave her a look and I understood, in my fog, that my mother simply wasn't ready to talk to me. Feeling shunned, I kissed her cool cheek and offered to shop for dinner.

"No, it's all done."

I offered to take Gorbi for a walk.

"That would be lovely," Mirella said, giving me a quick hug. "The dog park is across the street, you remember, don't you?"

"Get some sleep," my mother reminded me.

As soon as she closed the door, I called my father's number in Rocca di Papa. How could he be burping mineral water at a spa when his whole life was at risk of falling apart? If I'd thought my spouse of forty-two years was leaving me, I'd hide behind a car, a tree, spying on his every move.

I let the phone ring, imagining my father weeding in his beloved vegetable patch. Ten, twenty, thirty rings. I was about to hang up.

A woman answered. My heart knocked against my chest.

"I would like to speak to Console Gabriele Griffo," I asked formally, not wanting to give myself away.

"I'm sorry." She hesitated. "Il Console is not in. May I ask who's calling?" Her speech was educated, without a trace of dialect or a foreign accent. Not a housekeeper, then.

"When will he be back?"

Her breath caught after a second of silence. "He's on vacation in Spain."

I hung up, stunned. She'd lied, I was sure of that. The spa, now Spain. He was right in Rocca di Papa. I even thought I'd heard a man's heavier breath behind her own. My father was probably listening in on an extension.

I had caught him doing that once when my mother was on the phone. We were living in Boston. It was my freshman year at Barnard, and I'd just come home for Christmas vacation. In the bedroom, my mother was talking long distance to Mirella. Or so she had said at the time. My father listened in on the kitchen extension. When he saw me, he carefully placed the receiver back on the hook. He had looked too embarrassed for me to ask questions. I'd forgotten all about it.

Now he had another woman. It was that simple, that

banal. My mother betrayed just as I had been. My father—
I couldn't think of it. It was too repulsive.

I took Gorbi for a quick walk, then went back to the
living room and shuttered the windows. I'd chosen to
sleep on the sofa, which had also been Tamar's bed,
declining an offer to share Mirella's room. In that crowded
apartment I wanted a space of my own at least at night. I
unhooked my bra and stretched out. Gorbi pushed himself under the coffee table, where he had barely enough
room to curl up. Outside, the traffic was intense again,
everyone driving back to work after their long lunch
break. A different sound from New York traffic. The rum-
bling of scooters, the high swish of speeding cars, no
sirens. I fell asleep to its flow.

I dreamed of Tamar, my father relegated to a deeper
recess in my subconscious. I saw her pale, long face looking at me a few moments after she'd been stabbed. Except
that now each of her ears held three sets of gypsy earrings,
and her nose bore a single gold ring. She was walking
toward me. I backed away, saying no as if she had asked
me something. Tamar looked accusing. The scooter
droned in my ear. Carlo took her in his arms.

When I woke up, I was starved for a cigarette.

3

*Perhaps one of Rome's sweet charms is
that she reconciles the imagination to the
long sleep of the dead ... Thus the sharp
edge of pain is duller.*
  —GERMAINE DE STAËL, CORRINE, OR ITALY

"She was stabbed," my mother said, her crotchet hook
adding a lacy loop to the edge of the bedspread. "Don't
you think that unusual?" She bit off the white cotton
thread and slipped the crotchet hook into her sweater
pocket.

Now, a few hours later, sitting on the same sofa I had
dreamed on, with a dinner of pureed vegetable soup and
lemon veal cutlets just finished, I was listening to my
mother talk of Tamar's death to Mirella's son, Luca, and
his grandmother, Nonna Monti.

Luca leaned forward on his chair, pressing his lips
together. He had his mother's long, strong nose, but his
face was less angular than hers, and his thick hair—all of
one length, and bluntly cut at mid-ear—was a gleaming

chestnut color. His large, deep brown eyes were his father's legacy. That's the only thing I remember about Mirella's husband. When I first met him—I was six at the time—I pointed to his eyes and said, *"Bonbon di cioccolata."* Everyone laughed. I loved the attention.

Luca's expression had been steady throughout dinner. If he had been in love with Tamar, he wasn't showing it. Mirella had given him the news privately, in her bedroom at the end of the corridor. Then she'd told Nonna after seating her in her armchair by the piano in the living room. "Death sits on my shoulder as ugly as a crow," Nonna said with a shrug. She'd shrunk in the two years since I'd seen her. Her parchmentlike skin, folded around her piercing nose, was yellow and crusty. Her breath had turned rancid. But her spirit, as my mother said, was indomitable.

I thought of my father with another woman and shifted to worrying about Luca. Luca tended to be morose, communicating little to anyone.

"How many exams are left?" I asked him. He'd been studying architecture at La Sapienza, Rome's overcrowded university, for about ten years, which is only a little longer than the norm. I was trying to steer the conversation to lighter ground.

Luca raised five fingers.

"Fantastico!" I practically shouted. "In one year you'll be done."

Nonna clucked her tongue. I was holding her hand—she liked the "touch of young flesh." I needed to feel her dry, strong hand.

"The fact that Tamara was killed, does that make sense to you, Luca?" my mother asked, half-glasses perched on her nose. Making sense, to her, has the power of religious dogma.

"She didn't look as if she could have anything in that satchel of hers. She dressed poorly. And yet two *delinquenti* not only robbed her, they killed her. That's not your normal *scippo*!" Mamma looked around the room as she folded the finished bedspread over her knees. It didn't occur to her that she might be hurting Luca. Maybe she too was thinking of my father and that woman.

Mirella was fussing with some papers on the dining table, which doubled as a desk. "I finally got hold of Tamar's foster mother. All she's worried about is who'll pay to send Tamar back to Cleveland. 'There's just no way I'm going to fly all the way to Rome,'" Mirella tried to mimic the woman's American English. "'I told her to stay put with me. What she do, get shot by the Mafia?'

"Terribile!" Mirella shook out an old magazine. "Mrs. George Deaton suggested we bury her here. Mrs. George Deaton! Has she no first name of her own? Why do American women give up their names?" Mirella shook her hair. "Well, actually, I don't think there's a Mr. George around." She looked up. A bobby pin dropped down.

"The students are so upset about *povera* Tamar, they've canceled their party. Arthur thinks we should call an assembly." Mirella pronounced the name Artoor. "I can't find half the exam papers I have to grade."

Nonna grunted and let go of my hand. "They're on the bidet in the bathroom where you left them."

"Thank God." Mirella closed her eyes. "Sometimes the bathroom is the only quiet place."

"Who's Arthur?" I whispered.

"Un idiota!" Nonna lit her one daily cigarette, a Pall Mall that Mirella had asked me to buy at the duty-free shop at Kennedy.

"What do you think?" Mamma asked Luca. "Was Tamara carrying something special in that satchel?"

Luca sat back in his chair. "Her name was Tamar. She didn't like Tamara." His voice quavered.

"Mamma," I said, getting up. "Why don't we take Gorbi for a walk?" The dog looked up at the mention of his name, but he seemed placidly content to stay stretched out over Mirella's feet.

"No, I will not take the dog or you for a walk, Simona." My mother took her glasses off and looked at me with an angry face that now looked much older than her sixty-five years. She had lost weight since I'd seen her last year. Mamma was still thick and solid as she had always been, but her face now sagged. Skin folded around her neck like a scarf. Her eyes seemed to float over dark sacs. It finally hit home. She was suffering.

"I want to get to the bottom of this killing," she said, "and if that means ruffling a few sensibilities, I ask forgiveness in advance. What do you think, that the police are going to be kind and not ask all sorts of intimate questions they have no business asking? And after invading our lives for who knows how long, do you think they'll come up with the murderers? With this country going to pieces, our revered leaders taking billions of lire in bribes, colluding with the Mafia . . . " She frowned and looked at each of us as if to see whether we had caught the contradictions in her speech. An extremely private person, she was scared the police would hound her with personal questions.

"You don't think the police will care about an unhappy American art student," I finished for her.

"They won't!"

"Calm down, Olga," Nonna interjected. "Romans have been on the take since Romulus and Remus sucked that poor wolf bitch dry. We're not going to change anything." She did a slow reach to her skirt pocket. "I think the events of the day merit another cigarette."

"No!" Mirella flew to Nonna's side and grabbed the pack of Pall Malls from her hand. "You promised me!"

"*Dio Cristo!*" Luca threw his chair down and stomped out of the room. Mirella threw the cigarette pack at me and ran after him, Gorbi at her heels.

Mamma looked surprised by Luca's explosion of emotion. "The girl was murdered. We have to make sense of it."

"*Delinquenti!*" Nonna decreed, her milky eyes hooked on the Pall Malls in my hand. "The country doesn't make sense—why should that *sgualdrina's* death?"

"Tamara was not a whore," my mother said with a crisp edge to her voice. She turned to me. "Simona, in America you've gotten involved in nasty crimes. While you're here, maybe you can help discover why she died." She made it sound as if it were a matter of whipping up an omelet.

Nonna laughed. "Distract her, that's the trick. Now how about a cigarette?"

"Can't we talk, Mamma?" I asked, walking over to her. "Can't we just go somewhere and tell each other the things that need to be told?" Would I tell her a woman was at her house in Rocca di Papa, answering her phone? I wasn't sure. I rested a hand on my mother's arm.

She softened. "It hasn't been a very good homecoming for you. I'm sorry. But I'm not prepared to talk about myself yet. Not even tomorrow at breakfast. But you must know I never wanted to will you this." She gave me a quick hug. "I really didn't." She got busy readjusting her perfectly neat, barely gray short hair.

"Mamma, you didn't do anything! Why do women always think it's their fault?" I'd done that for more than a year after my marriage broke up. Now my heart was feeling that anguish all over again, this time for my mother.

I recognized her need to keep the event inside. For two weeks after walking in on my husband and my best friend in my own bedroom, I'd gone to every movie in town, seen the gory ones twice. It took me a month to tell my mother. We shared denial genes.

"If I can't smoke," Nonna said in a put-on helpless voice, "where are my *tarocchi*? I need my *tarocchi*!"

"Mamma, you didn't do anything!"

"My cards. Simona, get me my cards. They're in my bedroom."

I waved to Nonna. "*Subito*. I'll get them right away." I gave my mother a kiss.

"It's all so new," Mamma said in a whisper, breaking my heart.

"Talk to me. Let me help you. I've only got a week." I'd asked for emergency leave from my advertising agency.

"You're leaving before Easter?"

"Monday morning. Sunday I'll be with you."

"*I miei tarrocchi!*"

My mother shrugged me off. "Get her those blessed cards or let her smoke the whole pack."

Nonna clapped her hands. "I heard that. You'd like me underground, more than likely."

"When, Mamma?" I asked.

"Tuesday. I have an appointment in the morning, then we'll have lunch."

I laughed, happy to have a goal to carry me along. "Tuesday, it's a deal."

"What deal? Mothers don't make deals. They give orders." With a smile, Mamma took the pack of cigarettes from my hand and threw them into Nonna's lap. "I'm not trying to kill you, I'm trying to shut you up."

Nonna bared two glistening rows of false teeth. "I always liked you, Olga. There's no hair on your tongue. So tell the girl the truth and be done with it. And I don't want a cigarette." She slipped the pack back in her sweater pocket. "One a day's my limit. I want my tarot cards. They're under my pillow, Simona."

"What truth?" I asked. "You did leave my father? That's what you said over the phone."

Mamma nudged me to the door like a sheepdog with a stray lamb. "What I said is I need some time by myself to think, and if you don't get those cards to silence Nonna, the truth will be that I've gone crazy!" She pushed me out of the living room just as the doorbell rang. We both started at the sound.

"Olga wants to know who killed that girl?" Nonna shouted. "My cards will tell you!"

The bell rang again. Gorbi came bounding out of Luca's bedroom, barking. My mother held my arm for a moment, wiping her upper lip with a finger. Then she said, "Answer that, will you please?" in her best mistress-of-the-house voice. At the door Gorbi whirled with excitement.

I obeyed, thinking it was my father, knowing that's what she thought too. I was ready to pounce on him, hit him, kiss him, I don't know. I pulled the dog back and opened the door.

A man smiled at me. Not my father. He was in his midthirties, milky complexion, pink mounds for cheeks, round face with languid, almost black eyes, and a red voluptuous mouth.

He leaned down to pet Gorbi, confident in his movements, then stretched out that hand. The other held keys and the car radio. "*Commissario Perillo della Polizia Giudiziaria.* And you are?"

"Simona Griffo." We shook hands. I heard a sigh of relief from my mother. Gorbi licked the man's radio and wagged his tail against my legs.

"*Ah . . . bene!*" The commissioner slipped inside the apartment and closed the door behind him. "You are a key witness, but I would like first to speak to Luca Monti?" He raised his eyebrows at my mother, mistaking her for Luca's mother. She looked at him stonily.

Commissario Perillo smiled, his pink, full cheeks getting pinker. "Excuse me for the late hour." He spoke slowly and carefully, almost as if he were a foreigner. I had a feeling he was trying to get rid of the Sicilian accent that peeked through despite his efforts. He looked familiar, but I didn't know why.

"Why do you want to speak to my son?" Mirella walked out of Luca's bedroom, closing the door behind her. "He was at Poggio delle Rose today with my mother." She stood still, as if guarding the door. Rock music started to thump from behind her.

"You told Ispettore Rolfi he was the victim's friend, signora," Perillo said. "There is a great deal your son must know about her."

My mother jumped in. "Then there is something special about this case."

"Tamar was my friend too," Mirella said, coming toward us with quick, nervous steps. I thought of one of those mamma birds that leaves the nest, hoping the falcon will follow. "Question me."

"Is your son not at home?" He had to raise his voice above the music coming from Luca's bedroom.

"My son is tired and upset. Can't it wait?" She stopped before she reached him, examining his face with impassive eyes.

"Please," Mamma said, her hand stopping an inch short of the commissario's arm. "It's been a terrible day." The wretched look that appeared on her face could not be denied.

"Of course," Perillo said. "It is late."

I rubbed her back and felt her stiffen under my hand.

"Tell him to come to my office in the morning. Ten o'clock." Perillo furrowed black, beautifully combed eyebrows at Mirella. "You can follow at ten-thirty. That should give you enough time for Mass."

"Grazie." She visibly relaxed.

The commissario turned to me, heels lifting in unison. "Then since I am already here, Signora Griffo, just a few questions I needed to . . . " He stopped to stare at the oil painting behind me.

"I've seen this before." He looked puzzled.

"I copied Botticelli's portrait of Giuliano de' Medici," Mirella said, proud of her work. "I simply substituted my son's face. There is a distinct nose resemblance."

"I see," Perillo said, looking as if he didn't see at all. His glance dropped back to me. "Signora Griffo, I have already spoken to your husband in my office."

"Ex," I told him. "Out of my life forever." I added that for my mother's sake.

She was following her own thoughts. "You are investigating on Palm Sunday. This is an important case, then."

"Signora Griffo?" The commissario gestured toward the open living room door.

"I already told the local ispettore this morning everything I know, but if you want a repeat, let's get this over with." I led the way.

Perillo didn't follow. His eyes were on Mirella, who was still staring at him as if he might be a long-forgotten relative.

"Bacco!" Mirella exclaimed. "The god of wine." Perillo laughed and shook his curly black hair. "All you're missing are grape leaves in your hair."

My mother said, "Yes, of course. Caravaggio. You do resemble his portrait of Bacchus."

"I've been told that before." Perillo preened. "I made a special trip to Florence, to the Uffizi, to see it. I'm not quite as young as Caravaggio's sitter, but I hope more manly."

"Oh yes," Mirella said with a smile. "Much more manly."

"I'm exhausted." I was hoping to get the night over with.

"And I'm dying of boredom here, *cavolo*!" Nonna shouted from the living room. *Cavolo* is a euphemism for *cazzo*. The first means cabbage, the second penis. Nonna maintains they're interchangeable because they both give you gas.

"Bring that man in here!"

Perillo took a step inside the living room, nodded at Nonna, and swept his eyes over the hodgepodge of paintings. He pointed to Mirella's still life with red and yellow peppers. "That makes me hungry."

Nonna waved an arm. "It's the only thing worth anything in this room except yours truly. You don't look anything like Bacchus. There's no bloom of youth! My daughter sees paintings even in the toilet bowl."

"Nonna!" Mirella's hands fluttered to her face. Gorbi tried to ram himself past Mirella's legs and banged the door against the wall. Nonna clacked her teeth. Electric guitars were in full concert in Luca's room.

"We could go down the street to King's for a coffee?" I suggested.

Perillo patted the dog. "I prefer Giolitti's."

Yes! "Giolitti makes the best ice cream on either side of the Atlantic!"

"Ice cream it is," Perillo said. "My car is downstairs."

I ran to get Nonna's tarot cards while Mirella led the commissario back to the corridor, urging him to sit for her. She would paint him in the Caravaggio style, all shadows and light.

"I'm good at copies." She painted trompe l'oeil and portraits in the style of whomever to round out her teacher's salary. Her painting was not good enough to be her family's sole support. Nonna, every once in a while, threatened that she had scoops of money she was going to leave to the church if everyone didn't treat her right. No one believed her. My parents helped Mirella out during the hard times.

As I passed through the corridor again on my way to the living room, my mother was repeating herself. "It's very unusual, don't you agree? To kill the victim during a purse snatching? This is a special case. Tamara was very poor."

In the living room I bent down to kiss Nonna. She looked asleep.

"You are sadly wrong, signora," Perillo said in the hallway.

Nonna clasped my neck. "That policeman is a coward. Men always are. And don't worry about your mother. The cards say she'll be all right in the end. That's what counts. And you stay away from Carlo."

"Good night," I said, giving her another kiss. She had already forgotten me, too busy unwrapping the tattered silk that covered her beloved *tarocchi*.

"Shall we go?" I asked Perillo, closing the living room door behind me.

He kept his attention on my mother. "The simple *scippo*—where all that has been robbed is purse and dignity—is the norm, of course. But there have been cases of death."

Mamma looked skeptical. "Surely accidental."

"Ten years ago we had a case of a subway thief who used a razor to slash purses and people. Jack the Ripper we called him."

"I don't believe you," my mother stated.

I hooked Perillo by the arm and got him out the door.

4

The Roman world is falling, yet we hold
our heads erect instead of bowing our
necks.

—SAINT JEROME, LETTER 60

"Your father is not alive?" Perillo asked, dropping into a
metal chair inside the bar, an L-shaped room with a rust-
colored marble floor and glass-doored refrigerators tiered
with ice-cream cakes. He had already ordered at the
counter, where he was greeted with a lot of fanfare.

I scraped a chair back and sat down to face the glass
door and the lighted helm oak outside. It had gotten too
cool to sit on the sidewalk. The only other customers were
a family of four quietly lapping up whipped cream.

"My father's alive." In fact, I didn't want to think how
alive he was. The woman's voice over the phone had
sounded very young. "What prompted that question?"

"Your husband—"

I growled.

29

"—your ex-husband explained the composition of the Monti household. He included your mother."

"Salve, Commissario," a waiter said.

Perillo raised a hand. "Ciao, Mario." He turned back to me. "Strong women interest me. My own mother is the devoted kind, much like Signora Monti."

"Shall we talk about Tamar and what little I saw? I'll reiterate. I was tired, and the action of the thieves was so quick, I was barely aware that anything had happened. I saw the scooter flash by me, saw a lot of dark hair. I think the hair belonged to the guy sitting behind the driver. It was sort of flowing freely in the wind. At least that's how I remember it." I paused as the waiter laid a metal tray with our order on the miniscule round table. Perillo helped himself to his espresso. "I didn't see their faces. I'm sorry."

"Any idea what make the scooter was?" he asked, dropping four spoonfuls of sugar in a white cup half the size of a child's fist.

"I can't even tell a Cadillac from a Jaguar. Besides, one of the blessings of New York is not having scooters racing around you all the time. I've forgotten all the makes. Vespa, Lambretta, Honda—"

"M-a-n-a-t-a-n." Perillo concentrated hard on the pronunciation. He smiled. "I took my mother for a five-day visit two years ago. She liked the coffee shops best, all owned by Greeks it seems. Grilled cheese and bacon. Every Thursday lunch, that's what she serves me. Instead of *gnocchi*, which I don't digest. She thinks it's a Greek lunch."

Gnocchi, small dumplings made with flour and mashed potatoes, are part of the weekly Roman food ritual. Thursday, *gnocchi*. Friday, fish. Saturday, tripe.

"Your husband—"

I lifted my spoon full of blackberry sorbet and threatened his olive-green trousers.

"Carlo Linetti," Perillo corrected. "Carlo Linetti thought it might have been a Lambretta. He gave us a color. Do you remember the color?"

"I told you, all I saw was this flashing hair." I slipped sorbet in my mouth and wondered if Perillo's resemblance to Caravaggio's *Bacchus* was the reason I'd thought he looked familiar. I couldn't remember the last time I'd seen a reproduction of that painting. "And don't trust Carlo. He's a good bluffer. When the scooter passed by, I think his head was buried in the trunk of his car, which is a Fiat Spider. That make I recognize." Carlo had always owned a Fiat Spider.

"If Carlo had seen the scooter," I said, "he would have seen Tamar right away. They knew each other, he must have told you that."

Perillo suspended the white cup in front of his mouth. Those big black eyes of his looked as if they'd just spotted something odd. Behind him a well-dressed woman hurried in and asked our waiter about ordering for her boy's birthday party the next week.

"What is it?" I asked.

"You are still interested in Carlo Linetti, I believe."

"I have a very handsome lover in New York, thank you. I may even move in with him when I go back." I had no intention of moving anywhere except back to my Greenwich Village studio. When Greenhouse had asked me to live with him, I'd panicked. I wasn't quite sure why.

"Stanley Greenhouse," I added, liking the awkwardness of his name in Italian. I did not mention that Greenhouse was a New York City homicide detective.

"What held my attention was the girl's expression." I licked icy blackberry off the corner of my mouth. "She was thinking. Instead of screaming, or looking surprised, it was clear she was mulling something over."

"The identity of the killers?"

I shrugged. "Carlo told you she spoke before she died, didn't he? '*Doni.*'"

Perillo ordered another espresso. This time Hag, a decaffeinated brand. "A man's name? Perhaps she meant to say Tony? Difficult to assess. It could also be part of something longer. An ending. *Droni* for *ladroni*, for example."

That means big thieves. "*Droni* has an *r* in it, which she didn't pronounce."

"Americans are never very good with our rolled *r*'s."

"She said *doni.*"

"Your mother's daughter."

"I don't know how strong I am," I said, "but I'm certainly stubborn. And somewhat curious. Why does a police commissioner come to Mirella's house at ten o'clock on a Saturday night? Is my mother right? Is there something unusual about this *scippo*, beyond the fact that the girl was killed?"

"As I said, I live nearby. Via Ruffini. Right next to the local police station, in fact."

"*Me ne racconti un'altra.*" Tell me another, story being implied.

Perillo smiled. His lips were almost obscenely voluptuous. They made me think of a red plum. "The victim was an American citizen. The embassy has taken an interest. Also, this Tamar Deaton had a good friend in a rich businessman who has many dealings with our country."

"You mean he has friends in high places?"

"I hope not." He laughed. "These days high places means *Regina Coeli.*" Rome's main jail is called Queen of the Heavens.

I smiled politely. "I've been following the news in *The New York Times.*" The length of Italy was being rocked by the biggest scandal ever, which the newspapers had dubbed *Tangentopoli*—Bribe City. Up north, in Milan, an investigation, *Mani Pulite*—Clean Hands—was looking into the graft of the leading political parties. What government agencies and which politicians had accepted how much from whom for lucrative contracts? Down in Palermo, Sicily, the *pentiti*—Mafia repentants, a term that makes me think of the Inquisition—had just pointed the finger at Giulio Andreotti, perhaps the most prominent politician of them all, saying he had Mafia ties and that he had even ordered the killing of a nosy journalist. In Rome, the seat of the government, politicians pointed fingers, denied involvement, their faces bursting with lies and fears. I had come back to Italy in its moment of glory. Actually I was glad. After the cleanup, some new life might grow.

Perillo looked at my half-eaten sorbet cup. "Why did you not order ice cream? That is what you wanted, no?"

"I like this. I'm just tired." I'd eyed those lovely vats of walnut, banana, chocolate, cream, coffee, and then I'd remembered the doctor.

"Tell me why you changed your mind about the ice cream."

"Is it important?"

"Yes, to me, yes. Please forgive my prying." He edged closer on his seat, raising a finger in the air. "Human nature. That is important to my job. You wished the ice cream. I saw it clearly in your face. Your entire body leaned toward those vats. Then you stood up straight, anger on your face. Too much anger for it to be a question of weight, am I right?" He smiled, eyes narrowing with the effort. "Besides, you are even a little too thin. A corpulant woman has a great deal of allure. No, it was not a question of calories, am I right? That is all I need to know."

"You are right," I said. "And I think that is all I am prepared to say about it."

A month ago I had discovered a soft golf ball in my breast, which turned out to be a cyst the doctor had aspirated. "Nothing to worry about," he had told me after my first mammography, except that I had cystic breasts, which meant that cancerous cells might be splitting quietly behind a cyst and no one would find them until it was too late. Anyway, after two weeks during which breathing seemed an art I had never mastered, I was assured life would continue merrily if I got a mammogram once a year, if I visited the breast surgeon every four months, if I stopped drinking caffeine, took Vitamin E, ate lots of carrots and dark leafy vegetables, and drastically reduced my fat intake. Hence sorbet instead of ice cream. Thank God I had stopped smoking three years ago.

"I don't think my eating habits have anything to do with Tamar's death."

"Of course not." Perillo took out a tiny pocket agenda and carefully wrote a few lines. "Thank you. I am always a fascinated student of human behavior." The agenda went back into his pocket, and his eyes dropped to my cup again, which now held only one dark red melting scoop of sorbet. His nose twitched. "Signorina Deaton bled to death in less than a minute."

I pushed my cup away. "I didn't see blood until Carlo took his hand from under her armpit. How could she have bled to death?"

"The knife cut off her pulmonary artery. She bled into her lung."

"That was a fast autopsy."

"We can be efficient if given a reason." I restrained myself from making a face. "In this instance, there was no room in the morgue. The weapon was at least twenty-six centimeters long. That's ten inches." He lifted his spoon. "May I?"

"You can have the rest." He dug into my sorbet cup. "And I know centimeters. I haven't been away that long." Were all Italian policemen hungry?

"*Grazie.*" He dropped sorbet into his espresso and licked the spoon.

"Isn't it almost impossible to plunge a knife between ribs from a moving scooter? Ten inches deep!"

"It is what I asked myself. Do you think Carlo and Tamar were lovers?"

I bristled. "What are you getting at?"

"Perhaps the girl was killed while she was lying on the street."

"Impossible. I would have seen it." What an absurd idea.

Perillo studied my face. "You said yourself that you were tired. However, do not worry for your Carlo yet. If the young man with the long hair that you described was an expert of anatomy and the knife, then perhaps killing her from the scooter was not impossible, only difficult. A witness has told me that the scooter hovered for a few seconds, by which I suppose she means it stopped long enough to kill the girl. The witness compared it to a bee plucking pollen."

But flowers survived. He gulped his coffee. "Carlo denies a sexual relationship with the victim, of course, but perhaps he said something to you?"

"No, he did not, Commissario." I shot up from my chair. I had had enough of Carlo's "relationships." "I know nothing about my husband, and now it's time that I go to sleep. I was going to pay for my own sorbet, but since you've eaten half of it, you can. Thank you. If you want me to sign a statement, tell me where your office is and I'll be there at nine o'clock sharp." Then it hit me and I dropped back down.

"*Cavolo*, I said it, didn't I? I called him my husband."

"It in no way compromises you. Tell me, is your husband violent?"

"Leave Carlo out of this. He faints at the sight of his own blood. He doesn't kill his lovers, he cheats on them, and what would he want with Tamar's satchel?"

"I am contemplating the possibility that she was not stabbed for her satchel."

"Why not?"

"Your mother is basically right. It is not usual for *scippatori* to stab their victims. If the victim dies, it might be because she hits her head on the curb, or she is dragged by the motorcycle or the car. Yes, they now also use cars. An arm lashing out of the window, and if you don't let go, you end up under the tires. Now the girl did not look like she had even a thousand lire on her. And here you were stepping out of a car with a nice leather purse." He lifted my Coach bag—bought with a Christmas check from my parents—which I had hung over the back of the chair. He dropped it in my lap.

"A precaution needed even in the presence of a commissario." He looked regretful.

"When I stepped out of the car, the *scippo* was already in progress."

Perillo swooped air with his spoon. "Then why not snatch the purse of a very nicely dressed elderly woman who was standing next to Signorina Deaton, waiting for the light to change? An expensive Fendi purse that was a birthday present from her son.

"Don't you think it odd that the thieves should pick Signorina Deaton over this other lady who was encumbered by bags of food and would have been a far easier target than a strong young woman? Signorina Deaton was a meter seventy-five centimeters tall. That is five feet nine inches!"

"Maybe her height is what made them notice her."

"Does it not mean that a commissario who takes his profession seriously should look into Signorina Deaton's life, her friends, where she lived?" He dropped the spoon back in its saucer. His blue shirt was now sprinkled with coffee drippings. "Serious questions need to be asked."

"And you're starting with Carlo?"

Perillo nodded, pleased with himself. "He came to me first, which bears remembering." He patted the pocket with the agenda. "He claims to have known Tamar Deaton for over three months, and yet to the inspector he said one month. Why? This relationship with Signorina Deaton is not clear to me."

"Carlo's probably just as confused as you are. Women's bodily parts stress his brain. He's upset about Tamar's death. He got confused as to when he met her. That's natural enough." Why was I defending Carlo?

Perillo's tongue swept over his lips. "Perhaps."

I nastily pointed to the stains on his shirt. Perillo looked down and moaned.

"Sparkling water will take those stains right out, Commissario. Something I learned in America."

"No, no. My mother always uses salt." He waved his hand to call a waiter. The bar had run out of salt and offered sugar instead. Perillo ended up looking like a sugar doughnut.

"Carlo's not your killer."

"Drugs?" He licked his fingers.

"Drugs what, Commissario?" I wanted to shake that sugar right off him.

"Is, or has, your ex-husband, assuming that you would know"—he spoke slowly as if I did not speak his language—"been involved with drugs, either as user or seller?"

I sat, stunned.

"Both?" he added with a twist of the wrist.

"Stop picking on Carlo!" I finally said. It was my reaction that was surprising me, not Perillo's questions. I found myself wanting desperately to protect my ex-husband. At that moment I thought of him as a man who still belonged to me, with me. Everything that had been part of my life in Rome was attaching itself back to me: the desire to smoke, my mother, Mirella, Nonna, and Carlo, the man who had, for a long time, been the great love of my life. I felt responsible in a way I never had in four years of single life in New York.

Perillo was studying me, eyes curious.

"Tamar tried to fight them off," I said. "The guys were high on heroin. One of them used a knife to get her to let go of that purse. Isn't that the most likely scenario?"

"You have become American. You believe the straight path is the true path. You forget that we Italians are specialists in the science of *dietrologia*, looking at what is behind every word, every action. Tamar Deaton was as punctured as a colander and I am not speaking of her knife wound. She had no drugs in her body at the time of death, but she clearly was, or had very recently been, an addict." His eyes were sad.

"In the time I knew him, Carlo did not use drugs. I don't believe he uses them now. He's too sure of himself, too happy with the way the world is treating him."

"Ah, if you believe that, then you are not a good student of human nature. His eyes wander when he speaks, his fingers twitch."

"That's nervous energy. He's fine."

"Even now? His film editing career is not flowering, and I believe he did not want you to leave your marriage."

"Even now." I wondered why Carlo had talked about

our marriage with a police commissioner. Was he trying to drum up sympathy? Was his career foundering? He loved editing, he loved movies.

Perillo stood up. "I'll drive you back."

"No, thanks, I need the walk."

"Of course, it has been a difficult day." He stretched out a hand. "Thank you. Tomorrow morning, sleep late or go to church. Palm Sunday Mass is my mother's favorite. Our apartment is blanketed with the olive branches of past years. You and I shall talk another day. You will sign a statement the next time. I might even convince you to tell me more about ice cream. The *gianduia* here is the end of the world."

"I'm a vanilla and chocolate fan, with clouds of whipped cream on top." We shook hands. He sat back down and took out his notebook.

"Un'altro caffè Hag," he called out, making a scribbling gesture with clenched fingers.

"Si, si, we'll give you a check, Commissario, don't worry." The woman behind the cash register was knitting a red sweater. "We don't want to land in *Regina Coeli* for bribing you with sorbet." She winked at me as I walked by.

I swung back. "Carlo would never physically hurt another human being."

He looked up from taking notes. I imagined him writing, "witness needs to take a walk."

He waved me away. *"La notte porta consiglio."* Night brings counsel.

Stepping out into that cool Roman night, my body numb from lack of sleep, I did not know what counsel the commissario was wishing me. I only knew that I had defended my ex-husband with the same conviction I had shown one long-ago night, when I told my mother that my husband would never deceive me.

5

I do not think this idling can be called a waste of time.
—HENRIK IBSEN, CORRESPONDENCE

Mirella lives on the same side of the Tiber as the Vatican, in a fairly central area called Delle Vittorie—of the victories—because it once housed army barracks and many of its streets are named after World War I generals. Today it is known best by lawyers, thanks to its many courtrooms. No foreign guidebooks mention it. There are no art-filled churches here, no antiquities to be seen.

Delle Vittorie boasts some good stores; one excellent restaurant, Micci, which makes the best rigatoni with eggplant outside of Sicily; many blocks of large, sometimes elegant late-nineteenth-century palazzi, and some broad avenues flanked by trees. It is mostly residential, middle class, comforting, a little boring, and until this morning I would have said safe.

I walked back to the wide circle of Piazza Mazzini with its small park, which by day is flanked by yellow cabs and movers' trucks waiting for business, and paused in the bright light of an elegant shop window. Too tired to think clearly, I was suddenly scared. What had I come back to? Running away to New York after my marriage broke up, I'd gotten rid of family responsibility. I was too far away to help deal with the problems my parents might have. When I called home, maybe once a month, Mamma would declare that everything and everyone was fine, that I should not worry about anything. Sometimes she'd drop Carlo's name into the conversation. He'd taken her out to lunch. He'd given her a present on her name day, July 11, something I, of course, had forgotten to do. I always uh-huh'd my way out of further involvement.

In those brief conversations, with my mother protesting the cost and telling me I should write instead, Gigi, my father, would pick up on the other phone and whistle the first few bars of *Eine Kleine Nacht Musik*. As a baby I had been lulled to sleep with that music.

"Mi manchi," he invariably said.

"I miss you too, Gigi," I'd say. "Mamma too." But I didn't really miss them. At first I was too busy feeling sorry for myself, and then, when I began to settle into New York life, I relegated them to a life across an ocean, part of a past that none of my new American friends knew much about or could relate to. I came back to visit once a year, but my father knew I still felt skittish about being in Rome. After a couple of days which I jammed full of appointments with old friends, Gigi would take the family away. We'd gone to Provence, another time to the Amalfi Coast, Austria, Switzerland. Fun vacations that had nothing to do with everyday life. Once back in New York, my parents receded.

And now I was in Rome to immerse myself in their problems. That scared me. The woman who had answered my father's phone scared me. Tamar's death scared me. Perillo and his questions scared me. Carlo scared me.

I needed sleep.

I left the shop window with its apricot silk blouses on display and walked quickly along a row of helm oaks. The wide street was packed with parked cars. Under a muffler a cat in heat cried out. A black furry shape slithered past me. A waiter stacked chairs outside Antonini, a fancy bar with some of the best and most expensive *spuntini*— snacks—in town.

"*Buonanotte*," he called out to me.

"*Buonanotte.*" I passed the flower stand on the corner where, over four years ago, I had bought Nonna a bouquet of peonies the day I had my one-way ticket to New York in my pocket. Across the street was the covered market where I had bought the lamb roast for the farewell dinner Mirella gave for me. I inhaled, conjuring up the sweet smells of flowers and fruit, cheese and bread, that hung above the street each morning. I saw in my mind the one-legged war veteran caning chairs in the corner. I rummaged with my imagination through the tablecloths and underwear of the sidewalk stall. My old life was back, enveloping me.

"See you in the morning," a man's deep voice said. "Ciao, Gorbi."

"Ciao, Nikki."

I stopped when I heard Mirella's voice. An iron gate creaked open. A large dog slipped through and came to sniff my hand. I barely made out that Nikki was a German shepherd. The street lamps dipped into the trees.

The man closed the gate behind him and crossed the street, whistling. The dog went bounding after him. I opened the gate and called "Mirella?" I was stepping into a walled, block-long expanse of weeds and well-trodden earth that various neighborhood organizations were claiming as theirs. For years, the neighborhood dogs had been the winners. Mirella's building was across the street, behind the sycamores of Viale Angelico, the angelic street that in the past brought pilgrims to St. Peter's.

Gorbi butted against my knees with a slimy tennis ball in his mouth, begging me to throw it as far as I could.

"Ciao, Simona. Thank you for taking Bacchus out of the house." Mirella was sitting in what looked like an old, understuffed dark armchair in the middle of the dirt field. Only her face and hands were truly visible. "Nonna can be impossible."

I tugged the ball from Gorbi's mouth and managed to fling it all of twenty feet. I could have sworn I saw disappointment on his face.

"Was it gruesome for you?" she asked.

"No, just overwhelming somehow." I sat down next to her in a matching chair. "Ow." My rear end hit pebbles.

"Paolo, the man who just left with Nikki, got the armchairs for us. He loves to scrounge around for rejected junk." There was affection in her voice.

"A suitor?" My mother was always wishing a man on Mirella. She'd lived with only Nonna and Luca for twenty-eight years.

"I already have a suitor," Mirella said.

"Aha!" I took a deep breath. Mirella was wearing a pomegranate perfume made by a pharmacy in Florence that dated back to the Renaissance. For my twelfth birthday she had given me lace handkerchiefs steeped in that scent. "Who is he?"

"We're all having Palm Sunday lunch together tomorrow up at the farm. Nonna's idea. I want to cancel, but Nonna won't have it. You'll like him." She rested her hand on my lap. "Your mother wanted to wait up for you, but she was tired."

Beyond the wall of the dog park, nighttime traffic streamed gently. A colder breeze came in from the sea. I closed my eyes and leaned back. The smells, the sounds of Rome. Like it or not, I was home.

"Olga's convinced that Tamar wasn't killed for her satchel."

"Bacchus agrees," I said. "I think they're both wrong. We don't know what she had in that bag." I sat up. "Can we talk about my parents?"

"Olga made me promise not to." I felt a hand push hair back from my forehead. "Give her a little time. She's not ready for you or anyone yet." The hand stopped. "What did the commissario say?"

Maybe my mother deserved to be the first one to know about that woman on the phone, if she didn't already. I was also ashamed, I realized. "Perillo was asking questions about Carlo and Tamar. I know nothing. Carlo's been out of my life for years. Were they close?"

"She looked up to him. 'Carlo told me this, Carlo told me that,' that type of thing. Maybe she had a crush on him. Luca didn't like their friendship very much."

"At whose party did they meet?" Carlo hadn't given any specific details to Ispettore Rolfi.

Mirella explained that Carlo had edited a documentary on Italian museums that had been financed by Arthur Hensen, an American, CEO of Hensen Group International and also the owner of La Casa dell'Arte, where Mirella taught and Tamar had studied. Artoor, as she persisted in calling him, had given a party at La Casa to celebrate the completion of the film.

"Someone important from the Ministry of Culture came and thought the whole evening was excellent. It's the only word he knew. Carlo met Tamar that night. They were friends right away."

"When was that?"

"A month ago. Tamar videotaped the whole evening. We all had a wonderful time. It must have been very hard for you to walk away from Carlo. He has such a way about him. Tamar put it nicely. 'He makes me feel cherished,' she said."

"Yes, he does. Without discrimination."

"I'm sorry, Simona. I didn't mean . . . I really don't think Tamar meant it in a sexual way."

"Old story, don't worry about it. What is odd is that Carlo told Perillo he'd known Tamar for three months."

Mirella stirred. "Oh, no. I don't think so. He met her at the party. It was very clear they'd just met."

Who was lying? Did it matter?

"Tamar tried so hard to please everyone," Mirella said. "It was impossible not to like her or at least feel sorry for her."

"Nonna called her a whore." I was thinking how nice it would be to drop off to sleep wrapped in Mirella's voice and her pomegranate perfume.

"Nonna takes pride in shocking people, and she's jealous. She thinks Nonna and Mirella are all the women Luca needs in his life for now."

That didn't sound like the Nonna who had urged me to make a clean break to America, but then I wasn't a grandson. "Perillo said Tamar was a drug addict."

Mirella raised her head. "Was she? Was she really?" She sounded strangely hopeful.

"No drugs in her body, though."

"Then how did Perillo . . . ? Ah, the needle holes." Mirella sighed and dropped back down. "The drug problem here is enormous. The rich and middle-class kids are the worst. They have every opportunity and yet . . . It's terrible. I'm lucky with Luca.

"He's a good boy, but he's furious about Tamar's death. That's how he handles anything he doesn't like. He takes it as a personal insult. He got that from his father. I didn't want the commissario to see him like that. He might assume Luca isn't grieving. I know Nonna and I have spoiled him. He's as handsome as his father."

I had never warmed to Luca. He was too morose, too hard to draw out, and his leftist diatribes made my eyes glaze over. If I worried about him, it was for Mirella's sake.

"Perillo mentioned an American businessman who was taking an interest in Tamar's death."

"That's Artoor!" Mirella tugged my arm. "He's very generous, warm, like most Americans."

"He's your suitor."

"I think so. Yes. For the past year, ever since he's taken up residence in Rome, he has been—well, extremely nice. Artoor liked Tamar. He even mentioned once that he might try to adopt her. She adored him."

Gorbi barked at the far end of the park, digging at something. His white, spotted body gleamed in the darkness.

"Artoor was paying for her schooling, too. Gorbi! Please! The neighbors."

"Does the word *doni* mean anything to you?" I asked. "That's what Tamar said before she died."

"Oh, I am sorry, Simona. Shhh! *Zitto* Gorbi!"

I lifted my head. "Sorry about what?"

"Your present for your birthday. The eighth of March. I haven't given you one in years. Tamar called and told me she was bringing it to you from La Casa. It must have been in her satchel. Tamar was trying to tell you in Italian that she had your present."

"How sweet of you, Mirella." I was moved. "But I don't think Tamar was thinking of gifts at that moment."

Gorbi stopped barking and trotted our way, head held high, a trophy of some kind in his mouth. "Anyone named Tony or Doni in school?"

Mirella sat up. "Ah, yes, a name. That's a good possibility. Last year we had three Tonys. This year we have five Bills and one Tony who never came back after Christmas break. I'm sorry about the present." She waved the dog to her. "Tamar made a lovely sketch from a recent photo Olga lent me. You look like a Leonardo Madonna."

I laughed. "That's quite a feat."

I am a pleasant-looking woman when I smile, that much I will immodestly admit. I have an oval face, olive skin, lots of dark brown shoulder-length hair that refuses to fold in any particular way, average brown eyes that sparkle at food, romance, and sex. I'm five foot four if I stretch my neck. My weight is about right in Italy and five to ten pounds too heavy by American standards, depending on how down I am on myself when I think about it.

"Tamar must have been very talented," I said.

"She was the best student I have ever had and I only wish—Gorbi, what is that?" Mirella reached to Gorbi's mouth to remove his newfound toy. She screamed.

I jumped up. "Did he bite you?"

"No, I don't know. No." She was looking down at her hand. Gorbi proudly dropped his catch on his mistress's lap. Mirella shuddered and I bent over to see better. Her blue wool lap now held a long, bloody knife.

6

———— ◦❖◦ ————

. . . a love of "pranks," the more vivid the better, must from far back have been implanted in the Roman temperament with a strong hand.

—HENRY JAMES, ITALIAN HOURS

"I'm not taking this knife to the police!" Mirella shouted over the noise of the coffee grinder at breakfast the next morning. "They're going to think we killed her." She was dressed in a beige suit and floppy felt slippers, her gray hair free to fly around her face. Her green-ringed eyes were puffy from lack of sleep.

We were all assuming it was the murder weapon. The knife was exactly twenty-seven centimeters long. I'd measured it myself, careful not to touch it.

"That's what they'll think if you don't." I bit into a slice of white focaccia my mother had left for me before going off to Palm Sunday Mass. In Rome we call it *pizza bianca.* The slice was stale. She was already gone when I woke up.

"The Tiber's the right place for that knife, along with the rest of the garbage that's in there." Nonna was bent over her chair, sucking orange wedges. "Did you see the sea gulls? We've got sea gulls in Rome now, thanks to the garbage in the Tiber." Her teeth were in the pocket of her bathrobe. Outside the open window, a neighbor's mynah bird was whistling the building awake. We were facing a sunny courtyard filled with palm and fig trees and the one huge magnolia that wrapped around to frame the corridor window. From far away I could hear a concert of church bells.

The kitchen was a wide, cheerful room with old octagonal black and red tiles that wobbled on the floor, a long, gray marble sink by the window with last night's washed and dried dinner dishes, old cabinets fat with generations of off-white paint. The stove was covered in chipped white enamel. The refrigerator was new. The narrow windowsill carried the winter herb garden—basil, rosemary, oregano, and wisps of tarragon. On the walls Mirella had painted the hilly, olive-treed, vine-covered landscape of Nonna's *casale*, her small farm up in Magliano Sabino.

Mirella's son, Luca, sat in the kitchen below a cluster of painted purple grapes ripe for the picking. "Mamma, that knife could have been bought in any Upim or Standa." He was drinking caffèlatte from a cup the size of a crash helmet. "How can you be sure it's ours?"

"The handle." Mirella chewed her lower lip. She stood by the stove, making another small pot of espresso. "It's half-burned. Nonna did that at Christmas, don't you remember?"

"Mothers get blamed for everything." Nonna dropped a sucked-out orange wedge in Gorbi's open mouth. "You're the one who forgot it on the stove, and I saved it from complete incineration. Without me, Mirella would probably forget where she put herself. Which makes me love her even more. I like being indispensable."

Mirella squared her thin shoulders. "The handle even has a nick where Gorbi chewed on it."

"*Sicuro*," Nonna said. "He thought it was one of your burnt pot roasts. Throw the knife in the Tiber!"

Luca leaned back in his chair, cradling his caffèlatte cup. He was still in his pajamas and bathrobe. "Anyone could steal it. It's like Stazione Termini in here. People walking in and out all the time. Anyway, we don't know if this knife killed Tamar. It's just a bloody knife, that's all. There's a butcher down the street!"

"Your friends!" Mirella sat down on a stool, her face creased with worry. Gorbi hung a forlorn head over his corner bed.

"Oh, Luca," Mirella said, "you don't think …?"

"*Cristo*, Mamma, have a little faith. Anyway, my friends haven't been here in two weeks, not since Olga moved in." He looked resentful.

Nonna hooked him with a sharp glance. "You mean since that dirty American showed up."

Mirella waved a pot holder at Nonna, dropping it in the process. "I do have faith, Luca *tesoro*, but who else … ?" The coffeepot gurgled. Mirella clutched it with her bare fingers. "Ah!" she cried out.

"I'll do that." I picked up the crocheted pot holder and lifted the coffeepot off the flame. "The commissario is going to ask who exactly had access to this kitchen and the knife." It was now nine-fifteen. Luca was due at Perillo's office in forty-five minutes.

"When did any of you last see it?" I'd tried questioning Mirella last night. Once she'd recognized the knife, she'd been unable to speak. On the way home, I had a hard time convincing her not to throw it in the neighborhood dumpster.

"La notte porta consiglio," I'd told Mirella, repeating Commissario Perillo's words to me. The night had only brought scary thoughts.

"Luca, do you remember when you saw it last?" I refilled Nonna's cup.

Luca dipped the end of his *cornetto* in his caffèlatte. His face looked taut and tired. "Why should I remember a knife?"

"Well, I do." Nonna pointed her sharp nose at me. "That girl used it on Friday to make a mess on the piano, slicing up some crepe paper for the school party last night that Mirella insisted on canceling—"

Mirella whipped around. "The girl's dead! And I want to cancel today's lunch, too. The thought of eating is obscene."

Luca's face turned the color of mud.

Nonna ignored them both. "She probably took the knife with her to gut cats. The cats of Rome are disappearing. Anyone notice that? I used to feed at least thirty of them. Now I have only two. Someone's killing them off. If it were up to me, I'd gut the politicians."

I looked over at Mirella. Gorbi was licking her burned fingers. "We had the dinner on Friday, the day before you came," she said. "I must have used it then. Or your mother. She cooked veal roast. It's the only knife that cuts." She winced at her own words.

Nonna slipped her teeth in her mouth. "Tamar took that knife with her and gave it to some *delinquente!*"

"Quit hounding her!" Luca shouted, slamming the front legs of his chair down. "She's dead!"

"Shh, Luca," Mirella whispered. "Have some respect."

"I'm giving that lunch today," Nonna said. "It's my farm. I make the decisions. I expect all of you to be there."

Luca leaned into Nonna. "You're just old, nasty, and jealous." He was barely audible.

Nonna sipped coffee.

"Don't pretend you don't hear," Luca said, his tone turning ugly. "You've got antenna ears, Nonna. You listen behind doors. You can't fool me."

"*Basta*, Luca!" Mirella pulled him back.

Luca wrenched his arm away and left the room. He liked dramatic exits, I decided. Nonna smiled into her cup. She enjoyed the attention.

"Mirella, who was at this dinner?" I found myself hoping Carlo wasn't on the guest list.

"Everyone. You'll meet them today at the farm." She was patting Nonna's arm with an unhappy expression on her face.

"The farm is our meal ticket." Nonna's eyes glanced over the frescoed walls. "The only asset we have left."

"Carlo?"

"Yes, Carlo too," Mirella said. "Tamar wanted him here," she added quickly, probably lying, knowing how I felt about my mother still hanging on to him. "It was Artoor's birthday. Sixty-two."

Nonna slapped her hand on the table. "Today's my party!" She had that startled look the old often have. They are probably only trying to see better, but I can't help but think they didn't expect time to run out so quickly.

"Carlo is not invited," Nonna said. "You are."

"Thanks."

Mirella squinted at her tiny wristwatch and stood up. "Luca, it's time to go!" She started to clear the table. "Artoor's two years younger than I am. At our age I don't think it makes a difference, do you?"

"And he's centuries richer," Nonna added before I could answer. "Which makes a very nice difference. He'll buy you a new washing machine."

"You didn't ask him, did you?" Mirella widened her hazel eyes and her reach. "You didn't!"

"Let me, Mirella." I caught Luca's bowl. Was Commissario Perillo going to think Carlo had stolen that knife? "I'll clean up." Why did I care what Carlo did or did not do?

"Did Tamar have a present for Arthur in her satchel?" I asked.

Empty-handed, Mirella looked lost. "I don't know. Why?"

"If Tamar had only one present in her satchel, she'd have said '*dono*,' in the singular."

"Who knows what she said." Nonna raised an arm to be helped out of her chair. Gorbi barked and zipped out of the kitchen. "She had a terrible accent. I did ask him for a washing machine. An AEG, the best." A key turned loudly in the entrance lock.

"How could you?" All of Mirella drooped.

The key kept turning. Gorbi kept barking. Roman doors are strapped by foot-long locks to keep thieves out. To get in can require eighteen turns of two keys. Woe is you if you have to go to the bathroom.

"Someone has to look after you," Nonna said, hooking her arms in ours. "You're not very good at it."

My mother finally appeared at the kitchen door, a wrapped cardboard tray of pastries in her hand. Gorbi made a great fuss of sitting at her feet. "Mirella, you'd better run a comb through that hair before we go to the police. I have the car downstairs."

She slid the pastry tray on top of the refrigerator, safe from Gorbi, and took over Mirella's hold on Nonna. Mirella ran to her bedroom, accompanied by the dull sound of felt slippers slapping the floor.

"You're not staying here with me?" I helped my mother walk Nonna to the living room.

"The police station is a place I would not send a friend

off to alone." She knew about the knife and she was, once again, avoiding me.

We settled Nonna in her chair. Mamma dropped the Sunday *Repubblica* in her lap.

"No olive branch?" Nonna asked my mother.

"I didn't go to Mass."

"You didn't?" I felt like a disappointed kid.

She tightened her lips. "God and I are not exactly on speaking terms at the moment."

"I was sure you'd gone to Santa Maria sopra Minerva." Waking up and not finding her, I'd assumed my mother had gone to the church near the apartment in Via Monterone, in the heart of *Vecchia Roma*—old Rome— where we had lived between overseas posts. My father had sold the seven-room apartment when he'd retired to Rocca di Papa ten years ago. "You've got a home now with Carlo," he'd said a few months before my marriage broke up. "No use keeping empty rooms."

"No use at all," I said, aware that he needed the money from the sale to round out his civil servant's pension. My mother had said nothing, but I knew she was upset. Whenever she was in Rome on a Sunday, she went back to that church to sit in front of the Carafa Chapel with its graceful frescoes painted by Filippino Lippi. Afterward she always bought chocolates in one corner of the nearby Piazza Sant'Eustachio, then crossed the small cobblestoned square to have the best coffee in Rome at the Bar Sant'Eustachio.

Throughout breakfast, talking about the bloodied knife, the thought of my mother following her Roman Sunday ritual had reassured me.

She must have guessed my thoughts. "I went last Sunday. The Carafa Chapel is sheathed in plastic. Restorations."

"I could do with some myself!" Nonna snapped on the radio news.

Mamma smiled. "The coffee is still the best."

"Andreotti has just issued a statement that the accusations against him are totally unfounded and absurd." The deep voice of the announcer trembled with importance and drama. "Now it is up to the Senate to decide whether there is enough evidence for it to waive the parliamentary immunity of a man who has been prime minister of this country seven times, and allow the Palermo magistrates to proceed with the investigation."

Nonna laughed. "I haven't had such a good time since they got the Red Brigades."

My mother steered me back to the corridor. "Help them." Her face looked soft and tired. Needy.

"I came to help you."

"Thank you, but this girl's death is more serious. We're implicated now." She touched my cheek, a light caress I wanted to hold on to longer. Suddenly I thought I understood.

"You want solutions."

She stiffened, looking suddenly afraid. "I've never liked open-ended stories."

"I know." I hugged her. What was scaring her? My father? The police? I felt myself shudder and tightened my hold on her. "I'll try, Mamma."

"Mirella! Luca!" she called out, pulling away from me. "Don't forget to bring the knife!"

7

*She had always been fond of history, and
here was history in the stones of the street
and the atoms of the sunshine.*
—HENRY JAMES, THE PORTRAIT OF A LADY

"What is that stupid commissario going to do?" Nonna
asked once the front door had shut. She fingered one of
her coral drop earrings.

"He'll have the blood checked to see if it matches with
Tamar's. It might not, you know." I offered tarot cards to
keep her happy.

"As if tomorrow the sun isn't coming up." She started
shuffling. I went out to the phone in the corridor.

"I know what Tamar had in the satchel!" Nonna
shouted. I dialed my father's number. "Hold on, Nonna."
Gorbi whined, jerking his head toward the door.

"Come in here," Nonna yelled. "I can't shout at my age."
The radio was going full blast with the latest pop song.

No one was answering. I spotted Mirella's car keys on
the table. I hung up.

"Leonardo," Nonna said.

I wanted to take a fast trip up to the Alban Hills to see if my father was home, but I couldn't leave Nonna alone. I popped my head in the living room. "Who sits with you when Mirella's at work?"

"No one." The tarot cards were faceup on the coffee table. The top card showed the page of cups. "I get around fine. See?" Nonna stood up without the aid of her cane and walked a few slow steps, her head pointing at me at a forty-five-degree angle. "I walk those four flights of stairs every day. Keeps me alive."

I smiled at her. "Then why did you play helpless back in the kitchen?"

"See that page of cups?" Nonna pointed to the coffee table. "Upright it means good news."

"But it's reversed."

Her milky eyes managed to gleam. "Then a deception will soon be uncovered."

I laughed. "You're incorrigible."

"And never helpless," she added. "Now come in here and listen to me." She curved down on the piano bench, ringed, arthritic fingers clicking on the ivory keys.

I hesitated by the door. I could make it to Rocca di Papa and back in an hour at this time in the morning, before the crush of Sunday outings.

"Leonardo," Nonna said. "That *sgualdrina* found it." Her hesitant fingers were picking up a new song on the radio—Whitney Houston's "I Will Always Love You." It sounded odd sung by someone else, in Italian. Nonna followed the tune faithfully.

"Hey, you're good," I said, sitting down next to her on the bench. I couldn't leave her, not without checking with Mirella first. "Leonardo who?"

"I used to pick up all the songs before my fingers got

rusty. Luca's right. I have sharp ears. That's how I know about the Leonardo."

"What are you talking about?"

Nonna closed the lid over the keys. "Rotten piano! Made in Korea! There's never enough money in this house." She rested her elbows on the piano lid, her clouded eyes looking beyond me. "My father's father had a Steinway. As a little girl I used to think of it as a shiny black panther, the keys its teeth. So many teeth like these." She clacked her false teeth. "Such beautiful music that animal made.

"At the beginning of the century we had a hundred acres on Via Appia, you know. It was countryside and farms then, and ancient Roman tombs. None of these movie star villas. Gina Lollobrigida. Marcello Mastroianni. No movies either."

She had told me the story before, at her ninetieth birthday party, after Luca had played and sung from Mozart's *The Marriage of Figaro* for her. *"Aprite un pò quegli Occhi,"* he sang in a hesitant baritone voice. Open those eyes a little.

"I open them to the past now," she had said then. "The future is for Mirella and Luca, and I worry. My daughter is lost in oils and turpentine. Luca, lazy boy, has pine cones in his head. I have nothing to leave them except a set of good teeth and these." She had cocked her head to show off her coral earrings. They were not easily missed. Huge and heavy, a gift from her nursemaid, they'd been dragging on her earlobes since she'd been a young girl.

"The past looks better," she had said then, while birthday guests milled around her, drinking Asti Spumante and talking about their own concerns. I had sat on the arm of her chair and listened while she spoke of her grandfather and the wealth he had earned by hard work and a peasant's love of the land. Nonno Vincenzo had worn rags on his back and gone hungry, putting every lira he made from his vegetable garden and vineyards into buying *la terra*—a word that means land, earth and the dirt that comes from it. After her Nonno Vincenzo had amassed a hundred acres, he allowed himself the luxury of building a large, thick-stoned farmhouse facing the Appian Way, and had five sons, four of whom had died of typhoid along with his wife. His one remaining son, Nonna's father, stayed on the farm after marriage, as was the custom. Presented with only one grandchild, a daughter, Nonno Vincenzo bought a Steinway, his one concession to refinement. In the middle of her telling, Nonna had taken a sip of spumante and puckered her face. Mirella rushed to her.

"What is it, Nonna? Aren't you feeling well?"

"Rotten, cheap stuff!" Then Nonna had continued her story, not minding her daughter's chagrined look.

"I used to think the entire Appian Way was mine," Nonna said now, two years later, lifting the piano lid and playing Chopin. "The umbrella pines, the ancient tombs. I was going to make the catacombs my wine cellars. I even dreamed I would have a father-in-law who would build me a tomb as grand as Cecilia Metella's. I had pine cones in my head." She stretched her eyes wide open, once hazel like Mirella's. "Imagine wanting to die before your father-in-law."

"What did you mean about Tamar finding a Leonardo?"

Nonna gave me a stern look. She wasn't about to be budged from her track. "You might say I inherited stupidity from my father along with a few other bad things like stubbornness. It's all in the genes now, I read in the paper. That's unloading the barrel on someone else's shoulder, but then I don't mind blaming my father for my defects. He had many, charm being the one I didn't get. He left us when I was fifteen and Nonno Vincenzo was in bed, dying. Then he spent every penny of our inheritance. We lost the Appia land, the farmhouse. The Steinway went last. Then the war came. The First World War, the one no one talks about anymore." She closed the piano lid.

"The one good thing my father did for me was teach me to ride my bicycle on the cobblestones, in the ruts left by Roman chariots. It was a smooth ride, and I've been practical ever since. Something my good-souled daughter is unable to pick up, though I do love her, God knows. Now listen to me—"

Leaning on the piano, Nonna hoisted herself up. I pushed the bench back and let her make her way back to her armchair by herself. Nonna settled herself down and spread the newspaper open on her lap. For a moment I was sure she had forgotten her thought. Then she raised her chin from folds of flesh.

"That girl found a lost Leonardo drawing. Don't get that stupid look on your face, I know what I'm talking about. Luca and Tamar have been looking for it ever since that account book turned up in Principe Maffeo's archives. A drawing of Principessa Caterina. The one who got herself killed." Nonna stopped to suck on her lip, wet with saliva. I sat down on the sofa next to her and waited.

"Tamar was all excited on Friday. In Luca's room. They were buzz-buzzing like cicadas in August. I was perspiring from heat just listening to them. She found it all right, and that's what got her killed. You ask the American Croesus and the principe. I'll wager they're behind it."

I leaned back into the understuffed sofa, the stupid expression surely still on my face. A prince? A murdered princess? A Croesus? A lost Leonardo?

"I don't believe you, Nonna."

"The meek shall not inherit the earth." She plucked her teeth out of her mouth to signal the end of the conversation.

8

When we have once known Rome, and left
her . . . sick at heart of Italian Trickery,
which has uprooted whatever faith in
man's integrity had endured till now, and
sick at stomach of sour bread, sour wine,
rancid butter, and bad cookery . . . , we
are astonished to discover that our heart-
strings have mysteriously attached themselves to the Eternal City. . . .

—NATHANIEL HAWTHORNE,
THE MARBLE FAUN

Principe Maffeo Brandeschi held a green olive coated with
oil, chopped basil, and slivers of garlic in a teaspoon.
Everyone else was going at them with fingers. "Tamar did
discover an account book that has been stored in my
archives for almost five hundred years." He spoke in
English for the benefit of Mirella's friend, Arthur Hensen.
"A line in it may indicate that my ancestor, Lorenzo
Brandeschi, commissioned Leonardo da Vinci to paint a

portrait, presumably a betrothal portrait of his daughter Caterina." The prince owned Palazzo Brandeschi in the centro storico—the historical center of Rome—and rented out the ground floor to Mirella's school, La Casa dell'Arte. "I have not yet told the Belle Arti of this discovery."

Arthur Hensen nodded his approval. "You're hoping to find the Leonardo first."

The principe eyed him coldly. "No, I simply don't think my crumbling palazzo could take the weight of all those Leonardo historians." He smiled slowly, as if his facial muscles were not used to that friendly motion, and looked at each of us in turn. "I'd rather this information remain within our little group."

A man well into his seventies, Principe Maffeo did look princely. Tall and bony, with gray hair still streaked with blond grazing the back of his collar, a long chin, the white skin of an indoor man, and melancholy, shortsighted brown eyes. A little like Velásquez's King Philip IV, sans goatee and mustache. In Italy it's easy to see everything in terms of art. Mirella likes to say, "The art is real, the rest are props." As a little girl I used to keep a seashell in my bathroom so that I could fantasize rising out of the tub as Botticelli's Venus.

We were sitting outside Nonna's only asset, a small stone farmhouse atop a hill, just beyond Magliano Sabino, sixty miles north of Rome, near the border that divides the Lazio from the Abruzzo region. Below us was the valley through which the autostrada traveled to Florence and beyond. Behind us were the Sabine Hills. The sun was out, so were the Easter lilies growing in a trough next to the fading red entrance door. I took off my sweater.

"*Un ricordo*, a memorandum," Arthur Hensen said, his olive protruding behind a cheek. "That's what you need to find if you want proof that the portrait was commissioned." He was a short, compact man with a balding round head, a bulbous nose red from too much sun, and a large voice. "Contracts weren't used for portraits, isn't that right, Mirella?" He pronounced her name Myrela.

"*Si*, Artoor, you are a good pupil," Mirella said, putting a tray of bruschetta on the picnic table. I wondered about their future as lovers.

Principe Maffeo eyed his olive sadly. "I have my doubts that Leonardo painted a portrait of Caterina. By the time he came to Rome in 1513 he didn't like painting anymore. He'd been in ill health. The Pope was preventing him from skinning corpses to study anatomy. His Roman sojourn was not a good one. And the princess was murdered."

Arthur Hensen raised a large hand, as if ready to grab a passing cloud. "Just like Tamar. There's even an old Rennaissance ballad about Caterina, right, Prince?"

The prince lowered his eyelids.

"According to the ballad," Hensen said, "this Princess Caterina was a very spoiled young lady, like a lot of young Italians." He gave Luca a pointed look.

Luca lit a cigarette. "Ballads are fictions."

"I say where there's smoke, there's fire, not too popular an idea these days." Hensen flashed his wide, sun-red face at me. "The prince has been good enough to give Luca a job sifting through his archives, but it was Tamar who found the account book. The job was my idea, really. I plan to buy that palazzo and restore it to its former glory. It's only fair—"

"I have not sold it to you yet," the prince said.

"You mustn't, Principe Maffeo!" My mother's tone was indignant. "Your history is there."

What about the history you left up in Rocca di Papa with my father, I wanted to ask her. But who was I to judge? If the woman who had answered the phone was my father's lover, then my mother was only repeating what I had done before her. *If.* I clung to that word as if it were the only bush on the cliff.

"Principe Maffeo has already begun restorations," Mirella said. She smiled apologetically, as if she'd told upsetting news.

"A few patches here and there." Principe Maffeo's face was expressionless.

Mirella took a long gulp of water, spilling half of it on her flowered dress. "I've got a sore throat from having to yell my lectures over the noise."

"Sell the rubble and run with the money," Nonna commented. Speaking no English, she was following the conversation through Mirella's translation.

Hensen gave a satisfied smile. "Go ahead, do your patching, Prince. I'm a patient man. And when you sell, it's only fair you know what you've got, right, Prince?"

"I might not sell." The prince dropped the olive into his mouth.

My mother beamed her approval. She was wearing lipstick *and* rouge, a rarity for her. She had been the one to drive the prince up here. Hensen had come on his own. She was also overdressed for a day in the Roman *campagna*. She had on a light wool rust-colored suit that looked brand-new, a silk beige blouse, and her strand of pearls. She had, as always, an old-fashioned neatness, but today she had taken extra care.

Hensen dug fingers in the ceramic olive bowl, his eyes on me. "Did you know that da Vinci hired musicians to play and sing for the Mona Lisa while she was posing?"

"You certainly know a lot about art," I said.

"That's going to be my next business."

"It already is," Mirella said. "You own La Casa dell'Arte." With elbows planted on the table, Mirella leaned her chin on her overlapping hands. She was trying to relax from her meeting at police headquarters. Commissario Perillo had not arrested Luca, which is what she feared most. He had, she said on the drive up here, been surprisingly kind and had promised to call the minute he had the results of the blood analysis. Luca's comment had been, "I don't trust him."

"La Casa is a money hole," Hensen said. "I have bigger plans."

"Is that how you got to be friends with Tamar?" I asked. "Through the school?"

Hensen looked annoyed. "Hensen Group International gives lots of scholarships for La Casa. Bolsters our humanitarian image. You know, I wanted a portrait of my daughter Debbie, but she refused to sit for one. She thought I should donate the money to the ASPCA. Now she's acting CEO while I'm here and she's still giving me a hard time!" He laughed awkwardly.

"What does the account book say about Leonardo?" I asked Principe Maffeo. His eyes were getting so soppy from looking at my mother that I was ready to label him Tamar's executioner just to get rid of him.

"The interesting entry is dated February 26, 1515." He reluctantly shifted his gaze in my direction. "It reads, 'Thirty-two scudi paid to Messer da Vinci.'"

"Now that could be the right price for a preparatory drawing," Mirella said. "The account book for the previous year makes no mention of Leonardo, so it has to be a first installment. The principe kindly let me study it." She clutched her breast. "The possibility of a new Leonardo makes my heart jump out of my mouth."

Hensen's chin shot up, his eyes betraying excitement. "The prince has a portrait of Caterina done by Melzi, one of Leonardo's pupils who came to Rome with him. Not a good painter. What's interesting though is the date of that painting—January 1516, eight months after she died. How did he know what she looked like? Dad didn't have a snapshot around."

"Leonardo's drawing."

"Right on, Simone."

"It's Simona. The thirty-two scudi could have been pay-ment of a debt," I offered. I was having a hard time believ-ing in lost Leonardos.

The prince raised long hands to heaven. "I only wish a da Vinci drawing existed. There is no shame in saying that the Brandeschi family could use a weighting of the purse. We are not known for our good fortune." He looked at my mother as if she could change all that.

My mother did not have the good grace to blush. Instead she offered him a slice of bruschetta, thickly cut country bread toasted on the grill, rubbed with a clove of garlic, salt, and doused with extra-virgin olive oil. The stuff is so good I was sure the prince would take it as a love gesture. That's how I've always interpreted her food offerings. Whoever feeds you has a firm grip on your soul.

"Mamma, I would love some," I said loudly. My mother frowned. The prince, as I expected, had manners to go with the title. He gestured the bruschetta my way. Actually he didn't look like a prince at all. He had no authority or grace to his expression, and his clothes were old—a ratty olive-green sweater over brown worn-out corduroys. A retired grade school teacher is what he looked like.

I thanked him, avoiding my mother's face. "Luca, what do you know about the drawing?"

He was now with the farmer, Oreste, over by the pizza oven Nonna had built in the stone pigsty that probably dated to the fourteenth or fifteenth century. They were haul-ing out a pan of lasagne large enough to feed half of Rome. The long picnic table already held sleek green bottles of homegrown white wine that tasted of pure grape, wooden trays filled with salami, thick slices of dark mountain prosciutto, goat cheese that had been made with yesterday's milk, bread baked by Oreste's wife that morning in Nonna's pizza oven. For once my mother wasn't in charge of the food. She was too busy enjoying the prince's cow gaze.

Luca didn't answer me. His lips were sealed on another cigarette.

"Nonna said she heard Luca and Tamar talk about the drawing." I downed more wine. Wine has no fat.

Nonna, sitting at the head of the table in the narrow strip of shade her house provided, sucked on bruschetta. She wore her husband's stained fedora, calling it her *cappello di battaglia*. Her battle hat. Her husband had died thirty years before.

"Nonna makes things up," Luca said, not looking at her.

"When I die, which is soon," Nonna said to no one in particular, "I will take my money with me." She smiled, pleased with her threat, her lips shiny with oil.

Luca dropped the lasagne pan at Nonna's end of the table with a bang. I tried again.

"Is there a chance Tamar found the drawing somewhere in Palazzo Brandeschi?"

Luca glared at Nonna. "You don't have any money." He spoke in Italian.

"Luca!" Mirella's face crumpled.

"Of course I have no money left!" Nonna shouted. "I spend it on the rent, on food, so you can hang out with your friends and not even dream of getting a paying job." Nonna threw her bread crust at the fig tree behind Luca. "I make things up!" Gorbi lunged. "What was that girl tittering about then on Friday when the two of you locked yourselves up in your room? Don't give me snake eyes, I heard the key turning. Antenna ears, you said it!"

Mirella bent her head and pushed food around on her plate. Luca scanned our faces, his expression hard.

"She died," he said, reverting to English, "and one of you killed her. For a drawing, for money, I don't know why, but one of you did it!"

Hensen shifted his weight. "Come on, boy. That's a pretty heavy accusation."

"How else do you explain it?" my mother asked. Oreste hovered over her, serving the lasagne. "Mirella's knife killed her. I remember cutting the veal with it Friday night. When Mirella and I did the dishes, it was gone. Remember, Mirella? I asked you if you had put it away."

"*Cosa?*" Nonna asked, pulling Mirella's sleeve. "*Olga che ha detto?*"

Mirella shook her head, her face blank. "No, I don't remember, Olga. I'm sorry. We don't know about the knife. The commissario has to analyze the blood first."

"*Cosa?*"

My mother smiled, a smooth, automatic parting of the lips that she had learned to use as a diplomat's wife. "*Niente, Nonna. Sciocchezze.* I said nothing of importance. Mirella's right. We have to wait for the report." She looked around the table. "I was tired that night. I even had a bit too much wine. I was excited about Simona coming."

That's why you sent my ex-husband to pick me up. My palate burned with delicious lasagne. "The knife could have dropped in the garbage." I was trying to please her again.

"The garbage!" Mirella clutched Hensen's arm. "That's what the commissario suggested. His mother lost three forks from her wedding silver that way." She beamed at me.

"I have, too," Mamma said, her smile intact. "So many things." My mother never lost anything.

"On the other hand," I said, "one of the party guests is missing today." I silently bid good-bye to my food. Too much oil and cheese. "My ex, Carlo. If the knife didn't go in the garbage, he's a suspect, too." I didn't for a minute believe Carlo had killed her. I was only trying to relieve the tension.

"Carlo has nothing to do with this story!" Mamma eyed my plate. "Why aren't you eating?"

"Jet lag, Mamma. I'm out of it."

"Nice guy, your Carlo!" Hensen cracked. "Did a great job on my documentary. He liked Tamar! Why would he knife her?"

"Why would anyone?" Mirella asked. She clenched her fists. "But we must wait for the report. We must. There's still a chance."

"That you'll win the lottery. That knife killed her." Nonna curved over the lasagne that Oreste had just placed in front of her. "From the garbage to the Dumpster, from there into some gypsy's hand. Thieves, every last one of them."

Hensen laughed and patted Mirella's bare arm. Luca watched from the other end of the table, not liking what he saw.

"Glad you have something to laugh about." Nonna was peering at the tiny portion on her plate. "Oreste, I have not turned into a sparrow!"

"Tomatoes are bad for you," Oreste muttered. "The seeds get stuck in your gut and give you a stomachache. My wife cleaned them out, but you never know." His tanned, grooved face was torn between good sense and pleasing her. Nonna aimed her eyes at the sharp cleft in his chin. "*Eh, va beh!*" He gave her another spoonful.

"That the knife landed in the garbage Dumpster is a probable theory," the prince said, his expression noncommittal. "It can only have been a random killing."

"I would like to believe that, too," my mother said quietly. It was clear she didn't. "I wish you would eat, Simona."

"This commissario could be right on." Hensen had

stopped patting Mirella and was cutting the lasagne into little squares, to cool them off, I suppose. "Good to know he's
a thinker. You saw the guys on the scooter, Simone—"

"Simona with an *a* like Liza with a *z*."

"They didn't look like me, right, Simonaah?" He
grinned.

I nodded. "No. The only thing I saw was a lot of hair on
the guy on the back of the seat."

Hensen pointed to his balding head and laughed.

I had a sense of slim, young bodies. "The two muggers
could have been hired by one of you." I felt Gorbi's wet
nose nudge my knee.

"Simona!" My mother looked shocked.

"You asked me to help."

Everyone looked uncomfortable except Nonna, who
was noisily lapping up lasagne. Mirella had stopped translating.

I dropped a fold of pasta under the table for Gorbi. "It's
as plausible as the Dumpster theory." More plausible, I
thought. If Tamar had something worth murdering for in
her satchel. If. I was beginning to wallow in "If."

"I will help," Oreste announced in Italian, limping to
Nonna's end of the table. He asked forgiveness for eavesdropping. "I used to work with American GIs after the war. I only
speak a few words." He had everyone's attention. "Seegaret,
seegar, neelon stohking, Spaahm. But I understand."

"He got rich on the black market," Nonna said, eyeing
him with what looked like pride. Mirella translated to
Hensen. "Owns fifteen hectares of land. Pigs, chickens.
Olive trees, vineyards. He's even got a couple of sheep for
when his wife turns him down."

"To this wonderful family I sell the best and the cheapest."
He grinned broadly, displaying perfectly capped teeth. His
cheeks pleated.

Nonna snorted. "You don't sell me anything. I've got my own." She slapped his thigh. "What's your forked tongue going to spit out this time?"

Oreste drew himself up. All five feet four of him. "I will swear to the police that I have a knife just like Signora Mirella's. Burned, with a dog bite on the handle. And the knife is gone. Stolen right from my kitchen!" He lifted the lid from another pan filled with *carciofi alla romana*, cabbage-sized baked artichokes stuffed with mint, garlic, and bread crumbs.

"My wife will agree with me." Oreste had to be in his seventies. Short, stocky, strong, he worked Nonna's vineyards and olive trees, plus his own land down the hill. He would, my mother thought, die for Nonna. It was a romantic notion so unlike my mother that it had to be true. Why he was so devoted, I didn't know.

"The commissario will think it was me that killed her. I will do that. It is like being in the Resistance again."

Two ringed arthritic fingers reached into the pan and tugged at an artichoke leaf. "Don't be an idiot, Oreste!" Nonna slipped the leaf in her mouth and sucked on the soft end. "Serve the food."

9

A nut found itself carried by a crow to the
top of a tall campanile, and by falling into
a crevice was released from its deadly
beak ... the wall, moved with compas-
sion, was content to shelter it in the spot
where it had fallen; and within a short
time the nut began to burst open and put
its roots in between the crevices of the
stones, and push them apart .... Then
the wall too late and in vain bewailed the
cause of its destruction.

—LEONARDO DA VINCI, FABLES

"*Gesù Maria, che macello!*" my mother declared, bending
over to rustle fingers between old and new leaves. *Macello*
means slaughter and is another of my mother's disaster
words. She was hunting for wild asparagus.

"What *macello*?" I had followed her up the hill from
Nonna's farm after lunch while most everyone else was

snoring under the sun in dilapidated deck chairs. "The run in your stocking or that lovesick prince?"

She snapped up, holding three pencil-thin asparagus in her fist. "The knife!" She lifted a leg and spotted the run. "It was gone after dinner, and it didn't end up in the Dumpster." She licked a finger and applied her saliva to the end of the run just below her knee. "Gorbi had the good grace to spill the entire contents of the garbage can on the kitchen floor. Mirella and I mopped it up. There was no knife. On the floor or anywhere in the kitchen, and Commissario Perillo expects me in his office tomorrow morning. I have no idea what I'm going to tell him."

"If you don't tell him the truth, he'll end up thinking you've got something to do with it. How long have you known Principe Maffeo?"

"Everything is so simple for you, isn't it? You just follow your nose and don't care who you hurt. I will not betray Mirella. Let that stupid policeman think I killed the girl."

"Mamma, you're the one who sees everything in black and white. And nothing I do ever pleases you! And I want to know why that man looks at you like that!"

"Are you angry with me?" The asparagus in her hand trembled.

"Yes! *Gesù Maria macello* yes! I'm angry that you're living with Mirella instead of my father and won't tell me why. I'm angry that you ask me to help you in a murder case just to get me off your back. I'm—"

"That's not true! You said you understood."

"—angry that you didn't pick me up at the airport. Why in hell did you send Carlo?"

"He still loves you."

"Bull droppings, Mamma. It's over, *finito, basta,* no more Carlo. I'm in love with someone else now."

"The New York policeman." She started walking farther

up along the edge of the woods filled mostly with chestnut trees. "You're going to marry him?"

"No. He asked me to live with him." Why had I turned Greenhouse down? With him I was safe. "Maybe I'll do that." A blackberry bush caught my skirt. "How long have you known Principe Maffeo?"

"Don't give yourself away so cheaply." She was studying the ground, covered with violets and pink wild cyclamens, both flowers no bigger than a fingernail. "If you don't know your worth, why should he?"

I disentangled myself and scrambled after her. "There's nothing cheap about living with someone you love."

"At your age there is." I stopped. She had done it again. Made me feel no bigger than those flowers she was tramping on to get to her precious asparagus.

I looked back at the farm. Between the grapevines I could see the prince's head thrown against the back of the deck chair, open mouth just begging for a bee. Mirella was reading the paper underneath the fig tree, Gorbi stretched out at her feet. Nonna napped on the second floor.

I had taken her up to her old bedroom while Mirella and my mother helped Oreste with the dishes. Nonna had pointed to splotches of faded frescoes.

"Like Pompeii," she said. "Men doing women, animals. Peas everywhere." She laughed. *Pisello*, pea, is a euphemism for penis. "Makes for fun dreams." I could barely see the figures.

While I helped her undress, she told me that during World War I, before her husband's family had bought the property, the farm had belonged to two sisters. The sisters had the frescoes painted by a local artist. Both "exercised the profession."

"Like Tamar," Nonna added, pulling the white linen sheet over her cotton slip. "A drug-addict whore. Luca gave her up. Told her he had no use for her. Mirella was going to kick her out. We're better off with her dead." She'd closed her eyes and waved me away.

If I went to live with Greenhouse, what would my mother think of me?

Mamma dropped a hand on my shoulder. "Look! I'll make spaghetti with asparagus tonight." Her fist had filled up. "You'll eat that, won't you?"

"Nonna says Mirella was going to kick Tamar out of the house and that Luca had broken up with her. Is any of that true?"

Mamma has an old-fashioned face: white skin that she always keeps powdered, thin lips that have stayed red because she seldom uses lipstick, intelligent brown eyes, a tall, curved forehead with a hairline that starts far back. She is too asymmetrical to be considered good-looking. Her forehead is too high, the chin too square and long, her eyes too small. And yet, I have seen a photograph of her at eighteen, taken at a Venetian Carnival ball, in which she looks beautiful. She is wearing a nineteenth-century blue satin dress that flatters her. Her waist is squeezed into a corset, her hips are hidden by the width of the skirt, her straight hair is parted in the middle and sweeps down each side of her face to soften the jaw. She holds a fan up and her head is tilted flirtatiously. She looks happy, shining with possibilities.

Now, as I looked at her tight, worried face, I wondered what had happened to that softness. Had my father taken it away from her? Hadn't he always adored her?

"Friday morning Mirella told Tamara she had to leave," Mamma said.

"Why?"

My mother examined my face with her keen brown eyes. She was assessing whether to trust me or not, and I realized sadly that since my divorce, which she had adamantly opposed, we had come too far apart.

"If I'm to help, I have to know."

"Of course you do." She did not sound eager. "Tamara was doing drugs in the apartment. Mirella found a used syringe in her drawer and some drug . . . heroin, I think."

"Is Luca involved?" In the dog park, Mirella had pretended surprise when I told her Tamar was on drugs.

"Of course not!" My mother's mouth twitched. "But she was a bad influence."

"Luca's thirty years old!"

"Mirella worries. Every mother has to worry now."

"Did you worry about me?" The most I had indulged in was a few joints that nauseated me.

"During those four years you were in college in New York, always." I had gone to Barnard while my father was posted in Boston. Outside the classroom, I'd gotten a crash course in sex and American swear words. Inside, I'd gotten a wonderful education.

"If Mirella knew Tamar had gotten Luca into drugs, do you think she'd kill to protect him?" I linked my arm in hers as we walked back down the steep hill.

"Yes, of course. I would."

But Mirella isn't you, I wanted to say. She's much kinder. Weaker, too. "I don't believe Mirella would."

"She only looks frail," my mother said, stopping me before we were within earshot of the others. She leaned against a gnarled olive tree that looked old enough to have seen the birth of the eighteenth century.

"I don't like that American," she declared in a half whisper. "He's pretending to be in love with Mirella, but he only wants her knowledge of art, her ins with the museums and the bureaucracy. She's been helping him for a year, without a cent of pay except for patronizing little gifts. He'll set up his business and go back to America, and Mirella will be left with a dog's love. Luca detests him."

"Luca's Mamma's little boy. He's jealous."

Mamma steered a stray wisp of hair back to where it belonged. "I do not trust Signor Hensen." She held on to my arm for support. The incline was steep here.

"What business is he setting up?"

"He wants to run the Italian museums. Ridiculous idea!"

Sounded good to me. Maybe we'd have a few less thefts and kinder guards. And the museums would stay open beyond their two P.M. closing time. I said nothing.

"Tamara was blackmailing him."

"What?" I was going to have bruises for weeks from her grip.

"I'm not sure, but I overheard a phone call she made from Mirella's bedroom Thursday afternoon. I was so incensed that she'd gone in there that I listened at the door. She was whispering so I couldn't hear very well." She shot a guarded look at the farmhouse beyond my shoulder.

"They can't hear us either. Go on."

"First she said something about the documentary party at La Casa. Then she said something like, 'I know you want to see it, Art.' I had to stop listening because Luca came back in from walking Gorbi, but I think that—"

"What do you have there to show us!"

I jumped. My mother parted her lips in that diplomatic smile of hers. "Mr. Hensen, my asparagus. Wild and delicious. Do you have these in Minneapolis?" She showed him her fistful of spindly shoots.

"If they grow under ice and snow, we got 'em! We got wild rice, which beats wild asparagus in my book. I was in that business once." Hensen, still sleepy-eyed, had napped in the sun and the redness of his nose had spread over his face.

"What business are you in now, Mr. Hensen?" I asked. He looked perfectly innocent. Tamar's "I know you want to see it," could refer to many things that had nothing to do with blackmail. A drawing she'd done, an article that might interest him. Her body, if Nonna was right.

"Art, Simona. That's my name and that's my business." He brayed with laughter. A caterpillar legged it off his shoe, fast. "I get this dumb only when I have an elegant foreign lady looking at me like I shouldn't have come out of my good mother's womb." He was staring at my mother. Her expression was not pleased, and he looked angry. How much had he overheard?

"I don't like being made to feel like I'm a lesser human being, ma'am. So what'd I do?" Hensen crossed his arms and lifted his chin. "Did I pick up the wrong fork, chew with my mouth open, eat the fruit with my hands? Halitosis, body odor, what is it?"

My mother looked down on him, taking full advantage of her height and the higher slope she was standing on. "I do not agree with your assessment of the value of wild rice," she said in her careful, clipped English. "Wild asparagus are much better."

He gave her a close-mouthed grin. "I'd like to believe you. Why don't you and your daughter come to dinner at my place tomorrow night? Mirella's coming. So's the old lady and Carlo." He raised his eyebrows at me. "You don't mind Carlo? Let bygones be bygones, right? Carlo's a good guy and a crackerjack editor."

My mother, pretending that she needed support, grabbed my arm again. "We'd be delighted."

"Good!" He wasn't smiling. "I have an announcement to make that might make you change your mind about yours truly." He turned down the hill, his balding head barely clearing the vines.

"What announcement?" I asked.

"The contract." My mother looked stupefied. "He must have gotten the Ministry of Culture to agree to let him run the museums. I told him it was absurd to even think of it! They're going to let him commercialize our artistic patrimony. How did he do it?"

"Just like you've done everything in your life, Mamma. Never letting up."

"I wish that were true. Now what am I going to tell that commissario?"

"Everything. I'll come with you, if you want."

"I can manage alone."

You always have, I thought.

The thick, snarled traffic getting back to Rome was Hamptons, Long Island, bad. Sunday is the sacred day, especially for Romans. The pealing bells of Rome's more than eight hundred churches send the family—kids, mother, father, grandmother, grandfather—off, not to church, but to the countryside north or south of the city, or to the sea. Their aim is not to take a healthy walk to pick the minuscule pink-edged daisies that cover the fields at this time of year, or even to sit and enjoy the view that Henry James marveled at. Their aim is a table in a crowded trattoria with dogs and cats and children running around while everyone overdoses on homemade fettuccine, roast chicken, pork cutlets, baby lamb, all washed down by liters of wine and mineral water. Then a snooze in the car or under the shade of the tree as a radio announcer screams out the fate of a soccer ball and little girls huff with boredom and little boys dream of someday being the soccer stadium star.

As my mother wove slowly in and out of small towns and backways to avoid the worse traffic of the highway, I both huffed and dreamed. I huffed because my presence was no comfort to my mother, and a very young part of me dreamed that whatever problem—with her life or my father—had made my mother leave her home, I could solve it. I would solve everything for her. And I would start with Tamar's death, as she wanted me to.

I burrowed into the hard seat of my mother's brand-new blue Panda—a car that would turn into a twirling leaf if a bus should speed by—and put facts together. Like everyone else, I was convinced that Mirella's knife had been the murder weapon. According to my mother, the knife had not fallen into the garbage, so I ruled out the random-mugging-gone-nasty. The knife was Mirella's, and it had disappeared Friday night, which meant that only someone who had been in the apartment that night could have taken it. That someone could be Principe Maffeo, Arthur Hensen, Carlo, Luca, Mirella, Nonna, or my mother. Tamar had not come back to sleep there that night so she could not have taken the knife that killed her.

Six suspects. I ruled out my mother and tried to eliminate Mirella and Nonna, but I was trying to leave my emotions out of my reasoning, an effort that always gives me a headache. I put Mirella and Nonna back on the list. Then I thought of Gorbi. Maybe he'd grabbed the knife to lick off the veal juices in some private corner of that none too neat apartment. I suggested that to my mother and Nonna, who was half asleep in the backseat.

"And then what?" There was cold impatience in my mother's voice. She was tired, the traffic was heavy, I told myself. She had refused my offer to drive the car.

"Then maybe someone came into the apartment the next morning and found it. A delivery boy, a maid, the portiere. I don't know. A perfect stranger. Wouldn't that be nice, if it were someone you didn't know at all?"

Nonna snorted. "You want your barrel full and your husband drunk. Nice it isn't going to be. Life isn't." She was smoking her third Pall Mall that day, two smoked in the car. Mirella was in the Mini Morris in front of us with Principe Maffeo and Luca. I could see Gorbi's head drooping against the rear windshield.

"There was no delivery boy, no maid before Tamara was killed," my mother said.

"And now only the rich have a portiere to look after their buildings!" Nonna sent a veil of wonderful smoke my way. "We've got a buzzer that's so loud I'm going to hear it in my grave."

I leaned toward the driver's seat, pretending I wanted to look in the rearview mirror. The sky was darkening and the stream of cars had turned on its lights. It's a moment I find immensely sad.

"What if it's someone in the family?" I whispered to my mother in English.

"I can hear grass grow," Nonna whispered back.

I turned around. "In English?"

"No." Nonna tossed the cigarette out of the car. "Only Italian grass, and French when I feel like it. Sheet. Tamar's favorite word. That I know. Sheet. *Merde*. What did you say?"

"I was asking what was happening to our family."

"Stop planting carrots." Carrots are lies. "Luca and Mirella don't have the liver to kill anyone. If that commissario needs someone to blame, let him pick on me. And Simona, you stay out of it." Nonna's finger dug into my neck. "Friday night Carlo was playing man of the house, carving that veal roast Olga made as if he'd been a butcher all his life."

I swung my head around. "Carlo carving? Since when?"

"Nonna's the one planting carrots," my mother said. "I carved every centimeter of that roast. I was hoping to save some for you, Simona. You can't get good veal in America."

Nonna clacked her teeth. "They ate as if veal grows on trees!"

"You've stopped eating on me," my mother complained.

I didn't answer. We were passing the cutoff to Sacrofano, a medieval town I'd been to with Carlo on many Sunday outings. The cool air from the trees was now filling with the sounds of shuffling feet and tired voices. I thought I could still smell the fennel, the *porchettaro* used to stuff his roast pig. Carlo and I had made love in a small hotel there one afternoon, too hungry to last out the drive to Rome. The details of that memory tried to press themselves back into my brain. I fought them by thinking of the choking webs that families spin around each other. I had assumed that, by going to America, I had broken free.

"The first thing to concentrate on is motivation," my mother said as we entered the outskirts of Rome. Nonna snored in the back.

"Yes, motivation is certainly it." My tone made her turn to look at me. She knew I wasn't talking about Tamar's death.

"Go to Mirella's class tomorrow," Mamma said. "Talk to Tamara's friends. They will help."

"I know what to do." Why did her advice always sound like an order? "And why do you insist on calling her Tamara? The woman's name was Tamar!"

She pushed the palm of her hand hard against the horn as an Alfa-Romeo in front of her braked for a hooker standing under a huge sycamore, a signature fire burning at her feet.

"The name Tamar sounds as if the girl was missing a part of her soul, which she was." Honking, Mamma swerved around the car. The entire Viale Tor di Quinto was lined with sycamores, and *"lucciole"*—fireflies—the Roman nickname for the hookers warming themselves by a fire. They were another landmark that rooted me back in the past.

"I want everyone to be whole." She gave up honking the horn at the light. "Are you?"

"Yes, Mamma. I am." I put conviction in my voice. "The past is dead, long live the future. What about you? Can we talk about it?"

"I don't believe you. One can't just fly to another country and find a new identity."

"One can try, Mamma." Was she thinking of new possibilities for herself?

My mother frowned, pushing her face close to the windshield, like old people do when they drive. I wanted to lean her back and brush the loose skin off her chin.

On the left I could see Ponte Milvio, the oldest bridge of Rome, where Constantine defeated the Emperor Maxentius. As the light changed and we drove past the bridge, toward Mussolini's Foro Italico, I thought of the bridge's nickname—Ponte Mollo, the soft bridge. Soft because it had constantly needed repairs throughout the centuries.

Mamma and I were a little *mollo* at the moment, I decided, but we'd survive, too.

10

❦

You cannot take one step in Rome without
bringing together present and past, without
juxtaposing different pasts.
—Germaine de Staël, Corrine, or Italy

When we got out in front of the apartment on Viale
Angelico, I asked to borrow Mirella's car.

"I want to ride around nighttime Rome," I said. "You
know, reconnect." Mirella threw me the keys, which Gorbi
lunged for. Luca was helping Nonna out of our car. The
prince had been dropped off somewhere along the way.

"These asparagus smell good." My mother crinkled
the paper bag noisily and took a long sniff, her way of
calling attention to the fact that I was going to miss out
on her cooking.

"I'm not used to eating so much anymore."

"I noticed." She looked at me sternly for a moment.
"Why not use my car?"

"I like old cars," I lied. "I can bang them up."

"Don't you dare!" Mirella laughed.

I waved and slipped into the Mini Morris. Gorbi raised both neck and paw with an expectant moan. I opened the passenger door and let him leap in. I needed the company.

I maneuvered back and forth, trying to get out of the tight parking space with Gorbi spinning himself in a circle in the backseat until he found the right spot to settle into. My mother presided from the sidewalk.

"Where *are* you going?" she called out when the Mini Morris was finally free. I gunned the motor, pretending that I hadn't heard, and rattled out of there.

Up to the Castelli Romani, the Roman fortresses in the Alban Hills southeast of the city, where the aristocracy sought refuge in the Middle Ages while Rome drowned in anarchy. That's where I was going. To Rocca di Papa, the Pope's fortress, to be more precise. To see my father and that woman who had answered the phone.

I was off to find solutions. Taking my mother's car would have felt like a betrayal.

"First you have to concentrate on motivation," my mother had said. I couldn't begin to know what had motivated Tamar's death. I knew too little of the players, nothing of the world she had moved in. It would take time, and lots of questions. And my heart wasn't in it. My heart was with the picture of my parents I carried to America: Mamma walks with Gigi, my dad, a sweater impeccably folded over her arm, the other arm tucked in his care. He stands as straight as he can, to minimize the fact that he's several inches shorter. He wears his pants a little high on his waist, his perfectly ironed cotton polo lies tight against his sinking chest. He is getting old, but he looks proud, as if he's lived a good life. She looks, as always, somewhat stern, but satisfied, even pleased. Their arms stay linked, and I think I can always lean into them.

It took me forty-five minutes to get up to the *Castelli Romani* and I still had a steep climb ahead. Rocca di Papa is the highest of the thirteen villages, and crawls over the slopes of Monte Cavo. "Where the air is purest," my father had said.

"Where the biggest villa is owned by the butcher," Mamma had retorted, hoping to strike at my father's snobbism. She wanted to stay in Rome.

Maybe that is why she left, I thought, as Gorbi climbed in the front seat and nudged my face. I was beginning to regret the drive. What if the woman was there? Would I say, "Get out of my father's house, you whore!" What had I said to my best friend Daisy as her mouth shaped itself into a surprised O and my husband slid off her hips? Nothing. I'd just slammed the door and run hard down the stairs, down the street, as if I were chasing after a missed life.

Gorbi whined.

"What is it, baby? Bathroom?" I'd reached the lower and newer part of the village. My parents' house was farther up, at the edge of the medieval part of town. I turned into a narrow unlit street behind a restaurant and stopped the car. Gorbi leaped out. I was slower. He ran for a corner. Behind the garden gate, a cat hissed. I walked along the one block of the street, breathing in the crisp air. The back of the restaurant had a glassed-in terrace filled with diners overlooking the *campagna* below. I stopped to take in the breathtaking view of a distant lake of lights, the south side of Rome. It was too dark to see the real lakes, Nemi and Albano.

I had been in Italy almost two days and had seen little of my city. Appreciated even less. On the way here, only the sight of the Colosseum lit up for the night had tugged at some emotion which I refused to release.

"*Dai*, Gorbi, let's go." I heard the clatter of the restaurant's kitchen and longed for a glass of the cool white wine these hills are famous for—bad wine laced with good memories. Gorbi's nose was sifting through the restaurant's garbage.

"*Su, Gorbi.*" I pulled at his collar and looked up. Gigi, my father, was standing at the corner of the main road, a few feet in front of Mirella's car. He was in his waiting mode, arms crossed over his sinking chest. I used to fish for a smile from my mother by mimicking that stance. If he was waiting, he hadn't come alone. I held on tight to the dog, who slurped on something.

Gigi, short for Gabriele Griffo. I had called him that from the beginning, wanting, I think, to be no different from my mother. Gigi, my daddy.

"*Scusami,*" a woman said, joining him. He said something I didn't catch. My heart was making too much noise.

Whatever Gigi said made her laugh, and he opened his arm to her. She, slim figured, bleached blond hair sparkling under the restaurant lamp, took Gigi's arm. They walked away, out of my sight, and for a moment all I thought was that she was shorter than my father. He would like that.

I dropped down and put my cheek against Gorbi's ribs. I heard him chomp, felt his chest expand and deflate with each breath. I breathed with him and smelled the warmth of his lean body. And I cried. Gorbi gave me a tomato-sauced lick.

Back in Rome, I stopped at a bar behind the Colosseum and looked up my ex-husband's number. In my head, I saw lions eating up Christians. "Carlo, I'm coming over, and you're going to tell me all about Tamar."

———

"This is where I met her," Carlo said, after ordering a bottle of white wine from a black-clad girl who could have been Madonna's double. "She was sketching in a corner inside." We were sitting just a few blocks behind Piazza Navona, at an outside table of Jonathan's Angels, a piano bar. The dimly lit interior spilled sensually beautiful people out into the narrow street called Via della Fossa. *Fossa* translates into ditch or tomb. Either was appropriate.

"I noticed her because she looked like you." Carlo poured wine into our glasses. I bit into a pistachio nut, shell and all.

"The way Tamar held her head, she was instantly familiar." I had refused to go up to Carlo's apartment.

"She liked to hang out here with this lot. Spoiled brats most of them. Too rich, too pretty, too young."

"Noisy." A table of six was shooting rounds of laughter into my ear. Gorbi ducked under the table. He's a sensitive dog.

"She wanted so badly to be one of them," Carlo said, offering me a full wineglass. "And she took to Nino, the owner. He's a stuntman, trapeze artist, sculptor, painter. She was envious of his ability to change." Carlo raised his hand. "Ciao, Nino." A pigtailed, white-haired truck of a man flexed a sea gull tattoo in our direction.

"His American wife left him," Carlo said too casually. I gulped wine and scratched Gorbi's reassuringly soft ear.

"She took the kids with her. One of them is named Jonathan." Carlo had not wanted kids, which was fine with me now. "He misses her." Abandoned dog eyes.

"Tamar," I reminded him, preferring to look inside the bar with its Caravaggioesque paintings glowing lamp yellow. If I'd had Carlo's children, I would never have had the courage to leave him.

"Painted by the owner," Carlo said. "Imitative, like

Mirella's work. That was Tamar's assessment. I like the paintings myself, but then I can't even copy stick figures." He huddled closer.

What was he looking for? Pity? Wrong moment, wrong woman. "Tamar told Mirella she met you for the first time at the documentary reception at La Casa. You told the ispettore the same thing. Why did you both lie?" His cologne hadn't changed. Eau de cologne du Coq by Guerlain.

"Why did she do anything? She wanted a family. 'Starting off with a full tube of paint,' she called it. She thought she'd sprung out of charcoal dust someone had brushed off some bad drawing." Carlo's expression changed, became sincere, concerned. For a second I recognized the man I'd fallen in love with. My throat tightened. Wandering *coq*, I reminded myself. Just like my father.

"Why did you lie?"

Carlo pressed fingers in his graying hair. "Tamar was greedy. She sketched the truth to her liking, she railed against people, but she was intelligent, talented . . . " He had no intention of answering me, another one of his habits. "Give her a hug and Tamar's face would glow as if I'd stuck a candle under her chin."

"You like having that kind of power."

Carlo looked startled by my snarl. "Hey, we're on neutral territory here."

"I'm going to find out who killed Tamar and then I'll know why you lied." My mother was going to get Tamar's killer served to her on a platter.

"You sound determined."

"I am." Somewhere in that anger I knew the head I wanted was my father's, but I wasn't ready to face him yet.

"Olga would like that."

"Don't you have your own mother to chitchat with?" A

mother who had asked me to leave her house when I told her why I was divorcing her son. "I've developed a knack for blood, and I have you to thank for it." I downed my glass. Pinot Grigio, my favorite. It didn't help that Carlo had remembered.

"Olga and I are friends. She was very supportive of me after you left."

"Fantastico!" I held out the glass for more.

He smiled at me. He still had a smile guaranteed to make most women rush to his defense. It had no effect, I told myself. Neither did the round face that looks like it always wants to have fun, or the dimple on his right cheek, or the curly cheruby hair. He could join my father and the murderer on that platter.

"Tamar wasn't my lover," Carlo announced. He didn't refill my glass.

"You already said that. Who cares?"

"Olga hasn't left your father." Carlo was always good at understanding what was behind even the blandest of my moods.

I reached for the bottle. "What makes you know everything?" Gorbi pulled at his leash, raring to go. Clever dog. I threw him a pistachio.

"You shouldn't drink when you're mad." Carlo watched me pour, his smile still trying. I almost told him about the woman with my father. I was straining to unload the sight of those two, but instead I sat back on the plastic seat and watched the man behind Carlo stroke a woman's long black hair. She swayed, her eyes closed. His other hand was underneath the table.

"Wine and anger make you morbid and weepy. And I don't know why Olga's at Mirella's, but I don't believe she's left Gigi for good. They're too devoted to each other." He took the bottle from my hand. "They have a sense of duty to their marriage I've always admired. Why didn't we have that?"

Bad question. "Tamar was on drugs according to the police commissioner. That could be a possible motive for her death. She owed money, she stole drugs. Or did she really find a lost Leonardo drawing that someone desperately wanted?" I filled him in on Nonna's theory and the lunch discussion at her farm. "What's your guess?"

Carlo's face rucked up. "She was using when I met her. That's why I lied to Mirella and the ispettore. Tamar asked me to. She wanted to pretend we met when she was free of drugs. I found her a rehab center. I made sure she went."

"Since when have you become a Good Samaritan?"

He filled my glass, then rubbed the back of his hand against mine. "People change, Minetta."

"Don't call me that."

"You're Minetta to me." It had been the name of a cat he'd loved very much as boy. He'd refused any other.

"Well, now I'm Simona." When I'd first met him, I'd been charmed by that loyalty and happy to let him rename me to his liking. "Mirella found a syringe in Tamar's drawer at the apartment, which looks as if Tamar might have gone back to her old ways."

"I don't believe it. I won't."

"You never did like women slipping out of your grasp."

Carlo jumped out of his chair and plunged into the semi-darkness of the bar. Against one wall I could see a jumble of vases, tarnished copper pots, a few Art Deco lamps. The place looked like a monument to kitsch. The piano player banged out "Black Bottom." My father had taught me a dirty version of that song when I was still in grade school. "Lola, why aren't you in school? Under the sheets you're a fool." My mother didn't speak to Gigi for a week, but I had felt initiated into the adult world. Damn my father!

Carlo came back with a stunning tall blond woman wearing ironed jeans hemmed above the ankle, an Italian twist on the American classic.

"Simona, meet Lea." He moved back a chair for her, something he hadn't done for me. "Lea, tell her about Tamar. My word is dung."

Lea gave me a soft hand and a sad smile I didn't understand right away. "I'm Tamar's counselor at the rehab center. She'd been clean for two months." She sat down in one fluid motion and added, "The center's around the corner," as if she needed to justify her presence at this piano bar. "Tamar was getting happier every day, stronger. She loved staying at Mirella's house." She leaned into me, her eyes drinking me in. She made me feel as though I held something rare. It was disconcerting.

"For the first time, Tamar had a sense of family and it was doing her a world of good. She was clean. She was going to make it." Lea was about my age, but I sensed she was light-years ahead of me in wisdom. She exuded a calm strength that made me instantly trust her. It was her face, I think, square-jawed, with wide sculpted planes that caught the white light of the street lamp.

"With Carlo's help she would have become a good, solid person." Lea turned her face to him.

Carlo looked uncomfortable. "I just brought her to you, Lea. You're the one who helped."

"Are you sure she was free of drugs?" I asked. "Mirella was worried that Tamar wouldn't get through her exams, she was so nervous. That's why she took her in. She found heroin and a syringe in Tamar's drawer and told her she'd have to leave. According to Mirella's mother, even Luca had a fight with Tamar, gave her up as a girlfriend."

Lea looked at Carlo, a question in her blue eyes.

"Tell her," Carlo said.

She moistened her lips, clearly uncomfortable. "Tamar liked to manipulate people. It was part of her insecurity. Please don't judge her harshly. She'd had an absolutely frightful childhood!" Lea's broad face filled with dismay. "I don't think I would have survived." I wondered if she woke up every morning caring for the entire world.

"Tamar pretended to be nervous and upset so Mirella would take her in," Carlo said. "I told her it was pretty rotten." He shot Lea a glance.

"The girl had been denied everything," she said.

Carlo started playing with the label on the wine bottle, an old nervous habit. "I didn't think anything bad would come of it." Without thought, I stopped him with my hand as I had always done.

Carlo's expression softened. Lea looked at both of us. I hid my embarrassment by tugging at Gorbi with the offending hand. I'm sure that people around us continued making noise, but to my ear, or my heart, I should say, there was a beat of silence. In that silence I did not live in New York; I was still young, still married, still convinced that "we" was the hook I could hang my life on.

"Now Tamar's dead," Lea said finally, taking a long drink from Carlo's glass. An intimate gesture I registered. As intimate as mine had been.

"You don't think Tamar's dead because she went to live with Mirella?" I asked.

Lea shook her beautiful head. She had curly blond hair that fell on her shoulders like just-sheared wool. "I think she might have died because she wanted a family and she would do anything to get one."

"Blackmail?"

"It's possible. She reminded me of one of those street cats that stalk you with distended, starved eyes and when you reach down to touch it, it curls up into a hiss of sheer terror. I think Tamar was constantly frightened of being alone, but she made it very difficult for anyone to love her." Lea's face softened into sadness. "She detested being touched."

"Was Tamar desperate or crazy enough to steal a Leonardo?" I asked.

Lea's surprised eyes swept over Carlo's face. "Did she find the drawing?"

Carlo shrugged. "We don't know."

"She would have told me," Lea said. "Although it might explain her euphoria Friday night. I don't like to think she didn't trust me."

"What do you know about the missing Leonardo?" I asked Lea.

"I always thought that drawing was her little fantasy."

"Not so little." Carlo opened a pack of cigarettes. "A lot of money would be involved. Five, six million dollars maybe?"

Lea held out her hand for a cigarette. "Money wasn't Tamar's primary motive for searching for the drawing. At least not at first, I think. She said it would be neat to find something truly artistic, something she would donate to the Metropolitan Museum or the National Gallery. 'Gift of Tamar Deaton.' I pointed out that the drawing, if found, would belong to Principe Maffeo. That upset her for a few days, then she came back and told me she would find the drawing because the supposed sitter, Caterina Brandeschi, was her soulmate, maybe even her ancestor. It was a matter of fate." Lea's smile was gentle, motherly. "I think she fantasized about being a spoiled princess in Renaissance Rome. Leonardo and Raphael were both here at the time. Michelangelo had just finished the Sistine Chapel. That's exciting for an American art student."

"She once told me the missing drawing was going to

look just like her." Carlo dropped a cigarette in Lea's hand. He still smoked MS, the most popular state brand, popularly known as *Morte Sicura*, certain death, or *Merda Statale*, state shit.

"She came from northern New York State," Lea said. "One winter all she remembered eating was apples she and her foster mother had stolen from orchards."

Carlo shook his head at that deprivation. His surgeon father had taken good material care of him.

"How did she get from stealing apples to art student at La Casa dell'Arte in Rome?" I shook my head no to a cigarette. Carlo looked surprised. In his day, I'd been a two pack a day smoker.

"I didn't ask," Carlo said. That's how he'd accepted me when we'd first met. Without curiosity. "Personal histories spin false webs," he'd said, refusing to tell me about himself. "Why not discover each other by how we are together." The discoveries had been wonderful the first years.

Lea leaned her golden head toward Carlo's flashing Zippo and lit her cigarette. "That American who wants to buy the Brandeschi palazzo gave Tamar a scholarship."

"Arthur Hensen," I filled in. "Yes, he told me."

Lea waved her cigarette. "The 'Ensen Group Art Scholarship. Tamar was its first recipient, she told me. She was very grateful to Signor 'Ensen."

"Arthur Hensen mentioned that Caterina Brandeschi was also killed," I said.

"Shades of an idea for a movie script." Carlo tipped his chair forward. "Tell me more."

"Are you into screenwriting now?"

"The Italian cinema is dead. I'm thinking Hollywood. Was it a gory death?"

"I don't know." I turned to Lea.

She buttoned her green quilted jacket over a perfectly ironed white cotton blouse. "It's too long ago. I try to concentrate on the present and the future for my charges." She stood up. "Tamar came by the center from La Casa late Friday night. She'd been helping out with Saturday's school party, which wasn't like her, really. She didn't get along with any of the students there. Of course, being shunted from foster home to foster home, she never developed a sense of community. Friday night she glowed and said not a word about Mirella asking her to leave or that Luca had broken up with her." She dropped her half-smoked cigarette on the cobblestoned street and stepped on it. Her face had shuttered down.

"Do you know where she spent the night?" I asked.

Lea shook her thick head of hair. "I assumed at Mirella's."

"Carlo, do you know?"

He took a deep drag of his cigarette, then smiled at both of us. "No. I was her friend, not her keeper." The smile was too gentle, too smooth. He was lying, and I got the urge to clip off his long, thick brown eyelashes to get a better look at his eyes and find the truth.

"Tamar told me she had a gift for you, Carlo. Something that made her laugh. She wouldn't tell me what it was." Lea stood there, pulsing her thighs against the round plastic table, seemingly not knowing whether to go or not. "Let's hope it didn't get stolen."

"Carlo"—he'd stopped smiling at last—"did Tamar know you'd be at Mirella's Saturday morning?"

"Yes. I told her I was picking you up at the airport and taking you to Mirella's where we were going to have lunch."

"That explains why she said '*doni*' in the plural. She had your gift and mine in that satchel."

"That's a shame," Lea said. "Carlo loves presents. His

birthday is April . . . " She blushed. "How stupid of me. *Buonanotte*." She quickly slipped back into the crowded black cave of Jonathan's Angels.

"She's in love with you." I caught myself from saying it out loud, sorry for her and jealous at the same time. "Nice woman," I ventured instead, peering at Carlo for some indication that her feelings were reciprocated.

"The best," he answered with a sweet face that spoke of zero.

I drank more wine, the liquid now vinegary in my mouth. I didn't know what I had hoped for. Years had gone by since I had left this man, but Lea's love for Carlo upset me, as did my own proprietary gesture. I hadn't come to Rome to dredge up the past. I didn't want to. I was no longer in love with him, so what was I clinging to?

Tamar's killing. That was the event to focus on.

"Do you think Tamar was capable of blackmail?"

"I think she was capable of anything. She was that needy. Drugs made it worse for her."

"But you saved her?"

Carlo scraped at the wine label again. "Is that beyond the realm of possibility?"

"I guess I'm surprised by how much you were involved with her. Without being her lover, I mean."

Carlo hunched down, his face knotted with intensity. "Minetta, give me another chance. I still love you."

My stomach did a nauseating roll as if the ground were suddenly buckling. "I'm here for Tamar. Only for her. Please." I felt as if I'd lost my footing and suddenly had no father, mother, husband, no one and nothing to keep me from falling. It was a feeling Tamar must have lived with every moment of her life.

I grabbed Gorbi's leash. Holding on to the dog, I fled from Via della Fossa—the street of the ditch.

11

Wherever the Roman conquers, there he dwells.
—LUCIUS ANNAEUS SENECA, MORAL ESSAYS

The house was quiet except for the jingle of Gorbi's collar as he padded down the corridor to Mirella's room. I crept into the living room, dragging the phone with me. The sofa had already been made up into a bed. Sweet Mamma. I snapped on the light and started to dial. I got as far as 001-212 and then stopped. I couldn't remember Greenhouse's phone number. A blank. I tried remembering my office number. Nothing. Forget my apartment number; I have no idea what that is. Ever.

Don't panic, I told myself. You haven't lost Greenhouse, just his number. You can look it up in your address book. Look up Greenhouse's number? That was humiliating! I couldn't do it. Not to the man I make love with, the man I may want to spend the rest of my life with if I ever get over . . . over what?

What was I thinking about here?

The living room door inched open with a low groan. Gorbi jingled in, jumped up on the sofa, and tried to curl his fifty pounds tightly enough to fit onto my lap. I welcomed his warmth and looked at the time. It was seven P.M. on a New York Sunday.

He's at the movies with Willy. He's cooking for Willy. No, he's probably on the phone ordering steamed dumplings and moo shu pork from Columbus Avenue. Maybe Willy's saying, "Too bad Simona's not here to cook pasta, huh, Dad? I mean that's the only reason we miss her, right?"

"Pasta's healthier." Dad smiles.

I remembered the number.

We exchanged greetings and I miss you's. We had one of those terrible connections where my words echoed back just as he was answering. I told him about Tamar's death, speaking slowly. Being a homicide detective, he was more interested in my parents. I hedged. Greenhouse is not one to offer opinions easily, but in those few days when I debated whether to come to Rome or not, I had felt he didn't want me to go.

"Children can have a strong influence," he'd said cautiously. Assuming that he was thinking of the last years of his own marriage, when Willy was the glue that kept two unhappy people together, I had taken the comment as a warning not to go.

"Have you spoken to them?" he asked again. "Do you know what's going on?"

My parents' problems seemed terribly private in that moment, something not to be launched across an ocean, with the words hardly settling in Greenhouse's ear before they boomeranged. "No, not yet," I said, the lie lengthening the distance between us. "Tamar's death has taken the forefront." I explained about the missing Leonardo, gave him what I knew about the people possibly involved, told him of the Sunday lunch, the knife, even that Commissioner Perillo resembled a Caravaggio painting. I was trying to weave a rope of words to reconnect us and pull us together. When I had stepped on the plane at Kennedy Airport, I had felt solidly bound to New York, a city I thought I had almost conquered, a place I wanted to dwell in. Now, I didn't know. Even Greenhouse's voice, usually warm and comforting, sounded hollow to my ear.

The telephone, underwater cables, Mirella's old dial phone, Gorbi's weight numbing my thighs, they were to blame for this horrible sense of discomfort.

"What did you order for dinner?" I asked inanely. This phone call was going to cost the plane ticket back if I didn't shut up.

"You've seen your ex-husband?"

"Yes, he hasn't changed." I tried to sound reassuring even though Greenhouse is not a jealous man. "Let me say hello to Willy." Greenhouse complied without a word.

"I go back tomorrow," Willy yelled in my ear. He was in ninth grade at a Manhattan private school, struggling with the high school's expectations. He had just finished spring break. "They're going to zap me with papers and tests, and I bet you're having a great time. Dad's watching *60 Minutes* and I'm waiting for pepperoni pizza."

"That sounds pretty good to me." I knew nothing of sports or cars, and Willy was still too wary of my presence in his father's life to be comfortable talking about his feelings.

"Pizza's okay," Willy conceded. I could picture his freckled face, with cornsilk lashes hiding sweet, curious blue eyes.

"I bet your dad ordered extra pepperoni." I felt myself relax. I had rituals and itineraries in New York too, I realized.

It was just a matter of letting both countries, both sets of people and ways settle in and find their grooves in my psyche, just as Gorbi had done on my lap. Maybe the two lives would not weigh as much as the dog.

"Extra pepperoni. You got it on the nose." Willy laughed. Greenhouse always used that expression around his son, dotting Willy's nose with a finger.

"I miss you," I told Willy, finding it easier to talk to the son than the father. Willy had no one to take his place in Rome.

"You do?" With divorced parents, Willy doesn't want to be left out of things, hadn't liked my leaving for Rome. "Dad'll miss you," he'd said, careful to keep himself out of that emotion.

"I miss you terribly," I said over the phone. In Mirella's dark living room that held nothing of my past Roman life, I did miss them both. Gorbi pawed my chest, wanting attention. "I better say good-bye now."

Greenhouse came back on. "I'm sorry about your parents. I'm sorry about the girl's death. You must feel pulled in all directions, Sim, and I wish I could be there with you, but probably I'd make it worse." He stopped, maybe waiting for his words to ricochet back to the west side of Manhattan. I widened my eyes in the dark, as if that gesture would allow me to look into his kind, wise face.

"I love you," he added. "Come home soon."

"Thank you," I said, the words *home* and *love* dropping heavily into my ear. I did not trust myself to say anything else.

"When can I call you?" Greenhouse asked.

"I'll be in and out. It's not an excuse. I really will be. I'll call you."

"You're determined to find the girl's killer."

"Yes."

I expected the usual lecture about letting the professionals do the work. Instead, I heard him try for a chuckle. "That Roman nose of yours can't stay crime-free, huh?"

"I guess not."

"Be careful."

"Yes, honey, I will be. Thanks. I'll call you tomorrow night."

"Good. I'll be your comic relief, the commercial break between the drama. 'Mr. Clean gets rid of dirt.' Psychic dirt's a specialty." He was trying hard.

"You could do me a favor."

"Sure."

"Look into a company called Hensen Group International."

"What do you need?" He sounded eager.

"I wish I knew. Arthur Hensen mentioned a daughter he's not getting along with. She's acting CEO now."

"You think she enters into this?"

"No, but I'm curious as to why they don't get along. I think Mirella's in love with him, and if he's a louse, it would be nice to know."

"You can't get distracted in a murder investigation," Willy chipped in from an extension. "You gotta go straight."

"Willy, Italians don't know from straight. Unless we're giving directions. Then it's *sempre dritto* right into the Mediterranean."

Willy laughed. "You need me there. Send me a postcard of Michelangelo's *Pietà*."

"It'll be faster if I bring it."

"No, send it with a Vatican stamp for my collection."

"Will do."

"Sim?" Greenhouse's breath was strong.

"Yes?"

"Finding that girl's killer might add a notch to your detecting belt, but it's not going to solve anything personal."

"But she'll feel like she's in control of something," Willy the Wise offered. "I do that when I can't write a paper. I go out and play hockey. I'm good at it, I win, I come home and I get the paper over with. Just send me a plane ticket, Simona, and we'll get it licked in a couple of weeks."

Inside me a smile spread. "Last time it took us under a week."

"We've got to leave room for sightseeing and eating."

We hung up after more echoed good nights. Stretching alongside Gorbi on the sofa, I wished I were back in New York.

At nine o'clock the next morning my mother was on the bus that would take her to police headquarters—she'd refused my company—and Mirella and I were crowded into a small corner bakery at Campo dei Fiori, waiting for a long slice of the best white pizza the world can produce. She was filling me in on Leonardo da Vinci. "It was his second trip to Rome and he stayed three years—late 1513 to 1516. Giuliano de' Medici, his patron, put him up at Belvedere Palace in the Vatican. Lucky man!" Mirella was on her way to Piazza Farnese to teach an open-air class on Renaissance architecture. Tamar had been in this class and I'd tagged along, hoping to talk to some of the students.

"Leonardo didn't do much painting in that period. Vasari talks about two pictures, but he's an old gossip. Nothing's been found."

We were shoving our way up to the short counter where three men sorted out a cacophony of orders. Standing in line is an impossibility for most Romans. They take pride in chaos. The victory tastes sweeter.

"Could one of those pictures have been Caterina Brandeschi's portrait?"

"Vasari says they were for Baldassare Turini da Pescia, not Lorenzo Brandeschi. We do know Leonardo wrote a book during his Roman stay. He also designed a stable, worked on drying up the Pontine Marches, drafted letters complaining about a German workman assigned to him." Mirella elbowed for both of us. I was out of training and the smell of bread and pizza baking was weakening my joints. "Some historians think he was being petty, but things had to be hard for him. He was sixty-three, which was ancient in those times. Michelangelo had been Pope Julius II's favorite and now Raphael was Pope Leo's star, busy painting the Vatican rooms. Pope Leo X, Giuliano's brother." In that moment, talking about art history, she seemed her usual smiling, generous self.

"How do you remember all this?"

"I've been teaching it for forty years." Mirella handed me the thin pizza, warm, brushed with oil and crusted with salt. She had opted for tomato pizza.

"There's a Vasari quote I always tell my students at the beginning of the semester." She started to pay the cashier, but I managed to beat her to it. "Thank you, Simona. You are always sweet.

"The pope commissioned a painting and when Leonardo started by distilling oils and herbs for the varnish, Leo X supposedly said: 'Alas, this man will never do anything, for he begins to think of the end of the work before the beginning.'" She took a timid bite from a corner of pizza. "Most of my students don't get it." Suddenly she cupped my chin with her hand. "Are you tired? You must be exhausted. All this commotion on top of everything." She clucked her tongue.

I hugged her and we walked out into a hazy warm

morning and Campo dei Fiori—the field of flowers—a square that had started out as a meadow in the Middle Ages, had become a grain market and an important meeting place in the fifteenth century as the halfway point between the Vatican and the Capitol, and in 1600 had turned into a place of execution. The grim statue of Giordano Bruno, a monk burned for heresy, watched as we ate greedily. Now it was an open-air market, and at our end the piazza was covered with stands of azaleas, tulips, roses, and daffodils. Almost Union Square market, I told myself, thinking of the open market I went to every Saturday morning in New York even when I had nothing to buy. In New York, I was trying to be reminded of this very campo.

Vendors tried to hook shoppers with words.

"*Signo'*, look at these olives! As big and black as your eyes, *signo'*!" Mirella unlocked her bike from the lamppost.

"Have you seen these lemons?" another vendor cried out. "They'll give you the juice of love! Tart and sweet. Special price just for you, signori."

I laughed at the exaggerations, at the absurdities that are part of Roman life, and suddenly wanted Willy and Greenhouse with me so I could show them all of Rome. I took that to be a good sign.

I took my time following Mirella and her troglodyte bike, watching as designer-dressed women trailed Filipino maids and vied with women in housecoats trailing knit bags to get the plumpest, the shiniest, the most delicious of anything. I looked over to the far side, by the movie theater, for the stands filled with neat rows of fish. I remembered sardines looking like silver blades. But it was Monday. No fish.

"Is there any mention of the Brandeschi family in Leonardo's manuscripts or letters?" I asked, catching up to

Mirella. She was eyeing a window layered with antique jewelry.

In the clouded light of the street, Mirella's eyes looked tired. Her cheeks were colorless. "No, but there's a record of a visit Giuliano de' Medici paid to the Brandeschi palace in December 1514. If Lorenzo Brandeschi knew Leonardo's patron, there's a good reason to suppose he knew Leonardo too."

A bobby pin dangled from a straying gray strand. "I feel terrible about Tamar's death. We had an argument on Friday." She squeezed her eyes shut as if the light were too strong. "Nothing of importance, just trying to get her to clean up the mess she made."

I could have told Mirella then that I knew she'd found drugs in Tamar's drawer and had kicked her out of the apartment. Had Mirella been American I might have, but being up front or demanding clarity are not Italian imperatives. The wheel of our lives is so often propelled by the slow waters of implication and innuendo, by letting people keep their deceptions, their hard-built securities so that we may keep our own. It is built in the language itself, with its passive voice and spiraling sentences that inspire vagueness. Even declarations of love are not direct, which may seem odd in a country known for its passions. *Ti voglio bene* is spoken more often than *Ti amo*. I wish you well instead of I love you.

Mirella was worried about Luca, perhaps she even thought the drugs were his. I doubt she asked him directly. I don't think she would have known what to do with an ugly truth. By American standards, not facing up to reality or to one's inner demons is wrong, unhealthy. Maybe America is a country that believes there is only one truth. In Italy there are many.

I did ask her about Carlo's present. "Did Tamar mention anything? Maybe it's in one of her drawers." Tamar had not had time to remove her belongings from the apartment.

"I took everything to Commissario Perillo Sunday morning. She had so little. A few leggings, T-shirts, underpants, a small sketchbook filled with drawings of Rome. I wanted to keep it. No presents for anyone."

I wheeled around. "Do you think it's important?"

"For Luca, yes. As a keepsake. But it wouldn't be right." Mirella shook her fist, splotches of color marking her face. "I argued with her and the next day she's dead. That is terrible! Tamar yelled at me. 'You can't treat me this way. I have power now!'

"I paid no attention, but she was talking about the Leonardo drawing. Think of the millions of dollars it would fetch. To a poor girl that is immense power."

"That's power to most people."

"Not to me. That's something Nonna can never get through her head." Mirella clutched the oily pizza wrapper and stuffed it in her pocket. "The beauty of a Leonardo drawing is far more powerful." Wearing a long green canvas coat and holding on to that old black bike, she looked as if she belonged in a daguerreotype of Rome at the turn of the century.

"Did you tell Perillo what Tamar said?" I asked.

"I will now. He'll put more men on the case. That drawing is a national treasure. It musn't leave the country!"

"Are you thinking that Arthur Hensen is involved?"

Mirella stopped, her face flaming up. "Why not the principe? It would be his drawing after all. He would smuggle it out where it could fetch millions at Christie's." Behind her, at the far side of Piazza Farnese, the Palazzo Farnese spread out like a graying monarch. The haze gave the square a dusty, romantic look.

"Armand Hammer paid five million dollars for the

Leicester Codex. If Italy hadn't just had that devastating earthquake, the government would have bid, too and driven the price up much higher. And that's for a thirty-eight-page manuscript with only a few uninteresting sketches!

"A preparatory drawing in 1515 would be—" She nearly dropped her bicycle at the thought. "Leonardo had stopped doing portraits by that time. And so many paintings were lost, too. He did a portrait of Isabella D'Este that's gone. Lucrezia Crivelli is gone. Leda and the swan. The paintings we do have, we're not sure they're all Leonardo's." The coloring in her face had settled to a flattering pink. She even smiled, as if confident she had talked herself out of a hole.

Mirella had been thinking of Arthur Hensen, I was sure of that. With his interest in art and his money, he might be the kind of man who yearns to possess his very own Leonardo. I needed to find out if he would kill for that yearning.

A group of knapsacked students surged from behind one of the two covered fountains undergoing the slow process of restoration. The kids surrounded Mirella, their raised voices tumbling over each other. "I'm sorry about Tamar, Mrs. Monti." "My parents are freaking out." "What did she have in her bag?" "Is it true someone planned her death?"

"Couldn't you cancel the final exam, Mrs. Monti?" a messy-haired student asked, his shirttails hanging out of his jeans. He didn't suppress a yawn.

The short pudgy girl next to him stifled a laugh. Elbows jutted out to stop the laughter from spreading, which made things worse. The kids compromised with giggles while Mirella cooed with her soft, accented English, reassuring them that they were safe. Then she spread an arm up to the heavens. "I must give you a final exam." She looked genuinely sorry. The students' faces turned serious. The short girl apologized. They were nervous, not heartless. And Tamar had not been popular. I wondered if one of them could have been on that scooter. Maybe. So could any of the youth of Rome.

"And now to Michelangelo and Palazzo Farnese," Mirella announced. Students dutifully took out notebooks.

I grabbed Mirella's bike before it slipped to the cobbled pavement as she tried to extract a large book from her briefcase. My eyes scanned the most elegant Renaissance piazza in Rome. A vast expanse of cobblestone, two large, bathtub-shaped fountains now hidden behind wood planks. On the right a small modern church and convent, built where the Swedish St. Bridget died, beyond it a modest trattoria. On the other side, the restaurant Camponeschi, elegant and expensive enough to match the grandeur of Palazzo Farnese, which dominates the far end of the piazza. A beautiful palace, started by Sangallo and completed by Michelangelo, it has never warmed my soul. It is too large, too perfect, too self-important. The French chose it as their embassy in 1871, offering a Parisian *palais* in exchange. They closed it to the public in the sixties. Perhaps that's what I resent and prevents me from loving the piazza as I should. The great Salon d'Hercule and the Caracci gallery with its swirl of amorous gods and goddesses can be enjoyed only by guests of the embassy. The humble populace is allowed to see the courtyard for one hour on Sundays. When the doors of the palazzo open to let in a diplomat's car, Mirella and her students have tried to steal a peek. The concierge invariably yells at them. In French.

"Which students were friendliest with Tamar?" I whispered to her.

"Tom, the yawner, and Linda, with the Duke sweatshirt. He's so in love with her, he doesn't sleep. He's flunking, too." Mirella smiled at them, a wistful expression on her face.

"In the late fifteenth century," she lifted her chin and her voice, "houses began to reflect the status of those who owned them. In Florence it was the merchants who could afford to dress up their homes. In Rome only members of high ecclesiastical offices had enough money. To have space in front of your home was very important, a status symbol not unlike your American lawns. The more, the better, no?" The short girl laughed and drew mouths in her otherwise blank notebook page. Behind her, Linda ran through a stack of photos Tom had dropped in her hands. They were paying no attention to Mirella. I walked up, bike still in tow and introduced myself in a whisper, adding that I had been a witness to Tamar's killing. I hoped, in their eyes, that that gave me the right to ask questions.

"Did you see Tamar Friday night?"

Tom, blond, with cute good looks he was aware of, leaned into Linda, clearly resentful of the interruption.

"Yeah, I saw her," Linda said. Tall, with a long Modigliani face and dark, deep-set eyes, she looked relieved. "She was on a high or something, trying to help everyone out. Tom and I were in charge of getting the food ready for the party on Saturday."

"What is this?" Tom asked. "Was Tamar's death planned or something? Are you a private detective? We've already been questioned by this dweeby policeman in love with his eyebrows."

Linda laughed. "He kept rubbing them."

"I just have a healthy curiosity." I did not want Tom to start rumors that would scare everyone and solve nothing.

"You mean you like to snoop?" Tom shrugged. "Okay by me. Anything not to have to take notes."

"What did you tell Perillo?"

"There was nothing to tell him. Tamar was happy."

"Happier than usual?"

"Oh, yeah. She pranced around getting in the way while everyone was trying to clean up the place. Then she broke the only knife around and I got stuck trying to cut roast beef with scissors." Tom threw up black leather arms. "La Casa dell'Arte. Nothing works. Better known as La Casa dell'Farte." He laughed and looked at Linda for approval.

She ignored him. "Tamar was up and down all the time," she said. "Sometimes she'd love you and then *pow*, she'd be in a black sulk that made you want to get as far away as you could."

"Did Tamar say anything that night that might help find her killers?"

"No," Linda said, "but she did tell me she was going to change her last name, if that's any help. That was on Thursday when Mrs. Monti took us to the Vatican Museum."

In the background Mirella was talking about Alessandro Farnese, how he became Pope Paul III and endowed his children with many riches. A middle-aged woman carrying yellow streaks of forsythia had stopped to listen.

"She was acting funny," Linda said. "I was going to mail some letters at the post office there—Vatican mail is faster, you know—and I was writing my name on the back when Tamar popped up with this new name thing."

"Did she mail anything?" I asked.

"I don't know." An unhappy expression came over Linda's face. "The other kids were waiting for me downstairs so I left her there."

"Did she have anything in her hands?"

Tears welled up in Linda's eyes. "She had that satchel with her. All I know is she wanted to change her name and I didn't even remember to tell the policeman."

"Maybe she was getting married," Tom offered, reeling Linda in. "To that Italian guy." He jerked a finger toward Mirella, who was pointing out the changes Michelangelo had made to the Farnese façade. "Teach's son. Tamar got off on him. Now talk about brood mood. His chin's glued to his feet."

"Why are you always down on everybody?" Linda pushed him away. "Luca helped you Friday night!"

Rebuffed, Tom bent down to tie a shoelace that didn't need tying.

"Luca was at the school that night?" I had set out to talk to Luca this morning, but he was still fast asleep when I left. "Did he see Tamar?"

"No, she'd gone," Linda said.

"Did she sleep with you that night?"

"She never showed up in the dorm." Linda eyed Tom's bent back. "But I heard her call Luca before she left so I figured she'd gone back to his place."

"What was Luca doing at the school, then?" I asked.

Linda's hand reached down to ruffle Tom's hair. "He brought a sharp knife and helped Tom slice roast beef."

12

Fiat justitia ruat coelum.
Let justice be done though heaven should fall.
—ANCIENT ROMAN PROVERB

Linda remembered the burned handle. Tom remembered the nick. They had not made the connection to Tamar and hadn't told Perillo.

The sun came out of the clouds and Mirella, bicycle in hand, trudged her students off to see the Mannerist ornamentations on nearby Palazzo Spada. I called Nonna from the piazza bar and told her not to let Luca out of the apartment until I got there.

"Take your time. His alarm clock's the Gianicolo cannon."

I used to set my watch by that noon sound that has been plummeting down from Janiculum Hill since 1904. In the months before flying to America, the cannon's boom seemed to mark off the time I had left.

I walked briskly down to Largo Argentina, where what seems like half the city buses converge in front of a vast pit of temple ruins that used to be covered with cats and leftovers to feed them. While I waited I spotted only two kittens under what was left of a column. An American student offered milk. Nonna was right. The cats of Rome were disappearing. I paced as every bus but mine wheezed past me, a long flash of orange spouting choking fumes. A horrifyingly expensive, rare taxi was parked at the taxi stand across the street. It was as temptingly bright yellow as the newest New York cab.

The taxi stand phone rang. The driver looked with regret at the sports paper he'd been reading. I ran across the street and slipped into the backseat just as he was about to answer the call.

I made it to Mirella's in ten minutes. Twelve dollars worth of Roman miracle.

Unlocking the front door, I found Nonna pointing her nose at me from the living room door. "What do you want to wake him for?"

"I want to talk about Tamar." I was out of breath from running up the four flights. "Did the commissario call about the blood on the knife?"

"He didn't have to bother. We're not idiots."

"Then it's confirmed. It's Tamar's blood?"

"The sun rises every day, like it or not. If you're going to wake Luca up, make him some coffee first. He won't get up without his cup of coffee."

"I will not!" I marched down the corridor and knocked loudly on his door. Nonna grumbled something about having to make coffee at her age. Without waiting I strode in and opened the French windows and the double shutters to the balcony. The Monti heir was buried under clouds of pillows. I shook him until he groaned. Gorbi helped by jumping on the bed and curling on Luca's chest.

"Why didn't you tell anyone you had the knife?"

Luca blinked, ran a hand across tousled hair. "I was up all night working on a project. I need coffee."

I leaned against his drafting table and looked down on an architectural plan of a supermarket. "I talked to Linda and Tom this morning."

He shoved Gorbi off his chest. *"Allora?"* Gorbi resettled at his feet.

"Allora, why didn't you say anything about taking the knife to school?"

He shook himself awake and reached out to swing the door shut. "Which side are you on?"

"What do you mean?"

"Are you one of those do-gooders who goes running to any recognized authority to tell them all so that you can feel self-important?"

"Why don't you move out of that bed, get your damn coffee, and we can start over again with you being polite?"

"What business is it of yours what happened to Tamar? You didn't know her and you probably wouldn't have liked her if you did!"

"Why did you?"

"She had a skewed perception of things. A little crazy. Exciting. And she didn't hem me in or demand great declarations of love every five minutes."

"I imagined her insecure."

"Having a boyfriend wasn't that important to her."

"Friday night she called and told you she'd broken the school's only knife."

"'Tom's pissed,' is what she said."

"Hadn't you two broken up that day?"

"That doesn't mean we weren't going to speak again. She had her ideas, I had mine. Why do you care about Tamar?"

"Because my mother cares and so does Mirella and I

love them both." I knocked knuckles against the table. Gorbi cocked his ears.

Luca sat up. The torn T-shirt he was wearing read MIS-ISIPI UNIVERISTY, in keeping with Italian youths' love affair with the States. Thousands of misspellings are spawned by a thriving cottage industry.

"Right now I'll do anything to please my mother," I told him.

"I'm touched." His face was defensive. For a moment Luca reminded me of Willy, when I'd first met him, hell bent on disliking any girlfriend of Dad's. Luca wasn't fending me off, he was fighting the situation.

"I'm trying to help, Luca." I smiled, trying to reassure him. Luca was spoiled, but he was a decent human being, too. "I don't know if I'll go running to the police. Loyalty is a tricky issue when there's a murder involved. Why did you lie to Perillo? You were at Poggio delle Rose with Nonna all day Saturday. You were there all day, weren't you?"

"After the visit, I took her up to the farm. She wanted to check with Oreste about Sunday's lunch. I got stuck with sweeping the place."

"In the morning you stayed with Nonna and the sisters?"

Luca nodded, a distracted expression on his face. Gorbi lifted his head.

"Then even if he finds your fingerprints on the knife," I said, "which I don't think is likely after Gorbi's slobbered all over the handle, Perillo isn't going to accuse you of the crime."

Luca didn't answer. He was listening. So was Gorbi, head cocked at the door. Without warning Luca bounded out of bed. The dog barked. Luca threw open the door, looking harmless in his T-shirt and candy-striped boxer shorts.

"Buongiorno, Luca." Nonna stood, without blinking, offering a tiny cup of coffee.

Luca fingered the cup. "The coffee's cold because you've been eavesdropping for the last five minutes."

"You're welcome. The coffee's cold so you won't burn your forked tongue and why should I eavesdrop?" She tried to lift up her neck, but it quavered and dropped back to its usual angle. "I saw you walk out with the knife, Luca, *caro.*" She walked away, one hand holding on to the wall.

Luca sipped and made a face.

"Nonna's got nothing else in her life."

"I have no privacy! Everyone falls for Nonna because she's old. Can't she live by herself?" He let Gorbi slurp the rest of the coffee. "God no, that would be a scandal and there's no money. Old age home, even worse. 'How can you do that to your grandmother?' 'What would people say?'" Luca slipped on a tattered bathrobe and moved out to a balcony blanketed by potted plants in various stages of growth. They all needed watering.

I followed and looked out on sun-filled sycamores, the new leaves still unfurled. "The leaves are late this year," my mother had said this morning. "We had a cold winter. Everything's late except bad news. That always comes early." It was almost noon. The hum of traffic was steady, punctured by the broken mufflers of scooters.

"Nonna can't hear us here," Luca said. "She won't go near windows."

I didn't care if she heard us or not. "Why couldn't Tamar or Tom get a knife from Principe Maffeo? He lives above the school."

"He's locked all the doors. He doesn't like having the school there. Needing rent money has to be humiliating for him." Luca coaxed a new morning glory vine between the spokes of the balcony. "Then Tamar made things worse."

"How?"

Luca shuffled his bare feet. "Mirella likes you."

"I love her."

"She says you'd have made a great sister for me." This man was thirty years of age and not a day older than Willy. He was, at that moment, deciding on trust. I found myself liking him.

"I would have nagged you," I said. "No coffee in bed. University finished by now. A job, your own apartment with all the privacy you wanted."

"Have you tried looking for a job in this country? Tried to rent an apartment?"

"No." It wasn't much easier in New York, but I'd been lucky. "Pretend I'm your sister and tell me about Tamar."

"I consider Principe Maffeo a friend. I work for him now. It's dumb work, but I enjoy being in that crumbling palazzo with generations of family history flaking off the walls with the paint."

"A lefty like you isn't supposed to like degenerate aristocracy."

Luca smirked. "I'm a Roman first, cradled by history. And I like the man. Sometimes I even wish . . . "

"What?"

"I don't know, maybe that Mirella would get together with him. I'm not sure. He's a gentleman. Not because of his title. That's meaningless. He's a gentle man. Honorable. Everything my father was not. I think he'd make her happy. He's got no money though."

"And Arthur Hensen has tons."

"Arthur Hensen is ignorant, full of himself, and a true capitalist!"

"Which means what, Luca?"

"Hensen uses people for his own gain."

"What happened between the prince and Tamar?"

"She was fascinated by him and his title, by the palazzo. At first he let her come and go as she pleased. I think he was flattered, maybe lonely. Then Tamar decided she looked exactly like the Melzi portrait of Caterina Brandeschi."

"The one Arthur Hensen mentioned at lunch up at Nonna's farm?"

"Yes. Ugly portrait, but there is a resemblance. She thought she was related in some way and she started pestering Principe Maffeo to adopt her." Luca tossed his hair back to look at me. "You look like Tamar, too."

From his bathrobe pocket he pulled out a strip of three gray photos taken in a photo booth. He peered at them for a moment, his jaw clamped tight, then handed them over. In two shots Tamar was making faces; in the third she must have been caught unawares, her expression serious, pensive. The way I had seen her just before she died, as if a thought were just beginning to form in her head.

"Something about the eyes and the forehead. Your mother pointed it out."

Carlo had said something similar and I should have been flattered. Tamar was attractive. Instead I dreaded the thought of being like her. It was her desperate neediness, I think, not that she was murdered.

"Can I keep these photos?"

Luca frowned.

"I'll return them tonight, I promise."

"Keep them. Sentimental mementoes are worthless." Luca tightened his bathrobe belt until I thought his stomach would choke.

"Thanks. I'll return them tonight." I slipped the strip in the pocket of my slacks. "On Thursday Tamar told Linda she was going to change her last name. Could the prince have promised to adopt her?"

"No! He asked her to stop coming by. Then when I found the account book recording the payment to Leonardo—"

"I thought Tamar had found it!"

"She took the credit, thinking Principe Maffeo would like her more. She went a little crazy and started searching the whole palazzo for the drawing. That's when the upper floors of the palazzo became out of bounds. I think he didn't trust her to give him the drawing if she did find it. "

"When did this happen?"

"A month ago. Just before the documentary party."

"Then she couldn't have found the drawing. Unless the Leonardo was somewhere in the school."

Luca's expression clouded. "She had a copy of my key made. I had no idea until the principe caught her in the library on Wednesday night. He was furious. The next day I told Tamar I could not love her anymore. Love cannot be hypocritical. You know that too, Simona."

"I thought I did, but I'm beginning to wonder." At a distance of time, it sounded smug, a dictum rather than a personal belief. "Was the prince angry with you?"

Luca nodded. "He thought I let her in." He was clearly upset.

"The prince's trust is important to you."

A trace of a smile appeared in Luca's eyes. "Father figures are a bourgeois need."

"I would say a human need."

"And your need is to know what I did with the knife after slicing three kilos of meat?"

I nodded, smiling back.

"I left it at school. They had more food to slice on Saturday. Which means thirty-five American art students had access to the murder weapon."

"Luca, are you trying to protect Principe Maffeo? Is that why you didn't tell Perillo about the knife?"

"I'm trying to help my mother. If the police think one of the students killed Tamar, they'll make a lot of trouble. Hensen doesn't like trouble. Tamar overheard that his board is upset because the school is losing money."

"How did she overhear that?"

"She and Mirella painted his bathroom. If Hensen closes the school, Mirella is out of a job, with a pension that buys dog food. No one is spending any money on covering their walls with trompe l'oeil paintings or hiring sixty-four-year-old art teachers. Or thirty-year-old would-be architects. At least not for the kind of money that would support three people."

"I don't think lying helps. The newspapers might give a description of the knife, then someone at La Casa is going to make the connection." So far the papers had only printed a couple of paragraphs wedged between a kidnapping in Tuscany and a stolen Bellini *Madonna* from a church in Venice.

"They don't read Italian papers."

"One of them might. When Perillo finds out, it'll be worse. I won't tell him, but I'd like you to." My mother would never forgive me if I ratted on her best friend's son.

A thick curtain of hair hid Luca's eyes. "I don't know."

"Talk to Mirella."

"She'll start crying."

"She'll want the truth."

Below us a silver Alfa-Romeo charged the sidewalk to park. On the other side of Viale Angelico, three dogs chased each other in the dog park. Their masters huddled, alert playground parents.

"On Friday, did Tamar say or hint at having found the Leonardo drawing? Or anything else that might be valuable, maybe something she could blackmail someone with?"

Luca's chin snapped up. "Nonna's got senile dementia!"

"That's the last thing I'd say about Nonna."

He fumbled with his bathrobe.

"Did Tamar mention Leonardo in that last conversation?" I was sure Nonna wasn't making things up.

"I don't know. Maybe. Yes, we talked about the principe. Leonardo probably came up. She was obsessed with that drawing."

"But you don't think she'd found it yet?"

"I'd have made her give it back to Principe Maffeo."

"That would be a good reason not to tell you." I went back inside. Gorbi was fast asleep on the bed, a paw over the empty coffee cup. He hadn't spilled a drop.

"One last question, then I'll leave you alone."

Luca followed me in, exasperation on his face. "I now have four women in the house."

"What was heroin doing in this apartment? Tamar no longer did drugs."

"That really is none of your business. But just to clear the family name, no one in this house does drugs."

"Tell your mother that. You'll make her happy."

The time to visit the Vatican Museum is during the lunch hour. The mastodontic tour buses have gathered their fold and deposited them at cheap trattorias nearby, and in the summer, when the Vatican is open all day, the afternoon crowds are still huddled close to the Roman Forum, the Campidoglio, or some other glorious spot, fortifying themselves with the tourist menu for another onslaught of Culture.

At twelve-thirty the place was relatively empty.

Remembering childhood instructions from my mother which required that I perform some kind of penitence whenever I set foot in the Vatican, I refused the elevator and scaled the long winding staircase. I should have gone straight to the post office, but instead I paid the entrance fee, walked quickly down the vastly long map rooms, wound in and out of rooms laden with treasures, went up and down stairs, and finally came to the Sistine Chapel.

There are certain rituals I cannot do without when I come to Rome. Luca would call them sentimental mementoes. I call them landmarks of memory and life affirming—past life, that is. Something that I was apparently having a hard time giving up.

Michelangelo's Daniel was the man I sought, sitting up high to the left, a wide book open on one knee. He is writing something to one side. A wisdom? A secret? His face is serious. He is the prophet Daniel, interpreter of dreams. When I was six my mother had sat me down on a wall bench to admire, above us, the magical reach of fingers between God and Adam, maybe to envy the power that father transmits to son. Just as my gaze had shifted to the fresco of the prophet Daniel, my mother whispered that we, the family, were moving to Geneva, Switzerland, to Gigi's new post. I was leaving Rome for the first time. The thought frightened me and I looked up at Daniel's darkened yellow knee, at his larger-than-life blue chest, at his curly hair, noticing how young he was compared to the other prophets. I wanted to sit on his knee forever in this hushed shadowy place where God created earth and man. There I would be safe.

Geneva turned out to be fine. I learned to swim in its lake. I learned French. I made new friends.

Now Daniel's knee was golden yellow. His young face, cleaned, stunningly beautiful in its wisdom. I had good taste as a kid. I wondered what Tamar had thought of Daniel. She had been in far greater need of a welcoming knee.

For a few moments I luxuriated in the half-empty room, eyes glued to Michelangelo's ceiling. The grime-covered Old

Testament had been restored to a picture book of breathtaking vitality. With their refound sun-filled colors, the figures struck out at you in all their powerful glory. The ceiling would fill an atheist with awe. In this chapel Popes were made and Michelangelo, to strengthen the idea of man's need for leadership, had depicted man's fallibility, even showing Moses overcome by alcohol.

On the altar side of the room, *The Last Judgment* was covered up, the restoration not finished. Just as well. I was not ready for any kind of judgment. I gave Daniel a last look. Michelangelo had supposedly depicted him in the moment when the prophet is being inspired by an idea.

"From your brain to mine," I told my old beau.

At the entrance I picked up a postcard of *La Pietà*, as per Willy's instructions, and wrote "I miss you guys." And meant it.

"Francobollo da cartolina per l'U.S.A.?" I asked the postal clerk at the small Vatican post office off to one side of the entrance. She ignored my request for a stamp and continued counting money, her lips moving as a rubber-encased forefinger flicked down a three-inch stack of lire. Five minutes to two, the wall clock behind her stated. Closing time. I was hungry, confused about Tamar, and in half an hour I had a date with Perillo clear across town. Having no more money for taxis, I also had a long walk to the subway.

"Do you remember this girl?" I showed her Tamar's photograph between flicks. She frowned and went right on moving her lips. A colleague rustled something behind her. Mustached, past his prime, wearing a gray vest his wife must have knit for him in his slimmer days.

"Could you help me?"

He gave me my stamp, dividing his gaze between the photos and my chest.

"You're lucky," the man said. "I remember her."

The woman snorted between counts. "Thousands come through every day and Beppe remembers her." The finger kept flicking.

"Did she mail a package, a letter?" I paid the thousand lire. "Buy stamps?"

The woman slapped her money down. "That is confidential information!"

Beppe winked at me. I couldn't wink back; Flick Finger had me in her sights. I held Tamar's photos in front of my nose. Her face had not appeared in the papers. "She's my sister. I'll show you a letter she wrote me." I shook lire out of my wallet as if looking for a letter. "She said she mailed me a present for my birthday on Thursday, but it hasn't come."

"It's only Monday!" Beppe's eyes had shifted from my chest to the money on the counter. "We're fast, but not that fast." He leered at me behind that dyed black mustache as if to imply that he could be very fast indeed if only I would let him.

"Now she's dead and I want it." I appealed to both of them. "A sentimental memento, you can understand that."

"Nothing doing. I didn't see her. Beppe didn't see her. We're closed." Her face closed as if she'd pulled a screen down.

I skipped down the bronze-balustraded staircase and slowly strolled down to the corner where a stand was selling Michelangelo T-shirts. I rummaged through the piles. No Daniel. I held up a God and Adam and waited.

"Hands eager to touch," Beppe whispered behind me. He had doused himself with a sweet-smelling cologne that recalled moldy lemons.

I dropped the T-shirt and edged away.

"Why do you remember my sister?" He could be lying to keep me happy.

"My place's not far away." One of the perks of working for the Vatican—inexpensive housing. The Vatican owns half of Rome.

I smiled but didn't move. He tugged at his mustache. "She asked me how much it would cost to insure the package for a hundred million lire." That was about sixty-two thousand dollars, hardly the price of a Leonardo drawing, but better than nothing if she was so dumb as to risk sending it through the mail.

"That kind of insurance doesn't happen every day," Beppe said, sidling up to me again. "I started to look up the price for her, but she laughed and told me to send it as is. 'God's the mailman in the Vatican. You can't go wrong with God.' That's what I told her." He smirked, probably envisioning himself in the God role.

"Rome address? Thin, flat package? A cardboard tube? She had promised me a drawing."

His gaze dropped to my body. "You don't happen every day."

I opened my palm to reveal two ten thousand lire notes—about thirteen dollars—borrowed from Nonna. "Rome address? A tube?"

We clasped hands, both of us relieved. My body was forgotten.

"She spelled it Rome instead of Roma. I don't remember where in the city though. Not a tube and not flat. The size of—" He stiffened. Flick Fingers walked up and linked her arm with his.

"The size of what?" I asked.

"If you don't leave my husband alone," Flick Fingers said, "it'll be the size of my hand on your face."

She walked her silenced man away, throwing me a grin of triumph.

13

---

*'Tis pride, rank pride, and haughtiness of
soul; I think the Romans call it stoicism.*

—JOSEPH ADDISON, CATO

"You have an interesting mother," Perillo said while I signed my statement as a useless eyewitness to a murder. "This morning she was torn between truth and loyalty. Loyalty won out, naturally."

Perillo's office was a spotlessly clean cubbyhole full of yellowing files tied in neat bundles, a desk that could only fit at an angle, a chair, and a stool. He sat on the stool, eyebrows perfectly combed.

"How did you know?" I asked. At breakfast my mother had told me she was going to spend the remainder of her morning at the beauty parlor. In Rome, beauty parlors are closed on Monday mornings. I knew it, she knew it, but I pretended to accept her lie. I wasn't going to strip her of whatever defenses she was building, even if it meant that I was being shut out. "How can you tell when someone is lying?"

Perillo tapped his breast pocket, which probably carried his Human Behavior notebook. "When I asked Signora Griffo if the knife could have ended up in the garbage, her eyes gazed out the window."

"There is no window here."

Perillo raised a finger. "Exactly. Lies have big imaginations. They conjure up many ways of escape."

I made sure my eyes stayed on his round Bacchus face. I had said nothing about Luca taking the knife to La Casa. "Tamar may have sent my ex-husband a supposed 'present.'" I related what Beppe had told me, omitting the bribe. It would have been redundant.

A manicured finger traveled the ridge of Perillo's eyebrow. "The Leonardo drawing?"

"Why not?"

"If it exists and she found it."

"A lot of ifs I admit, but Tamar trusted Carlo. Maybe she thought he would keep it safe until she decided what to do with it."

Perillo looked doubtful.

I threw up my hands. "Maybe she just sent him a real present. His birthday's coming up." Carlo had always liked to make a big fuss over his birthday.

"I will inform post office headquarters." He took out an old-fashioned key from his jacket pocket. "Not an efficient place these days with the threat of privatization, if it ever was." Perillo locked his drawer and stood up.

I stood up, too, thinking I was being dismissed. "Are you getting close to solving the case?"

Instead of answering, Perillo ushered me out of his office. Ten minutes later we were on Via Nazionale at the imposing *Palazzo delle Esposizioni*, a spacious, early-twentieth-century building that had once been the Modern Museum of Art and now housed an exhibition titled "All Roads Lead to Rome?"

"*La mamma italiana*, she is the best," Perillo said, gazing up at Francesco Clemente's *Four Fountains*, a ceiling painting that consisted of four women's legs seemingly dangling toward us, their genitalia in full view. "She is the most fiercely protective, the most loyal."

I directed my eyes toward a painting of a green front door at the top of the marble staircase. It felt safer. "*La mamma americana*, she is perhaps not so good." Perillo slowly twirled, chin up to the sky. "I have solved the mystery of the victim's dying word. 'Toni.' Her adoptive mother. Toni, short for Antonia. Not a gentle woman and yet, in pain, Signorina Deaton called for her mother."

"Foster mother, and they didn't get along."

His chin dropped, his eyes noticing the green door at the top of the first flight of stairs. "When one is dying, animosity is forgotten, forgiveness is asked. The mother–child bond is difficult to sunder. Even foster mothers."

"Why did you bring me here?" He had insisted on paying for my entrance fee.

"To answer your question. These artists"—he waved a short arm around the spread of large rooms—"they use different symbols to evoke our city. Milna Kunc, the she-wolf. Jeff Koons shows a marble cat, Alex Katz, black lines for winter trees in Villa Pamphili, Mario Ceroli, the exterminating angel of Castel Sant'Angelo cut out of—"

"What are you getting at?"

Perillo's finger came up again. "In this show there are so many different symbols of the city, each symbol born of the artist's particular perspective of our city. This display of perpectives inspires me." He followed me to the wide staircase and peered up at the green door. "From a distance it seems real, no?"

"Yes." And very much shut. "You haven't answered my

question." We slowly climbed. "Are you any closer to solving the crime?"

"Before I answer, I must hear your perspective." He was short of breath. "You have seen some of the American students this morning, can they be killers? I think not. A stabbing during a purse snatching is not an American method. It requires expertise with Roman traffic, with the city's streets, with those infernal scooters. An American would use a car, drive her out to the country at night, then shoot her. Americans are much more involved with guns. The Wild West is their tradition."

Italian hogwash! "Commissario, if you want my viewpoint, you shouldn't interject yours."

His chin scooped down in chagrin. "Pardon, but I am seriously interested."

"I'll say that none of those students killed Tamar, because I don't think Tamar knew her assailants. If she had, she would have said something besides 'Toni.' I also don't see an art student hiring a killer, but I am naive and maybe . . . have you checked into their backgrounds?"

"I've sent a fax. My men have spoken to all of them. They are good kids. I do not expect that direction to yield fruit."

"How did you know I saw the students this morning?"

Perillo spread his hands.

"Don't tell me. I think I know. A middle-aged woman carrying forsythia."

"The forsythia she bought on her own."

"Are you following Mirella? Me? What are you doing?"

"My job. Gathering perspectives." Perillo stopped at the landing and examined the green door close up. "The illusion is over," he said. "Now we have painted wood. This door will not open." He wheeled around, suddenly energized. "I find interesting the perspective of Aldo who works for the principe. The knife, our all-important symbol in this case, was in the school, not in the garbage, he tells me. Your mother need not have been so loyal. Or you."

I studied an interesting blemish on his forehead. It was about the size of a pepper grain.

"Luca brought it to the school." Perillo was now bounding up the stairs. "Perhaps Luca also took the knife from the school."

I followed him with less enthusiasm.

"Tamar did not know her assailant!"

"That is not necessarily correct." He tapped his breast pocket, as if it were the seat of his knowledge. "The shock of recognition can produce denial. She might have preferred to evoke the image of an unpleasant foster mother rather than to accept the betrayal of a lover. Mothers are useful that way."

Double hogwash! "Luca was at Poggio delle Rose with Nonna when Tamar was killed."

"And now Luca is in the office adjacent to mine, answering some new questions."

"Is that why you brought me here? So I wouldn't see him?"

"One of the reasons. You would be upset. That would cloud your perspective."

That word was getting boring. "Yet you told me."

"The ear is kinder than the eye."

"My ex-husband is off the hook?" We were now in one of the upstairs galleries looking at a black and white photograph of Anita Ekberg kissing Fellini's cheek. Carlo had started his film editing career as an assistant on *La Dolce Vita*. From there he had moved down to spaghetti westerns, too impatient to become head editor to stay on as an apprentice to a genius. He had never worked with a great director again.

"The only thing I understand about Fellini is his women," Perillo said, drumming a finger against his red lips. "All mother figures. That is why he is obsessed with the female breast."

He tore his eyes away from the famous Ekberg cleavage and resumed walking. "No one is off the hook. That answers your first question, too. I have many suspects, I have none. First I must establish why she was killed. A lost Leonardo? Blackmail using the Leonardo? Something else? Your mother mentioned a certain conversation she overheard. She is not loyal toward Signor Hensen."

He made my mother sound petty. "She has good reasons. Who exactly is this Aldo who works for the principe and knows all about the knife?"

"I thought you knew him, being such a friend of the family. He is the farmer's son."

"Oreste?" Nonna's devoted farmer.

"Yes. Everyone is somehow connected, which I find curious. Luca and Aldo I find very interesting."

"What are you going to do?"

Again he didn't answer me. He offered to buy me ice cream instead, studying my face as he asked, as if he could discover just why I refused to eat ice cream and by understanding, know me. I declined politely, a cold empty space forming in my chest.

I burst out into daylight and the confused traffic of Via Nazionale, a shop-filled street that climbs to Piazza della Repubblica and the railroad station nearby. I felt uncomfortable, blaming the long, narrow room I had left Perillo in. A room lined with small paintings, each a sight of Rome so exquisitely done it would wrench the heart of the most indifferent emigré.

"All Roads Lead to Rome?" the show asked. I could only answer yes.

On the bus back to Mirella's, the commissario's words intruded on my nostalgia. "Aldo and Luca." "Very interesting." What I felt was dread.

Nonna was alone in the apartment, except for two police inspectors with a search warrant. They'd been at it for two hours. They were now removing the lining of the living room sofa.

"That's vile," I said loudly. Gorbi was locked up in the bathroom, barking frantically. "Couldn't you wait until she had someone to keep her company?" I'd wasted words with Perillo while Nonna watched her home being desecrated. "What are you looking for? There's nothing here." I flailed arms to no effect. "You've got the murder weapon. What else do you want?" Bloodstained clothes? Cash? Another body?

"I want my blue button," Nonna said from her armchair, cool as could be. "Look what they found behind the dresser." She raised a pair of dusty kid gloves. "Lent them to Mirella and didn't see them for the rest of the winter."

"Nonna, this is terrible! I'm so sorry."

"I'm not!" She hooked a finger at the inspectors. "The button's the size of a phone token. Midnight blue. The five of cups came up at my lunchtime reading." She flashed her teeth at me. "Upside down, which means the return of an old friend. Haven't seen that button in two years. Don't look so worried." Her eyes slid to the men bent over the sofa. "*Idioti,*" she mouthed, her jowls trembling.

White dog hairs clung to their slacks as the inspectors pressed, poked, and squished the upholstery. I hoped they'd both choke on hair balls. I felt tricked by Perillo, personally violated. My suitcase lay open on the dining room table, Tampax scattered out of its box. I also felt guilty, as if it had been up to me to protect all of them from this shame.

The sofa yielded a comb and some change. Nonna laid cards out on her lap as if they might tell her where to find the missing button as the two men, both dressed in wrinkled olive-green suits, went for the dowry chest.

"What a waste of time!" I straightened out the clothes in my suitcase, half tempted to throw them all in the washing machine. How dare they? The Tampax I stuffed in my pocket.

"*Cazzo!*" The balding man dug his arm in the chest. "*Cazzo,*" he repeated, as if he'd lost his penis and hoped to conjure it up out of Mirella's trunk. For epithets, Italians prefer male genitalia to excrement.

I moved closer. "What is it?"

"You tell me." His gloved hand held up a long, black wig.

"Hair," Nonna said. "You could use some of it."

I tried for an impassive stare while my stomach churned. Balding started to say something. His partner stopped him with a hand gesture, his eyes on Nonna.

I rushed in with explanations. "Mirella Monti does portraits in the Renaissance style." I pointed to the brocade and velvet cloths Balding had spilled out of the chest. "She uses wigs, costumes, whatever will help create the right effect." I smiled at them. I had convinced myself.

"No button?" Nonna asked.

Balding shook his head and dropped the wig into a paper bag. His partner wrote out a tag. From the bathroom, Gorbi yelped.

"What are these men doing here?" my mother asked from the doorway. I had been too upset to hear the loud key turns. "And why doesn't someone free the dog? He doesn't bite." She held a big hatbox in her hand.

I pecked at my mother's cheek and ran to the bathroom, glad to have a job to do. Gorbi slathered me with saliva, then careened down the corridor to the living room. My mother was throwing out words like *rights, villainy, cowardice*. She even brought up the Inquisition. The men wisely did not answer. I took refuge in the kitchen to fortify myself with an orange. I hadn't eaten anything since the pizza in Campo dei Fiori.

The phone rang. I ran to get it in the corridor. Gorbi rushed out, thinking it was play time. I tripped on the telephone cord, hit my knee against a chair, and lost my orange. Gorbi caught it; I answered the phone.

"Mrs. Monti, this is Deborah Hensen." A brusque American voice. Arthur Hensen's daughter? I rubbed my knee. Maybe he had a hidden wife.

"I'm not Mrs. Monti. Would you like to leave a message?" I turned on an opaline lamp. Outside the window at the end of the corridor, the magnolia tree was turning a deep shade of purple.

"Have Mrs. Monti call me." She rattled off a number. Before I could ask her to repeat it, she added, "Collect if she has to. Tell her one thing for me. Not to even try to palm off a fake Leonardo on my father. She's got all she's going to get from him." She hung up, and I had no telephone number. Which was a good thing, I decided. Gorbi wagged his tail and spit out orange seeds. My knee hurt and my mother loomed with her hatbox. She hated hats. The whole day wasn't making sense. Daniel wasn't doing his job.

"Who was on the phone?" she asked as she always did.

"What's in that box?"

The two men came out of the living room and trudged to the door. "We'll be back," Balding said, clutching the bag with the wig.

"Wigs cost money," Nonna yelled. "I want it back! And I've counted every pot on the terrace. Someone give me a cigarette." She fumbled in her sweater pocket, retrieving a scrunched pack.

"They're going to the terrace?" Mamma turned back into the living room. I followed her in, my mind already suppressing the unpleasant Deborah Hensen. I could hear the policemen scratching around above us. They'd found a wig, a prop of Mirella's. That's all they were going to find.

"Why?" my mother asked. "What are they looking for?" Nonna frowned at a tarot card that depicted the moon, a crooked cigarette hanging from her mouth. "The lost Leonardo. Someone get me a light." A box of kitchen matches bulged from her other pocket.

My mother dropped herself on the sofa. "This is absurd!"

I sat next to her, explaining what had happened with Luca and the knife, Linda telling me, Aldo telling the police, how Luca was at that very moment being questioned by the police again. Nonna watched me with cloudy eyes, the moon card trembling in her hand, Gorbi at her feet. The cigarette stayed unlit. I fiddled with the lid of my mother's hatbox while my mother wondered at the stupidity and corruption of all Italian authority.

"We are back in the Middle Ages!" she declared, clicking on the gilt table lamp that had once been an altar candlestick.

I lifted the hatbox lid, she slapped my hand. "You're not a child anymore, Simona. You don't have to open every package you see."

"Then don't treat me like one." Inside the box was a perfect replica of my mother's hair. "Why the wig?"

She frowned. "You know what beauty parlors cost nowadays."

"I don't." I have my hair cut by a friend in the office who likes the challenge of a straight line, something she hasn't mastered yet. "The last time was my wedding day, and you paid for that. Waste of money."

My mother smiled, surprising me, and reached out to touch my drooping locks. "When the nurse first brought you to me, your head was already thick with lovely hair. You got that from your father."

Ah yes, the father. He had yet to be dealt with. "What did I get from you?"

"To hell with your hair!" Nonna threw down her deck of tarot cards. Gorbi's head shot up, cards cascading over him. "What are they going to do to my Luca?" The cigarette fell out of her mouth. Gorbi shot out of the room, barking.

"Signora?" a man's voice called from the hallway. The policemen were back.

My mother raised her head in annoyance. "The dog doesn't bite!"

"La prego." The voice was dire.

We both stood up and went to the living room door.

"Check that they didn't steal any plants," Nonna called out.

My mother and I stared at the front door. At Balding's partner. The hall lamp doubled in his glasses. Gorbi whined and sniffed at his hand. He was holding a wrinkled, dirty khaki cloth satchel with a Goofy sticker peeling off the flap.

"You found nothing, of course," my mother said in a perfectly controlled voice. "Perhaps you would like some coffee. Please." Mamma and I hustled him into the kitchen, beyond Nonna's hearing.

"Do you recognize it?" he asked.

My mother nodded, her face set in stone.

Tamar's satchel. I slipped my arm around her waist. "Where did you find it?"

"Wedged between two wisteria pots." He looked disappointed, as if he too had hoped to come away from this apartment empty-handed. "I called you out in the hallway because I didn't want the old lady to get a shock." He offered a receipt for both wig and satchel. "Coffee won't be necessary, thanks."

"I had no intention of offering you coffee," my mother said, "although I suppose Nonna would miss the odor." She folded the receipt neatly and slipped it up the cuff of her blouse where she keeps things she wants no one else to see. "Simona?"

I set out to make coffee, again glad I'd been given a menial task. The satchel disappeared in a black garbage bag which the policeman dropped over his shoulder, away from Gorbi. "There won't be fingerprints. Not on cloth."

Was he trying to reassure us?

"What will you do now?" Mamma asked. She looked worn out.

"They have to return my key to the terrace!" Nonna shouted from the living room.

"I report, the rest is not up to me." He dropped the terrace key on the kitchen table, gave a quick glance around the frescoes. I suspect he was uncomfortable with the expression on our faces. "Nice walls. Makes you think it's Sunday in the country, eh?"

He patted Gorbi's head. "Nice dog. I have a mutt at home." He edged to the kitchen door, not turning his back to us. "I found her tied to a tree on the autostrada last August. Right after the sun set, you know, that in-between time that's sort of spooky. Five minutes later I'd have missed her. She's black as night."

We followed him out into the hallway, Gorbi's nose pointed up toward that ugly load on his shoulder. "When

I brought the mutt home she drank a bathtub full of water. Now she's my best pal. Good evening. That's her name. Good evening." He slipped out the front door, head lowered. He was trying to apologize.

I picked up my purse from the corridor table. "Let me borrow your car, Mamma."

"Where are you going? You have to get dressed. Dinner is at eight."

"Dinner?" I started to lower my voice to tell her how absurd she was to think anyone was going to Arthur Hensen's for dinner tonight.

Nonna suddenly stood by the living room door, commanding in her ninetieth birthday party dress, a long, black velvet gown trimmed with cream-colored lace. She waved the moon card. "An engagement dinner!" Her eyes shone with a fierce light. "*Finalmente!* That American is going to propose to my daughter. I can die in peace."

"Don't you dare!" I told Nonna. Too much was happening already.

My mother smiled, clearly not believing a word. "Is that what your cards told you?"

Nonna threw the moon card on the floor, her face flushing with anger. "The wolf and the dog baying at the moon. That's bad luck for someone I love, but I won't believe it! Not tonight! Not Mirella!" Gorbi pawed at the card and wrapped his mouth around it.

"Don't worry, Nonna." Mamma smoothed hands over her skirt. "The police found nothing."

"Of course they found nothing!" Nonna snatched the card from Gorbi's mouth. "That is not what I worry about!"

Mamma's face flushed. She eyed my slacks. "You look so much nicer in a skirt, Simona." She doesn't like lying and works out the guilt by venting pet peeves.

I ducked past Nonna, told her she looked beautiful, and snagged car keys from my mother's purse.

"Slacks are not becoming on you."

"They're comfortable." In the corridor I clasped the phone book and stuck it under my arm. Gorbi circled my legs as if they held the hope of freedom. "No, *bello*, not this time."

My mother looked at Nonna for help. She didn't want me to go because she didn't want to be faced with the implications of that satchel being found on the terrace, faced with having to continue her lie to an old woman who only lived for her family. But my mother couldn't bring herself to say, "I need you here," and I resented it. Besides, I wanted to check on Luca.

"Simona inherited your big hips," Nonna said drily as I blew them both a kiss at the door. "Let's hope that's all she got. What happened to that coffee you promised, Olga?"

As I closed the front door, Gorbi dropped his head in desolation.

14

Rather by conferring than by accepting favors, they [the Romans] established friendly relations.

—SALLUST, THE WAR WITH CATILINE

I drove up the Cassia, a narrow, treacherous, uphill street choked by traffic that was built over the ancient Roman road that led to Florence. The rolling countryside dotted by a few grand villas became, with the postwar boom, crammed with foreign private schools and clusters of upscale apartment buildings layered by plant-carpeted terraces. Trees had been left as props along the road to give the idea of country living. In the distance, the Sabine hills helped the illusion.

The Tarelli sisters' oasis was called Poggio delle Rose—the hill of roses. The roses weren't in bloom yet. I checked my watch. The trip had taken me thirty-two minutes in five o'clock workday traffic. Early on a Saturday morning, Luca would have needed twenty minutes at most.

I parked in front, passed a flowering weeping cherry tree that looked incongruously delicate against a wide eight-story apartment house, and pushed the buzzer. I had called from Mirella's corner bar, using the phone book I'd stuck under my arm, confused enough to think I was back in New York where a public phone book is almost impossible to find. I reminded Pia Tarelli, the older sister, that I had met them briefly at Nonna's ninetieth birthday party.

Monica Tarelli offered coffee and homemade butter cookies, and we sat in a large, comfortable room with a glistening marble floor and richly carved oak *boiserie* on the walls. At one end, a grand piano Nonna would have envied stood draped in deep blue damask. Monica was telling me how upset they'd been about the American girl's death. Nonna, whom she called Professoressa Monti, had told them all about Tamar. Monica was somewhere in her late fifties, with bleached blond hair neatly coiffed around a soft moon face and a beaming smile.

"As I told you over the phone," Pia said, sitting upright next to her, a darker, older, more suspicious version of her sister, "a student is coming to be tutored for *la maturità*." Italians call their high school diploma "maturity," with the conviction that thirteen years of schooling make you ripe for life.

"I wanted to ask about Luca."

"I only have a few minutes." Pia sat on the edge of the beige velvet sofa. She was dressed in a dark brown suit, a color that did not flatter her olive skin.

"I have the entire afternoon." Monica gestured to her leg, wrapped in ace bandages and propped on a needle-point stool. "Phlebitis. I've been standing all my life." She smiled and reached in the small pocket of her pea-green faux Chanel suit. "I own a boutique here in Poggio delle Rose, just by the pharmacy. Here." She held out a card, which I took. "For a Monti family friend, I take fifteen percent off."

"What exactly do you want to know about Luca?" Pia tapped a cigarette on the coffee table, then pushed it between her lips with a rapid, brusque gesture. Over the phone I had explained that I was trying to help Mirella make sense of the murder. "An ispettore from the Giudiziaria has already been here."

"Luca was here all the time," Monica said, "that's what we told the ispettore. He had dirty shoes. I had to wipe down the entrance again, which isn't easy when you're trying to keep your leg up." Monica laughed and bit into a cookie. "Hmm." She stopped chewing and narrowed her eyes. "Try one, Pia, this is a better batch than the last one. My sister is very demanding when it comes to sweets."

Pia kept her gaze on me. Her wary expression looked as comfortable on her makeup-free face as a beloved old hat. I wanted to tell her the truth, that Luca was in danger, that even if she had sworn that he'd been with her all morning, the police would be back to crack the alibi. I wanted to make sure they couldn't. It was a tangible reassurance to take back to my mother, Mirella, and Nonna. And yet I hesitated, as if I were facing a blank blackboard and I hadn't done my homework. Pia's hard edge was familiar and inhibiting.

I turned to the sweeter Monica. "The girl was killed at ten thirty-eight—"

"Oh, Professoressa Monti was here at ten precisely. She's always punctual." Monica blew her sister's smoke away from her face. "Somehow visiting in the morning re-creates the classroom. She was our math teacher in high school, you know. The best we ever had."

Monica crunched into another cookie. "That's what Pia teaches. Math. She has the professoressa to thank for that."

She looked at her sister, pride warm on her face. "The boutique would fail if you didn't keep the accounts."

"Luca stayed the whole time?"

Monica opened her mouth.

Pia leaned forward, dropping a hand on her sister's arm. "Why does it matter?" She had intelligent deep brown eyes that were friendlier than she wanted them to be. "He had nothing to do with the killing."

"The police aren't as convinced."

"The police are only good at shooting their own toes." Pia moved a pillbox a few centimeters. Half the glass coffee table was covered with silver pillboxes, all of them gleaming. "What does Luca say?"

"That he was here. But he's young, and I don't see him sitting here with three women reminiscing for an entire morning."

"We do not waste our time with the past."

"Luca went to the pharmacy for me," Monica said. "That kept him busy. They weren't supposed to come on Saturday. We'd made a date for Palm Sunday, to watch the Pope on TV." A huge TV loomed in one corner, dimly reflecting us.

"Who changed the date?"

"Luca called on Friday," Pia said, dragging on her cigarette. "His grandmother forgot that Mirella had planned a lunch at the farm. He asked if Saturday was all right."

"Which it wasn't," Monica chipped in. "I do the ironing on Saturday. But with someone of the professoressa's age, you never know if you're going to see them again. We had to say yes." Monica bit into another cookie. "She had a heart attack in June."

"I didn't know that." Why hadn't my mother told me?

"Monica," Pia said quietly, churning out her cigarette.

"I don't remember it being a secret." The blush on Monica's face made her suddenly look ten years younger.

"Nonna got over it," I said, taking a nibble of a butter-laden cookie. "That's what counts. How long did Luca stay at the pharmacy?"

The doorbell rang. Pia half lifted herself up from the sofa, as if not sure whether to go to the door or stay to monitor her sister.

Monica shook her head, her brown eyes defensive. "If the police come back, they're going to find out he went there. And I can't go to the door for you. My leg. My leg can't take it." She looked as if she might cry. The doorbell kept ringing. "Do answer!"

I stood up. "Shall I?"

Pia strode off with a warning glance at her sister.

"She doesn't like me to eat so much." Monica pushed the plate of cookies away and tapped her hip. "I swell out of my clothes."

I sat back down.

Monica said, "The pharmacy is just down the street. Five minutes at the most."

We listened. The front door opened, the student and Pia exchanged murmurs. Footsteps sounded along a hard floor, one set bearing down hard, the other shuffling.

When all I heard was my own breathing, I asked, "Was Luca really gone only five minutes?"

Monica smoothed a lacy tea napkin on her pea-green lap. "The professoressa called us Saturday night. It was late, after eleven. She told us about the death, told us the police might come by."

"Nonna asked you to lie?"

She looked at the wall of transparent floor-length drapes. They had turned a pale orange with the setting sun. "Would you please open the doors? I like to see the sunset."

I did as she asked. The covered terrace was big enough for a metal table and two small armchairs. Large terra-cotta planters filled the corners with jasmine. Even the leaves were spotless.

"Thank you. Pia likes everything closed."

I sat down again, this time closer to Monica, in the warm groove Pia had vacated. In another apartment someone started listening to the last act of *La Bohème*, my father's favorite. "Nonna told you to lie?"

"She didn't have to. We did not speak to the police about the pharmacy, but if they come back, they might find out and then it will look worse. The pharmacist is German. Signorina Sondheim says Italians have no backbone. She came here for the sun. Once I took her a plate of my homemade fettuccine. She prefers potatoes."

Somewhere beyond the terrace Colline, the philosopher, was singing a dark bass good-bye to his old overcoat.

"Luca came back after five minutes?"

"Yes, of course." The opera was holding her attention. "Five minutes." I couldn't tell if she was lying.

"When did he go? When he first came or later? Do you remember when?"

"Late." Her voice tightened. Someone turned up the volume and *La Bohème* surged into the room. "I'd run out of my anticoagulant and he offered to go."

"Can you pinpoint the time?"

She raised a small, carefully manicured hand, the fingers covered with rings, as if fending something off.

"Eleven."

I stopped to listen, too.

"Mimi!" The tenor cried out in an anguished climax. Mimi was dead!

Monica shuddered. "I automatically cry at this point."

She dabbed her eyes with her tea napkin. "My sister was an opera singer."

"That's right, I remember. She sang from *Madame Butterfly* at Nonna's ninetieth birthday party." Pia's sweet, trembling soprano had surprised me. It contrasted with her tight face and sturdy body. "Cat in heat," had been Nonna's curt comment.

" *'Un bel dì vedremo.'* It's her best aria. The grace, the suffering is still all there." Monica smiled, her full cheeks cresting. Her round eyes gave her a mildly surprised look, as if life hadn't quite met her expectations.

"For two seasons the critics loved Pia. I have all her reviews, her opera programs. Then we lost our mother to angina, our father had already died when we were little girls." She gathered cookie crumbs, pushing them into a crease of her skirt. "Pia lost her voice. The professoressa convinced her to teach math. She'd been so good at it in school."

"I'm sorry."

"The doctors said the cause was a long-standing bronchitis. I say her heart broke. Mine did, but I had nothing to lose except joy. We never left each other after that." Monica leaned forward and carefully placed her leg on the carpet. She stood up gingerly, her gathered crumbs falling to the floor. She would have to sweep again.

"I'd like to show you something."

We slowly walked out on the terra-cotta tiles of the terrace. The opera was over. The sun was spraying us with that apricot light that is particular to Rome. It was a moment that should have been devoted to some life-affirming epiphany, not a murder.

"What time did Nonna and Luca leave?"

"Eleven-twenty. That's when I go to the boutique." She leaned over the railing, arms crossed. "I love it out here in the open. Pia could stay in a cellar for all she cares about living things." Monica pointed to the distant sunlit horizon wedged between twin buildings. "My Sabine hills. I tell the professoressa I can see her farm from here. She pooh-poohs me, but then she's a math teacher. Pragmatic. I say a little imagination is like a spoonful of that coagulant the pharmacist feeds me. Imagination lets the blood get to the heart. She won't come out here to see my hills." She looked disappointed.

"She's afraid of heights."

"Windows. Snipers shot at her in September of forty-three when they were taking over Rome. They wounded a friend of hers. She hasn't gone near windows since then. I think that's why her eyes clouded over. They don't get enough light."

Monica leaned forward and pointed to the grassy knoll at the entrance to her apartment building. "That's what I wanted to show you. The weeping cherry tree." The slender tree swooped flower-filled branches to the ground. "I show that tree to Pia when she gets bitter. She doesn't understand that you can weep and flower at the same time. She thinks I'm being sentimental." Her cheeks bunched up into a smile again. "Well, there's nothing wrong with that."

"No, there isn't." I shook her hand. On an impulse kissed both her cheeks. "Thank you for being so open with me."

She looked embarrassed. I said good-bye and left her on the terrace. When I came out of the building, I went up to her tree and smelled a faint trace of sweetness in the pink blossoms. From the terrace, Monica waved approval. I waved back.

The pharmacy was on the other side of the horseshoe road, two minutes away. A rose-bearing trellis framed the entrance, instantly reminding me of my parents' house. Next to it was La Boutique di Monique. Beyond the store, a bar.

The chimes went off as I walked in. I didn't like going behind Monica's back, but I had convinced myself that checking Luca's alibi would solve everything. Signorina Sondheim, tall behind a handsome wooden counter, was listening to a string of symptoms from a small, nervous man. She looked infinitely patient. In Italy the *farmacista* commands great respect as the saviour, comforter, dispenser of suppositories, unguents, a series of shots—the quick fix to health. The *medico* is feared. Doctors represent real sickness, the kind that can leave you dead.

I strolled to one end and gazed at rows of creams. An old wire-haired dachshund came ambling after me. A poster showing a knock-'em-dead rear end swore the end of cellulite. I stooped down to pat the dog and scanned the lower shelves, trying to avoid the black phone looming in the corner. There were creams to beautify my face, smooth my neck, soften my hands, enlarge my breasts, flatten my stomach, firm up my thighs. Nothing to bind families.

I faced the phone, reached in my pocket. If I didn't have enough change—this was a long-distance phone call after all—I would wait. If my father answered, I would make a date for an explanation some time in the near future. Next year, on another trip.

I found the change. I had no excuse.

"*Posso esserle d'aiuto?*" Signorina Sondheim had not lost her German accent. She was at least five foot nine, with a swimmer's shoulders and short gray-blond hair that fell in strands behind her large glasses.

I raised a finger and tried to give her a courageous smile. "In a minute I'll need lots of help."

I dropped coins in, I dialed, the phone rang. A long time. He could be in the garden, up to his knees in manure maybe. Why didn't he have an answering machine? I could speak without fear of reply. Ask him

to leave a message on my machine. Even better, let the
machines sort it out.

There was no answer.

I picked up a jar of the moisturizing cream my mother
used and strode to the counter. "The Tarelli sisters sent a
young man here on Saturday morning to pick up some
medicine."

"Yes, I remember." Signorina Sondheim wore a doctor's
white frock and a heartening smile that was now disappearing. "Is there a problem?" She rung up the sale.
"That'll be seventy thousand lire."

More than fifty dollars. I tried not to flinch. "Well . . ."
I was embarrassed. At the price and at the possibility of
lying to this woman. I handed over my credit card.

She frowned. "Did he steal something?"

"No, nothing like that. I was just wondering what time
he came in here?"

"Eleven-thirty. Signorina Monica was right behind him
on her way to work, with her usual offering of cookies.
She owns the boutique next door."

She wrapped the cream and slipped a rubber band
around it and the receipt. "Do you need a bag?"

"No, thanks." Spending fifty dollars on a cream didn't
seem so bad. I had good, solid news to bring home. Luca
had left the women at eleven, probably hung out at the bar
to kill time, then shown up at the pharmacy just when it
was time to pick Nonna up again. Tamar had died in front
of my eyes at ten-thirty-eight. Luca was in the clear. I
signed my credit card slip.

A bar boy came in with an empty tray, a white dish
towel hanging from his belt. "Mamma needs some aspirin.
Her cramps are bad." He dropped a half-eaten pastry in
front of the dachsund's nose. He was about fourteen.

"Here you are, Tonino." Signorina Sondheim threw him

a packet. "She can pay for it later." The boy rushed out. "Monica Tarelli can thank Tonino for her medicine. Your young man took his time."

I clutched my credit card. "Half an hour. Is that so bad?"

"You mean an hour and a half. I'd just made my tea. I always have tea at ten. Signorina Monica called not five minutes later, telling me a young man was on his way. It's prescription medicine. I can't just hand it over. At ten-thirty I sent Tonino over. Phlebitis is not to be taken lightly." She lifted hair from behind her glasses, revealing friendly hazel eyes. "You cannot rely on Italian men."

"Thank you." She'd just torn Luca's alibi to shreds. I had no reassurance to offer anyone. "You've been a great help."

She nodded. "Use that cream three times a day. Your skin is parched."

So was my mouth.

15

A tasca vota nun ce vo' rattoppo.
An empty pocket needs no patching.
—ROMAN PROVERB

"Get dressed, Simona." My mother looked into the shaving mirror and clipped on pearl earrings. She was standing in a white silk slip in front of an old steamer trunk that now served as a closet/dresser. "We're all going to Arthur Hensen's for dinner. I ironed your dress. You'll look nice in that." She's a great believer in the bolstering abilities of external appearances.

"This is absurd!" I sat cross-legged on the cot, slathering her cream on my face. "Luca could be a killer and we're pretending nothing happened?"

She gestured for me to quiet down. Next door I could hear Nonna ordering Mirella to pin her hair back.

Luca had called Mirella from a pay phone just before I got back to the apartment. The police had released him after five hours of questioning; he was at a fellow architect's house to work on his supermarket project and didn't plan to come

157

home until late. Nonna had shouted, *"Polizia idiota!"* to the ceiling and lit a celebratory cigarette. Mirella had laughed, then cried when my mother told her about the police finding Tamar's satchel. They had huddled in the bathroom with the faucet turned on, as if they were in an old John Le Carré novel. Nonna still knew nothing.

"Don't tell Mirella anything about Luca's bad alibi yet," Mamma said. I'd brought her the news first. "Arthur Hensen promised us an announcement tonight that would redeem him in my eyes. Perhaps he will prove his great American business acumen and announce he has Italian art in his hands. Or"—she pressed a white powder puff against her nose—"this could be an important evening for Mirella." I thought of the white rose my father always gave Mamma on her birthday. She would lift it up to her nose and invariably say, "Sweet, but not necessary." Her eyes always smiled.

"Nonna could be right about that engagement," my mother said. "She has an uncanny knack for guessing things." Mamma wasn't smiling now.

"Great timing for a celebration," I said.

My mother replaced the powder puff in its box and stepped into the skirt of her navy gabardine suit. "Luca may be lazy, morose, selfish, but he's Mirella's son, and therefore not the killer. Up at the farm you said this could be a hired killing. Alibis don't matter very much in that case."

"Maybe, but why did he lie? He must have gone somewhere, someone must have seen him."

"Oh, no doubt, he's a very handsome man."

"Who do you think hid that satchel up on the terrace, if not Luca?"

"Someone who wants to hurt Mirella or give Nonna a heart attack. You wouldn't need a key. The lock upstairs is easy to pick."

"Whoever it was had to get in the building first."

Mamma slipped on an underblouse with sweat pads sewn in. "The children on the ground floor leave the *portone* open half the time."

"Maybe someone wanted to get Luca into trouble. Did you know Nonna's already had a heart attack this summer?"

"I knew." Mamma buttoned the jacket of her suit. She looked tailored, efficient, even formidable. I was in sweats with a centimeter of cream on my face, huddling in the corner of that storage room turned into an emergency bedroom. The space was stuffed with artifacts of Monti life: suitcases, schoolbooks, old toys, a tattered poster of an ocean liner, Luca's childhood skis. Mamma's artifacts were reduced to a suitcase and a few clothes. She had left a sunny bedroom always filled with flowers in Rocca di Papa.

"You know everything," I said, fighting back an urge to pound the pillow like the five-year-old Simona, who out of frustration, or loneliness, or whatever ails a child, would pummel goose down onto her parents' bed, only to be scolded with a *"Gesù Maria!"* Mamma would quickly sew up the split seams of the pillow and say not a word to my father.

"I'm kept in the dark," I said. "Your rules aren't fair. We should stay right here, all of us, and talk openly about Luca, about what is happening to you and Gigi. Commiserate, hold hands, come up with a line of defense, call a lawyer, call Gigi. Share something!"

Mamma sat on the cot and clasped my hands, her face immensely sad. "This is a terrible moment for the Montis."

"For you, too."

"Yes." She let go of my hands to pluck at her skirt.

"Your skirt's perfectly clean!"

Mamma looked up. "Tomorrow is Tuesday. I have a morning appointment. Then we'll have lunch at Babington's. Its Englishness reassures me." Babington's Tearoom, flanking the Spanish Steps, has been around since 1896 and is one of my mother's favorite places to rest her feet after window-shopping on nearby Via Condotti. She likes its wood-paneled darkness, the prim atmosphere, the silver service, and the elegant people who speak only in soft voices. The tearoom is a throwback to an era she is at home in. I find Babington's pretentious, stuffy, and horrifyingly expensive.

She gave me a half smile. "We'll have a Blushing Bunny."

That's toast with mushrooms, creamed cheese, and grilled tomatoes.

"Ugh!" I edged closer to her. "I called Rocca di Papa this afternoon. Gigi didn't answer. I know he's not at a spa." I didn't add how I knew.

"No, he never was. He left for Florence this morning for a few days. He's looking into something for me."

"Then you speak to each other!"

"Of course we do. We've been married forty-two years. Except I didn't tell your father you're here. Please forgive me." She lifted my hair with one hand as if to weigh it. "I wanted to keep you to myself." She gave a small laugh, my hair still in her hands. "Very selfish of me."

She was protecting me. "I'm flattered."

"I've always been convinced"—she dropped her hands, clasping them on her lap—"he's the one you love most." She gave me a small, shy smile, presenting me with a vulnerability I had never imagined.

I hugged her tight. "Don't be silly, Mamma. I love you more." Gigi had dropped candy in my pockets, taught me to dance the cha-cha when I was five, to twist when I was eleven, and thought I should never, ever cut my hair. To him, I needed no correcting. But at that moment, hugging her while she kept her hands clustered on her lap, how could I not love my mother more, convinced as I was that my father was the villain?

"I hurt for you," I told her.

"It's the mother who is only as happy as her unhappiest child, not the other way around." She pushed me back gently and stood up, an embarrassed expression on her face. She had wanted more than one child, my father confessed to me once when he wondered why Carlo and I had no children. Gigi, whose mother had died at his birth, had refused.

"I didn't want to lose her," he said. "But it musn't stop you from having at least one."

"Why should you hurt?" my mother asked now. "You know nothing. Now get dressed or we'll be late."

We got through dinner relatively well. We ate on a ten-foot-long *fratino*, a thick oak refectory table that gleamed darker than the terra-cotta lozenges under my feet. Above us, oak beams had been holding up the roof of this vast penthouse since the sixteenth century. Around us, thick walls with a rough, stark white finish showed a few Dürer landscape drawings, a Titian head of a man, a Perugino Madonna.

The food was brought up from Sabatini downstairs in Piazza Santa Maria in Trastevere and was *squisito*—delicious. I ate with no thought to cells splitting up to attack my breasts.

Spaghetti alle vongole veraci, "genuine" clams with rough shells no bigger than a thumbnail sautéed in oil and garlic and topped with specks of parsley. *Pesce spada alla griglia con ramolata*, thin slabs of grilled swordfish coated by a sauce of olive oil, capers, parsley, and anchovies. Small boiled potatoes.

Carlo mentioned the delicacy of his liver.

"What's your liver got to do with anything?" Arthur asked, urging us to take seconds. He looked comfortable at the head of the table in a tall leather-backed chair that came straight out of a medieval castle. In his gray suit, white shirt, and subdued tie, he was ready to run a meeting.

"It's the national organ." Nonna spit a caper onto her fork. "Where the rot sinks."

Mirella nudged her with an elbow.

"Has the Ministry of Culture agreed to let you run our museums, Signor Hensen?" my mother asked.

"Not yet." He grinned at her, his teeth bright against his sunburned face. His bulbous nose was peeling. "That doesn't mean I'm sitting on my rear end like most of your countrymen, if you don't mind my being blunt. I'm working my way through a maze of hallowed marble corridors, and once Hensen Group International is in charge, we're going to turn the art of the Pitti and the Uffizi into greeting cards, calendars, jewelry, posters, books. Anything that sells." Arthur signaled his waiter for more wine. "Sixty percent goes to the Italian State, forty to HGI. That's more than fair, don't you think?" He panned the table with his eyes, seeming to require approval.

"Very generous of you," Carlo said.

I nodded to be pleasant, while having visions of Michelangelo's *David* flaunting his attributes on toilet paper. My mother's expression was outrage. Nonna didn't look much better. She set off for the bathroom for the second time during the meal, refusing any help.

"Waiting makes me pee," she explained in a loud voice, glaring at Arthur.

Mirella twirled her hair, a sad expression on her face.

Our host persisted. "The museums will generate more revenues by staying open longer and offering tourists Italian take-home art. Everybody will be happy." He stopped to sip wine. "Look, the merchandising operation of the Metropolitan Museum generates annual revenues of over eighty-five million dollars, and in good years they have a net income of over five million dollars. And that's only one museum. Italy's got to get moving."

"The money will be good," Mirella said, trying to sound cheerful. "It will fund scholarly works, new restorations. It will pay for added security. So much gets stolen."

"Simona believes my birthday present is going to be the missing Leonardo," Carlo said. "By mail. Incredible, no?"

I shot him a killing glance. He was supposed to have kept his mouth shut.

Arthur laughed and turned his glistening red face to me. "What gave you that idea?"

"It was a joke. Carlo likes important presents. I was making fun of him."

"Why send it to him?" Mirella seemed intrigued.

"I love packages in the mail," Carlo said. "I used to make Simona send me all my presents."

I looked for distraction. "Who did that drawing?" Mamma frowned as my finger pointed at the narrow wall of the arched entrance. Properly reared children do not point.

"Tamar Deaton knew how to use a charcoal pencil, if nothing else." Arthur picked up a spoon to help him twirl his spaghetti. "That's a portrait of Myrela. Tamar gave her a proud look that's unusual for her. It's kind of sweet."

Mirella spilled oil on her aqua silk dress. I did the same, in solidarity I told myself. My mother looked away. The white-gloved waiter offered flour, which reminded me of Perillo.

Dessert was a bombe of mocha ice cream from where else? Giolitti's.

"Hensen collects drawings," Carlo whispered with a conspiratorial wink as we rose from the table.

"I would never have guessed."

We walked back into a sunken living room where mosaics replaced the terra-cotta floor and two marble torsos held the glass coffee table on their cut-off necks. Three white linen sofas formed a wide U at one end of the vast room. Beige and tan silk pillows perched in their corners. An intricately carved travertine fireplace was large enough to sleep in. Mirella, my mother, and Nonna sat on the same white linen sofa, erect, waiting behind a wide spray of mimosa on the coffee table.

"Espresso for everyone?" Arthur asked, his waiter hovering behind him. Mirella and I declined. Mamma and Nonna said yes, with Nonna bringing out a fresh pack of Pall Malls from her cavernous purse and jiggling it on her knee as if she were placating a baby.

"You ate tonight, Simona," my mother said. "It's brought color to your cheeks." She looked pleased even though the food wasn't her doing.

"Simona looks wonderful," Carlo said, then laughed to break the tension. I was appropriately embarrassed. And flattered. "Look, Minetta, there's something I'd like to show you."

I turned to face Arthur. "What I would like is to see Tamar and Mirella's fresco."

"Sure, just off the library." Arthur offered an arm.

I slipped my hand through. Nonna glared, her mouth chewing at her impatience. I was taking the announcer away.

"*Torniamo subito,*" I told her.

Carlo prepared to follow. I wheeled around. "I said we'll be right back." I didn't want to hear him call me endearing nicknames again, and I did want Arthur Hensen alone.

My ex gave me the you've-got-me-all-wrong smile. "I thought you'd like to see the tape of our party."

"No."

"Tape coming right up," Arthur said, walking me briskly across one side of the living room. Carlo followed. The "library" was short on books and long on photographs, mostly of himself on the golf course, deep-sea fishing, skiing, slamming a tennis ball. Always alone.

At one end the bathroom door was open. I saw frescoed walls and another bowl of mimosa on the marble sink.

I stepped inside. The Roman *campagna* had been painted on the walls, with crumbling ruins, the aquaduct in the distance, poppies in the fields, a yellow glow coming from an unseen sun.

"Very pretty," I said. In one corner, just above the rim of the bathtub, a naked red-haired girl dangled a leg as if she were about to step into a bath. Tamar's signature.

"I got the idea at the Louvre." Arthur appeared in the doorway. "Corot painted a bathroom about like this one. Myrela and Tamar finished the work last week. Cost me an arm and a leg. Find the tape yet, Carlo?"

We stepped back into the library. Carlo tapped the cassette on the palm of his hand, an expectant look on his face.

"One lousy tape of a great evening," Arthur said. Carlo hesitated, waiting for me. His dependency had hooked me when we'd first met. It made me feel loved.

"We'll be right in," I told Carlo, suddenly wishing Greenhouse were here with me, telling me he loved me with his quiet, honest expression. Greenhouse, who was emotionally independent and yet wanted to live with me. "Five minutes."

Carlo spun around on his heels as if I'd given him an order and strode back into the living room. "I need some camomile tea," I heard him say. "My liver's really acting up."

16

*The mole . . . lives as long as it remains in
the dark, but when it emerges into the light
it dies immediately because it becomes
known. So it is with lies.*

—LEONARDO DA VINCI,
TALES AND ALLEGORIES

"Now what is it you want to talk to me about?" Arthur's
blue eyes went flat.

"Tamar."

"That's right. I'm supposed to be a good friend of hers."
His features slackened as if he had expected a different
question. One related to Mirella, perhaps.

"That's what the commissario said."

"Nervous little guy, Perillo. He sat on my terrace, twid-
dling his eyebrows, tapping a notebook against his knee.
He kept asking me why the terrace was so bare. How that
helps his murder investigation, I don't know. But I told
him, and I tell you—Tamar was no friend of mine."

"Mirella said something about you wanting to adopt her. Is that true?"

"All right. I have to admit"—Arthur's hand shot up to hug his balding head—"I have to admit that I was taken in by her at first. I like to get to know the HGI scholarship students, give them a tour of this apartment, let them know what they can aspire to if they put in a lot of hard work. Tamar put me in my place right away. Said artists work for art, not money. She reminded me of Debbie, my daughter. I was having some problems with her back home. Debbie's a very headstrong woman."

His gaze dropped to his desk, a smaller *fratino* with large lion paw legs. Next to the fax machine a brass frame held a large picture of a mud-spattered Debbie in shorts and a T-shirt, one foot triumphantly planted on a soccer ball.

"She'd just won her first tournament. A twelve-year-old kid already winning."

I remembered his daughter's phone call. I'd forgotten to tell Mirella.

"Now she commands a work team of her own and insists on being called Deborah."

"I hope everything's fine between you now."

He clasped his head again. "She's proud of her old dad except she's not too hep on the art stuff. Thinks my money would be better spent on hospitals. You know, her mom died of breast cancer."

Those two last words dug hard into my chest. "I'm sorry to hear that."

Arthur turned away, opened the French doors and stepped out onto the wraparound terrace. I followed. A striped awning protected us from the light rain that had just started to fall. There were only a few roses in giant terra-cotta oil jars. "Has your daughter met Mirella?"

"Debbie's never come to Rome." The regret in his voice

was palpable. "I tried telling the commissioner that I like to keep the terrace more or less bare so it doesn't take away from the real sight." He gestured down to the piazza. "He didn't buy that. Said something about solitary souls. Well, he's dead wrong. I love company."

I scanned the lighted piazza, one of the most celebrated open spaces of Rome, looking for Perillo's forsythia lady. At one end was the restaurant Sabatini, where on a hot May day Carlo and I had celebrated our fifth wedding anniversary and watched a sweet-looking American boy fall in the ancient Roman basin of the central fountain. Carlo had outrun the parents to fish him out. That afternoon while we kissed and stripped each other of clothes, we muttered about having a baby. At the last hot minute Carlo produced a condom.

"Why did you change your mind about adopting Tamar?" My eyes preferred the painless sight of the medieval basilica of Santa Maria in Trastevere at the other end of the piazza. Its twelfth-century gold mosaic glows in the morning sun and makes living in Rome all the more beautiful.

No forsythia lady.

"Tamar was greedy," Arthur said. "With all her talk about art for art's sake, she wanted in. I should have known that right from the get-go." His eyes flicked over to the library door. I heard the long peep, then the whirr of a fax machine.

"She called you on Friday."

"No." The wind changed direction, sweeping a mist of rain on our faces. "Hey, those five minutes are up." Arthur wiped his face with the back of his hand. "Myrela is going to think you and I have something going, right?"

I didn't move. "My mother overheard Tamar offer you something you had to see."

"Your mother—"

"Your announcement!" Nonna stood in the open door-way. Arthur jerked around. Next to her, Principe Maffeo held my mother's arm.

"It is getting late," my mother said.

"Arthur, this is a bad dub." Carlo walked out from the dining room door holding up the tape. "The colors are off. Where's the master tape?"

For a moment, surrounded by so many people, Arthur looked trapped. Then he raised a hand, an exaggerated grin plastered across his face. "Hello, Prince! Glad you could finally make it. You missed a great meal."

Carlo insisted. "Where's the master?"

"In your hand. What the hell do I know? That's what I paid for."

Nonna clapped her hands. *"L'annuncio!"*

Arthur stopped in mid-stride. "The only *annuncio* I'm going to make is for cognac. Anybody joining me?"

Un macello, a slaughter. That was my mother's defini-tion of the evening. Arthur answered no more questions. Nonna refused to speak. The waiter offered after-dinner drinks that only Arthur accepted. Carlo replayed Tamar's tape again "for Simona's benefit," shaking his head at the quality. Principe Maffeo talked quietly of a new show at the Schneider gallery to Mirella, who kept nodding her head as if she were listening. My mother examined the texture of her navy skirt.

The tape turned out to be a jerky procession of students laughing and waving into the camera, with Arthur popping up to palm his head and introduce the mournful represen-tative from the Cultural Ministry to every grown-up around. Carlo followed like a puppy, looking sweet and terribly young. Mirella wove in and out of the camera in a long, gray silk dress that matched her hair, reassuring everyone with a pat and a smile. My mother and father appeared only for a moment, both looking stolid and bored. I wanted Carlo to replay those seconds, to see if perhaps my parents had begun to smile, or touch, before Tamar had turned her camcorder away. I did nothing except press myself close to Mirella on the sofa, as if our bodily warmth would supply us both with reassurance.

At home Mirella cried only when she saw that Luca was fast asleep with Gorbi sharing his pillow. She took a silent, sad Nonna off to bed. I decided to save the news of Deborah Hensen's insulting phone call for a new day. My mother declared herself too tired to talk and waved good night.

I closed the living room door, settled in a corner of the sofa bed, and unfolded the sheet of fax paper. Nonna had slipped it in my hand in the car on the way home, saying, "The rewards of bad muscle control. Give me a translation in the morning. To me. No one else."

After I read it I understood that she'd picked up the sheet in Arthur's library on her way to the bathroom. The fax was in English.

1. NEED ANSWER ASAP RE: DILLER LETTER. WE RISK LOSING DEAL.
2. BOARD VOTED TO CLOSE LA CASA END OF SEMESTER. MINE WAS THE SWING VOTE.
3. IF YOU SPEND ONE CENT OF COMPANY MONEY ON A LEONARDO, REAL OR FAKE, YOU'LL BE REMOVED FROM BOARD. DON'T WASTE TIME TRYING TO FIND OUT HOW I KNOW ABOUT THE DRAWING. ALL YOU NEED IS ONE MORE MISTAKE. ONE.

DEBORAH

I crept out into the hallway and snuggled the phone under my arm. Slipping into bed I untangled the fifteen feet of phone line and dialed Greenhouse in New York.

No answer.

After dialing every ten minutes for over an hour, Greenhouse finally picked up.

"Your answering machine doesn't work!" It was now three o'clock in the morning, Rome time, nine P.M. in New York.

"I turned it off. I didn't want you to waste your money. Let me call you back. It's cheaper from here."

"No, you'll wake them up."

"How are you? Things any better?" This connection didn't echo. In fact he sounded as if he were next door and I could run out to hug him. I had a sudden urge to make slow, reassuring love until all questions had been pushed out of my head and I fell asleep. I told him about seeing my father with a woman.

"What does your mother say?"

"I didn't tell her."

"Then how do you know it's this terrible thing? Maybe she's a friend who can tell him what women want."

"What do you mean?"

"Maybe he's the one suffering. Maybe your mother has someone else."

"No, she doesn't," I said automatically. "You're thinking like a man."

"I am one."

Was that why she wasn't telling me? Where had she been this morning? What appointment did she have tomorrow? Tonight the prince had told her how well she looked, his eyes moony. She'd quickly glanced at me, her face stern.

"Maybe it's something else all together." His voice was

warm water lapping my skin. Greenhouse has had that physical power over me since I met him.

"You're jumping to conclusions, Simona." He said it sweetly, trying not to hurt. He happened to be right.

"I have good reason to this time." Having answers makes me feel secure, and I never mind discovering I am wrong, simply trading one answer for the other.

"Not everyone's a cheat, honey. Maybe that's difficult for you to see right now, with your ex-husband around."

"I guess."

"Willy's asking questions about our relationship. If we love each other we should live together. That's how he sees it."

I wanted to give both of them a sloppy hug. "Willy likes things clear-cut." I wasn't ready to say, "I'll come live with you," so I told Greenhouse about the satchel being found, Luca's missing alibi, the knife being at the school, about Deborah's fax.

"That squares with the information I have. HGI is a diversified holding company, and it's not doing well. I've got my notes right here." I heard him take a breath, imagined that wonderful silver-haired chest expand. Why wasn't I back in New York where I could rest my head in the hollow underneath his ribs?

"Last year consolidated revenues fell seventeen percent to under four hundred million dollars and led to the first operating loss in over fifteen years."

"Arthur calls himself a fixer-upper." I wasn't quite sure what a diversified holding company meant.

"That's exactly what he is. His group buys tottering companies, gets them going again, and then sells. Except they got caught with too many companies just as the economy changed. Deborah Hensen wants her father out and is spreading the rumor that he's a doddering old man."

"He's not, but can she oust him?"

"If she swings certain board members her way. Her mother left her almost as much stock as her father has. Together they have the majority, but they haven't seen eye to eye since Dad left Mom."

"Aha, another case of the cheating male."

"Don't do your usual leap. The facts change according to who's doing the talking. My source—he's a reporter for the *Minneapolis Tribune*—gave me both sides. Dad Hensen left Mom Hensen and a year later Mom Hensen died of cancer. The daughter and some friends of Mom, who was a beauty and big in the charity circuit, claim that Dad walked out when he heard Mom was sick and both her breasts were going to be cut off."

"Mastectomy, please." I hadn't told Greenhouse about my cystic breasts, afraid he'd think less of them.

"Sorry. I'm reading from my notes and that's what my source said."

"What does Arthur Hensen claim?"

"He refused to speak to the press about it, but according to my source the country club locker room gang claims Hensen left before she was diagnosed. And she was too angry to take him back when he did find out."

"Another woman?"

"No woman ever showed up at his side."

"How did Deborah Hensen get to be acting chair?"

"Dad. He's been trying to make up to her ever since his wife died."

"A guilty conscience."

"A father who loves his daughter."

"Okay, thanks. Now I know why she thinks he's gutless, why she hates him, why he'll probably never marry Mirella. But I don't have any idea who told Deborah about the Leonardo and why Arthur announced an announcement—whatever it was going to be—and then changed his mind."

"Sim, let it rest. Just figure out what's going on with your parents and come home. I miss you. I don't want you to be in any danger."

"I know nothing."

"Sim, I wish you'd let me call you. It'll only ring for a second."

"I do pay my own way in life." Barely. I found his worry naively old-fashioned. Sexy.

"I'm going to sell my body to one horny NYPD detective." For another ten minutes I whispered to Homicide Detective Stanley Greenhouse exactly what I planned to do to earn my money, starting with his toes, slowly working my way up, getting snagged midway over certain protrusions, finally winding up with his head pressed between my breasts, while I kissed his hands to soppy softness. It was a silly game that made us both concentrate on what had always functioned in our relationship. We finally hung up. I got up, undressed, opened the French doors to the balcony to let the cold night air of Rome cool me off.

I was in some in-between place, I realized, physically standing on the shore of the past, the shore of the future only a vague, scary outline. Half my heart was here with my family, with Carlo. I didn't love him anymore, but I was mired in regret. All I felt was that those years had gone by and had only produced a deep ache. Remember the good times, I told myself.

But if I did, real hurt would start up again.

Why couldn't I simply move on?

I shivered and reached to close the doors of the balcony. On the street below, a woman slipped behind a tree. This time no forsythia.

17

---

*Ruins and basilicas, palaces and colossi,
set in the midst of a sordid present. . . .*
—GEORGE ELIOT, MIDDLEMARCH

Only Nonna and Gorbi were in the house when I woke up. She was sitting in her usual chair in front of the piano in the living room, tarot cards floating on her lap, her head reaching down over her chest. Gorbi had folded himself on the sofa behind my legs, snout dropped over my waist. They had both been watching me sleep.

"It's more fun than waiting for death," Nonna said, eyeing the coffee table. I had left the fax folded under the glass ashtray. "Translate for me. What's it say about the Leonardo? Does Hensen have it?"

"Not according to his daughter. She thinks Mirella is trying to sell him a fake." I got off the sofa and lay down on the carpet, Gorbi trying to lick my face.

"Her father is going to marry my daughter and if the woman doesn't like it, you know what we say in Rome? She can console herself with garlic!"

177

I did fifty stomach crunches, groaning myself awake, debating whether to tell Nonna about the school closing. I twisted my head her way on a lateral crunch. With someone's fortune spread out on her lap, she looked sibylic. Wise.

I stood up, flushed, out of breath. "Hensen Group International is going to close La Casa. I'm sorry."

Nonna sucked on her lower lip for a few seconds as if tasting herself would give her strength. "What else did the note say?"

"Daughter doesn't like Daddy. She wants to kick him out of the company."

"He has enough money not to work. Say nothing to Mirella about the school. Yesterday was bad for her. Destroy that fax." She reached for it.

"No, you don't." I slipped the fax out of her fingers and plunged it in my pocket. "This is going back where you found it."

"Folded in four? He'll know we took it."

"We? Don't worry. I'll take care of everything."

"I have lost faith in those words."

"Where is my mother?"

"She had an appointment."

"Why all these appointments?"

"Olga wants you to meet her at Babington at one-thirty."

"Where's Luca?" His bedroom door was open. I stepped over wet towels on my way to the bathroom. I knew Mirella was off to the Capitoline Museum for her last class before spring break. "I thought he slept until the noon cannon." At the corridor window, the magnolia branch was black with rain.

"At the university," Nonna shouted. "His supermarket project is due today. He got the ace of pentacles."

I showered quickly, skipping half of my body. I had

made an appointment to meet Principe Maffeo in his palazzo at ten and I was going to be late. I was annoyed I'd overslept, missing everyone. I scrubbed my head hard as if to clear it. I was missing things from the beginning of my visit. The surprise of being dropped back into my past had put me in my own time warp, short in years but as wide as an ocean when it came to feelings. So many muddled feelings that I couldn't think with assurance.

Not that I ever do come up with forward-moving, declarative thoughts. I push and pry, stumbling upon truths rather than plucking them out of dark corners. My strength is persistence, not vision. I have convinced myself that there is some honor to stubborn determination, but this time I was waffling.

I got dressed, pulling on last night's gray skirt with a blue sweater Mamma had knitted for me at least ten years before. Outside, it was still raining. A cold wind was seeping through an inch of open window.

"What's the ace of pentacles mean?" I asked Nonna back in the living room as I toweled my hair dry.

"Success! Bliss! Luca will get thirty with honors for that supermarket." That translated into an A plus. "And you'll catch pneumonia going out with that wet hair."

I dropped down in front of her. "I'll catch pneumonia from bacteria, not wet hair. Nonna, lying for Luca is no good!"

Her eyes seemed transparent this morning, as if she had left them out in the rain to clean. "He is my child's son. I will defend him as strongly as my daughter does. Luca was with me Saturday morning, except for the ten minutes it took him to go to the pharmacy for Monica's medicine."

"That's not what the pharmacist says."

"The word of a German is not worth the spit it's coated with."

Instead of arguing, I made coffee. Coffee is *'na mano santa*—a holy hand. It cures all ills, or at least the social ones. Take a sip and the world seems to straighten itself out. Without your help. My holy hand was going to be decaffeinated (doctor's orders), a blasphemy for Nonna. I wasn't going to tell her.

"I didn't know Oreste had a son." I dabbed blusher on my cheeks in the hallway mirror, waiting for the familiar telltale smell of ready coffee.

"Aldo. A good-for-nothing. Mirella thinks he needs affection. Affection is her cure-all. She got him the job with Principe Maffeo."

I brought two cups of coffee into the living room. If I was going to be fifteen minutes late, I might as well be thirty minutes late. I was beginning to think like a Roman again. "Are Luca and Aldo friends?"

"Aldo's head is only good for holding his ears apart. He's not fit company for Luca." She slurped from her cup, stopped, sniffed at the coffee.

"I've lost the touch," I said.

She nodded. "Why are you asking about Luca?"

"Perillo mentioned him. I wondered if he was involved."

"Aldo wouldn't know the *Mona Lisa* if I rubbed his nose in her smile." She lowered her cup. The coffee had stained her mouth like lipstick, giving her a coquettish look. "Let Perillo worry about the Leonardo. You take care of your mother." She removed her teeth and I got no more out of her.

It had rained all night, and that morning, as I got off the bus and walked down one of my favorite Roman streets, a dark sky opened up to splashes of blue and sun washed the sides of buildings, restoring their ripe peach color. Palazzo Brandeschi is on Via dei Coronari, the street of rosary makers, flanked by Renaissance buildings that house small, precious antique shops and a few encroaching junk shops. It's a narrow, perfectly straight street which leads to the Sant'Angelo bridge and the Vatican on the other side of the Tiber.

My father likes to say: All roads may lead to Rome, but in Rome all roads lead to the Vatican. He had led himself to Florence. Mamma refused to explain why.

The entrance to the palazzo was on Piazzetta San Simeone, facing a pale pink side of the stern, newly restored Palazzo Lancellotti. In contrast, Palazzo Brandeschi was a dark gray, cramped, four-story building with fading grisaille work. A large, green rubber pipe ran down from a third floor window, looking like a long stack of garbage pails. Renovations had begun. A bright blue and white sign by a side door announced La Casa dell'Arte. A corner of the building held a glassed-in fresco of the Madonna. Shrouded in a painted brocade gown that had lost its gilt, her hand raised for eternity, she had a puzzled look on her face, as if she didn't know whom to bless. Underneath her, a torn garbage bag spewed soup bones. Across the street, a Hare Krishna center offered vegetarian cooking.

Principe Maffeo was waiting for me on the first-floor landing. I ran up the scooped stone steps worn smooth by five centuries of feet and apologized for being late.

He clasped big-knuckled white hands over his waist, looking incongruous in blue jeans and an old navy mock turtleneck sweater that Italian fishermen wear. "*Subito.* That is a favorite word in Rome. Make a request and you will inevitably be told, 'right away!' This being the eternal city, our sense of immediacy is somewhat prolonged."

"Then I'm forgiven." I asked him about Tamar—my calling card into any conversation.

"The girl disarmed me with her obvious need to nest in a warm corner." The stairwell was dank and somber, with threadbare wine-dark tapestries covering the two-foot-thick walls. What little I had seen of Mirella's school downstairs was a blinding white to dispel the gloom.

"Then you and Tamar were friends?" I wanted to verify what Luca had told me without revealing my source. My excuse for the visit was the much-talked-about portrait of Caterina Brandeschi by Leonardo's pupil, Francesco Melzi. The painting hung just behind the principe's grave gray head.

"The girl had no restraint. I live alone. I enjoy my privacy. She could not understand that. We parted inamicably, which I regret only because she is dead. One likes to think the dead are friends, lest they wreak some terrible revenge."

"You are superstitious?" I stepped to one side to see the painting.

"No." He followed my gaze and turned, lifting a heavy hand toward the dimly lit portrait of his ancestor. "Although according to the ballad, my tragic ancestor avenged herself in a terrifying way."

Caterina Brandeschi looked pretty despite Melzi's flat, graceless painting. She had a lustrously white oval face, heavily lidded sensual eyes, and the budlike lips typical of Renaissance paintings. Bright red hair was parted in the middle and pulled tightly back; a string of seed pearls was barely visible across her high forehead. She wore no other jewelry. Dressed in black, with a dark background, the white face with its cap of red hair seemed to float toward me. Not a painting I'd like to encounter at night in the dark bend of a staircase.

"How did she die?" What reminded me of Tamar was her pensive look. She was mulling something over.

"I'll tell you over coffee."

The prince made it himself, turning on fluorescent lights in a yellowing marble kitchen that had gilt moldings on the ceiling and had once been used as a music room. The original kitchen had been on the first floor next to the stable, both now part of La Casa dell'Arte. He had no decaffeinated, and out of politeness I pretended it didn't matter. I was, I have to admit, just a little daunted by his title. I was also remembering Greenhouse's words. "Maybe your mother has someone else."

The leaded glass window let us hear the rain ring out on the cobblestones of the narrow courtyard. A student yelled for an umbrella. A girl answered back. I casually asked about Aldo. Was he hired recently?

"Yes, a few weeks ago. As an assistant mason. Can you not hear them?" He cocked his head. The thick walls released a faint sound of hammering. "Aldo, however, has not shown up. The head mason has informed me that he is helping his father kill a hog this morning." He inhaled deeply through his patrician nose. "I have for years been a vegetarian."

"Has he been friendly with any of the students? With Tamar, for instance?"

"I stay away from the school as much as possible. I have asked the masons to do the same." Principe Maffeo reached for the silver sugar bowl in a tall glassed-in cabinet. Its sheen surprised me.

"I appreciate silence," he said. The prince did a careful half turn. All his movements were slow, as if he had nothing in life to press him forward. "The police suspect Aldo?"

"They find him interesting."

The prince's finger swam in the air between us. "You are clever, like your mother. You ask about Aldo to establish my alibi. I was out of Rome on Saturday. Commissario Perillo knows all the details. I am not your killer."

"Of course not, but we might be dealing with a hired killer. Maybe hired only to steal a drawing. At the last minute, he gets carried away."

"I have hired only masons. They work with bricks." The prince waved for me to follow. "Whoever he was, hired or not, and assuming the killer is a he, he would have had to know the girl had the drawing with her. If it is a drawing we are talking about." With two cups on a plastic tray we crossed the ballroom, a long, icy cold room with dust motes dancing on the geometric patterns of the marble floor and three chandeliers covered in dust cloths dark with soot.

"Would the girl advertise her prize?" the prince asked.

On the ceiling, clusters of gilt rosebuds and lightning rods represented Beauty and Strength—the Brandeschi motto—and half-naked nymphs floated down from a leak-pocked sky.

"The killer didn't have to know," I said. "He just had to think he knew." Occasional silver streaks, all that was left of once-mirrored walls, picked up varied slivers of our bodies as we walked by. My Greenwich Village studio would have fit into the room ten times. "If not a Leonardo, what else could she have had worth stealing?"

"Cash. It is the most sought-after commodity."

The dining room was as cold as the ballroom, and the nymphs had put on clothes and offered baskets of cascading fruit. A peach looked as if it might fall on my head any second, and I wondered how this palazzo weighed on its owner. Would he ever have the courage to walk away and start life somewhere else, as I had? For a second, I imagined my mother in these rooms, mistress of the house. She liked things clean and neat. She would hate it.

We settled in a small den, stacked from floor to ceiling with modern books. "I broke up some of the rooms," the prince said. "And lowered the ceiling. Unfortunately my aristocratic title gives me no discount on heat. Or on taxes. Unless I restore my entire palazzo."

"It would help to find a Leonardo, then." I sat on a shredded damask armchair.

"You are correct." He offered me sugar, which I declined. "However, I have not found it and I am conflicted as to whether I want to." He stirred his coffee. "The commotion in the art world. The media. Scholars polluting my privacy."

"Do you have family secrets you wish to keep hidden?" I asked lightly.

The prince half smiled. Again I got the impression that facial expression was unfamiliar to him. "Secrets are the cement that holds up palazzos. At least that's what novelists would like us to think. Caterina Brandeschi must have had hers. She was killed on her wedding day. Stabbed in the heart like the American girl. You came to hear about Caterina, did you not?"

"I came to help my mother. She wants a quick solution to Tamar's death."

"Olga is a great woman. She—"

"Are you going to sell Arthur Hensen your palazzo?" I didn't want to hear about my mother, not from this man.

He stiffened. "In a moment of weakness I told Arthur I would consider it. Now I have changed my mind."

"May I ask why? You have no heirs."

"I wish to live here for the rest of my life. At my death it will go to the Italian State. They will paint it pink or yellow as they are slowly doing with all of Rome. 'Ice cream colors,' *The Economist* calls them. I find them youthful.

"Perhaps the palazzo will become a student center. I like the idea of young people, although I do not enjoy their noise. I hear the students in the courtyard with those impossibly loud American voices. With no sense of the weight of history. I shall miss them, however."

Miss them? Did he know HGI was going to shut down La Casa? "Is the school closing?"

His eyes squinted. "Of course not." He did know. It was clear from the awkward look on his face, the sudden need to rub hands over long-boned thighs. How had he found out?

"It's Easter time," he said. "In two days they'll be off, traipsing over the rest of Italy."

I let it ride, shy about discussing filched information with a friend of my mother's.

"Are you still actively looking for the drawing?" I asked.

"I don't actively look for anything. The American girl foraged everywhere until I stopped her. She may have found it Wednesday night in my library."

"Hadn't the library been searched before then?"

"Hmm." He uncrossed his legs. "Yes. Luca had seen to it. The furniture was moved, the flooring examined. Every volume opened in my presence, each page leafed. There are at least a thousand books."

"That seems to exclude her finding the drawing that night. Why did she come back, then?"

"I don't know, but she told me I was a stupid old man not to want her as my daughter." He brushed a large hand over his face. "I have no children. No wife." The light from the window cast an ashen shadow over his face. He looked as if he had lost at the gambling table.

"I met your mother at Easter time, when I was a university student. Just before the war. There is a small Brandeschi Palazzo in Venice. It has since been sold. It is odd that we should have met again at Easter time." His expression softened, aging him. "I have always thought very highly of Olga, but at the time my mother . . . " He softly dropped a hand on the armrest.

I felt heat on my cheeks. My mother, daughter of store-keepers, would not have been the proper bride. For a second I thought of the possibility of being Principessa Simona Brandeschi, calling this palazzo home.

"Pine cones in your head," Nonna would have said. His daughter would have been someone else entirely.

"Your father is a very lucky man." His jaw slackened; his eyes sagged. Principe Maffeo's love for my mother was palpable, maddening.

"You should have fought for her!" I wanted to shout, then embarrassed, feeling a traitor to my father, I veered away by asking about the Caterina legend.

"Tragic," he said. I did not know if he meant the legend or his own missed opportunity.

Caterina was killed on her wedding day, he repeated, stabbed on the corner of the palazzo underneath the fres-coed Madonna. The ballad blamed the groom, a Lancellotti living across the piazza, who six months later married into the Orsini family, a far richer and more potent name than the Brandeschi's had ever been.

"We have only one cardinal in our family," the principe said without a trace of irony. "No popes."

One of the groom's servants, found with the knife under his bed, was tortured, then drawn and quartered, but the Roman *popolino*—the "little" people—came up with other versions, all of them recorded in the many verses of the ballad. The servant was in love with Caterina and killed her out of jealousy. The groom's mother, dead set against this demeaning marriage, had the girl killed. Caterina's own mother had stabbed her, her daughter pregnant with her father's seed. The father had her killed, afraid that the Brandeschi name would be dishonored once the groom discovered his bride was no virgin. Caterina's revenge had been to get them all killed off by the plague within two years. Only her father survived her wrath, the ballad said.

I listened while Principe Maffeo's face came to life with his storytelling, both of us engaged in a timeless Roman activity: sitting and talking about nothing particularly useful, cups of coffee in our hands, while outside events unfurled of which we knew nothing.

In Viale Parioli, my mother sat in an office and listened to her options.

In Florence, my father gulped a coffee with an old friend and asked advice in full view of the famous copy of Michelangelo's *David*.

In Piazzale del Verano, Luca, a grade of thirty with honors for his supermarket project in his pocket, left the morgue to accompany Tamar's body to the airport.

In Via San Vitale, at police headquarters, Perillo interrogated the German pharmacist.

In old Rome, the killer waited.

18

---

*My heart, I believe, ceased to beat for a
moment, and it was as much as I could do
to sustain myself from falling down upon
the ground in a swoon.*

—LADY ANNA MILLER,
LETTER FROM ITALY (1776)

I remembered the fax as I watched Nina, the blond owner
of the Osteria dell'Antiquario, bustling to wipe her tables
dry, layers of checked tablecloths thrown over her shoulders like a shawl. Now that the rain sky had retreated,
Piazzetta San Simeone had turned into a bewitched spot,
lighted by the Roman sun. I greeted the owner.

"*Simona! Bella mia!*" Nina ran over, waving her wet
towel and hugged me, smelling of rosemary. I felt instantly
guilty that I wasn't eating at her place.

"You haven't changed a bit!"

I explained that my mother was waiting for me; I
promised to come back. The food was homey, the sun glorious. After my separation I'd gone to live on a nearby side

street, on Via di Panico, an apt address under the circumstances. Osteria dell'Antiquario had been my second home.

I thought of Carlo and remembered the fax. I wanted him to return it to Arthur, saying he'd picked it up accidentally. I didn't want to be responsible for a deal falling through or for Arthur not knowing his school was being closed down. I had hoped to send Arthur an exact replica from a copy shop, a clean, unfolded sheet, but then I looked at the fax again. The date, time, and the sender's number was clearly stamped on it. Carlo would have to do. I called Carlo from the Osteria. Could I drop by for just a second? I was in a hurry, but I needed a favor.

The idea of a favor seemed to delight him. "*Subito. Subitissimo.*" He mentioned spectacular views.

I reminded him that I had little time and hung up. I had an hour and a half until my lunch date with my mother. I was pretty sure I didn't want to spend it with Carlo.

Nina stopped me outside. "I saw you come out of Palazzo Brandeschi. I wouldn't go there if I were you. An American student got killed."

"That's not where Tamar got killed."

"Ah, you know about it. Well, I think Caterina's revenge—" She let go of my arm and eyed an American couple contemplating the sky and the empty tables. Nina pointed to the sun. "*Bello!* Good for you." She hustled to a table and pushed two chairs back. She patted her stomach. "*Buono.* Cheap."

The American man laughed and sat down. "Come on, Ethel, plop! My feet are killing me. *Dos* glasses *blanco vino, por favor.*"

"Honey, that's Spanish." Ethel checked her chair for dampness and sat down, her green Michelin guide soldered to her hand. "*Due bicchieri di vino bianco, per favore.* That's the correct way to say it."

Nina had already gone back inside. She can understand an order for wine in any language. I followed.

"Did you know Tamar?" I asked.

"She ate here sometimes. At night. Always by herself. She paid in drawings. My husband says they're worthless and I'm crazy, but how could I turn her away?" She was filling a liter bottle with white wine from a barrel. She winked at me. "They start with two glasses, then the Roman stupor sets in and they drink this clean. Never fails."

"Why couldn't you turn Tamar away?"

"She said my cooking was as good as her mother's. Besides, she reminded me of you." She hurried outside with me in tow. "Allora, today I cook *spezzatino con patate*—beef stew with potatoes—*pollo alla cacciatora*, hunter's chicken, and rigatoni with *salsiccia*."

I went back inside to the kitchen. Her husband, a big man with a blowfish head, did the cooking.

"Show me the American girl's drawings," I asked.

"You want to buy?" He did not remember me.

"Maybe."

"Well, you're too late. The teacher bought all six of them this morning when I was bringing the vegetables in from the market."

"What teacher?" A huge colander full of half-cooked rigatoni sat by the sink, waiting to be plunged back into boiling water to be finished off according to demand.

"The pretty gray-haired lady. The one with a bike left over from the Roman Empire."

Mirella.

"What kind of drawings were they?"

"Heads. That girl had a way with them. She even did me. The moon man. I sold that, too. I prefer ten thousand lira notes with Leonardo's mug on them any day. Last one

she left was last Wednesday. Best of the lot. A self-portrait
I think."

My pulse did a skip.

"Gino!" Nina called out from the dining room. "*Un riga-
tone e un pollo!*"

"*Subito!* Don't tell Nina. She'll want to buy new tablecloths."

I put the unpleasant thought of Mirella possessing the
Leonardo out of my mind and sauntered toward Carlo's
apartment. America slipped off my back as I looked into
remembered shops with baskets of geraniums hanging outside to celebrate the upcoming antiques fair. A woman I had
seen every workday morning on my walk to the bus sat
where I had left her, by the window of her English antiques
store, smoking her usual cigarette, her champagne toy poo-
dle on her lap. Her hair was redder, her dog younger.

The corner bar had been spruced up, my building
painted a bright ocher, its balconies lined with cyclamens.
A fancy pink bow on the *portone* announced the birth of a
baby girl to a family living there. The mailman walked by
and nodded. I was a familiar face, but he did not place the
face with a name and an address. He did not know that I
had been gone four years, living in a very different country
that urged me to be dynamic, assertive, happy, to hold my
life in my own hands.

I looked at my reflection in the window of my old pots
and pans store. Had I changed? And if I had, why did I
have such a stake in keeping my parents chained to an
ideal of my own making? At Babington my mother was
possibly going to tell me Gigi had deceived her. Or that
she loved Principe Maffeo. Or that she was bored with
married life.

I dropped my head against the window, still wet with
rain, and suddenly wanted ten years to rewind, to when I

was still married to Carlo and Rome was my home, to when my parents would meet us for our monthly dinners at Piperno's in the Ghetto and we would feast on artichokes and codfish fried to a crisp without a thought of harm coming our way.

"God damn Carlo!" I said out loud. Pointing the finger brought comfort.

Carlo lived on Via Paola, part of a small area that had been the center of banking in Renaissance Italy. His apartment was in a narrow sixteenth-century building next to a trattoria. A busload of German tourists swarmed on the sidewalk, waiting to file in. Behind them, on the other side of the Tiber, loomed Castel Sant'Angelo—Hadrian's tomb and fortress to the popes. On top, the angel who supposedly saved sixth-century Rome from the plague, sheathed his sword as if his work was done. At the other end, beyond the wide Corso Vittorio Emanuele II, the white façade of Saint John of the Florentines looked like a freshly painted backdrop stolen from the opera house. Spectacular views, Carlo was right.

The front door of his building was missing a lock. A sign posted on the door told me the priest would come by on Easter Thursday to bless the house. The four mailboxes had no doors. A small, cobwebbed grate above the door gave no light, and I managed the steep stairs thanks to a naked lightbulb hanging above Carlo's door atop the first flight of stairs.

He had left the door ajar for me. I walked down a long room, narrowed by built-in closets on one side. Wooden beams squared off the high ceiling in chessboard-style partitions. The only natural light came from two windows at the end. It was a Roman version of the Soho loft.

The smell of burning coffee made me smile. Carlo always forgot his coffee on the stove, his mind jumping ahead to some other perceived need.

"Carlo, the coffee's burning!" I passed a dark bedroom created out of black modular furniture. How many times had I called out that phrase?

The kitchen was tiny, with no windows, hemmed in by flimsy plaster walls. A New York kitchen, I thought, turning off the gas. Two brown and white cups, the kind bars offer, were waiting on the stainless steel sink. I filled only one with coffee, put in two sugars and took it with me to the end of the one long room. How many times had I taken Carlo coffee?

A film script lay sprawled on a small round table. Indian cloths draped three sagging sofas. An earthenware lamp sat on the floor, the light bulb on. Rectangles of light spilled onto the floor from two French windows. Dribbles of tomato sauce marked a recent meal.

The room needed a cleaning badly, but then so did my place in the Village. The apartments were not unalike. Both studios, although Carlo's was much bigger; both with the slipshod, transient quality of someone who hopes "better" is tomorrow.

Across the street, above Carlo's empty balcony, a woman peered at me from a window above the English Methodist Church. Her emaciated, ashen face was topped by a badly made wig. A very sick woman, that much was clear. When my eyes met hers, she retreated behind a curtain. How many women had she seen in here? A banner across her room declared, "God is with you!"

"Coffee's getting cold!" I stumbled over the phone line. With my eyes I followed it up narrow wooden stairs to a dark, low loft. Sauce dribbled along the way.

"Are you in the bathroom?" Why was there such

silence? I looked at the still wet spots. My heart skipped a beat. The color was wrong!

I ran up the eight steps to the loft, the coffee cup forgotten in my hand.

Carlo lay on the floor between two beds.

I screamed, spilling coffee over the blood on his shirt. I threw myself down on my knees and cupped my hand over his heart. It was still beating.

I hugged him, grateful for his life, in my hysteria not even thinking of using the phone that sat on a sharp marble end table only inches away. Caressing his cheek, crying, I told him everything would be all right.

When I finally called 113, the siren's wail had already turned the corner.

The ambulance came from Santo Spirito Hospital just across the river. Carlo had hit the back of his head. There was blood on the marble end table.

"Na brutta botta," a burly, raucous-voiced attendant said while I filled out a long form in triplicate. An ugly blow.

"Can't this wait?" I asked, fumbling in my memory for Carlo's long-dead father's name.

"Don't worry, he's stable. Ciccio's giving him a healthy dose of oxygen. You can thank the lady across the street." He pointed to the window. "With her cancer, she's a regular at Santo Spirito. She knows about dying."

"Carlo isn't dying!"

"Who said he was?" The attendant wiggled fingers at me to hurry up.

Under allergies, I wrote tetracycline. I knew there was something else, but I couldn't remember.

"Someone bopped him in the nose." The attendant took the form. "And his gut. He's got vomit in his mouth. Ehi, Ciccio, what's the number for getting beat up? I'm gonna play Lotto." His companion called the police.

I followed the stretcher down. As a neighbor held the street door wide open, I noticed blood on the stairs. He had been hit in the narrow entranceway. His mailbox was the only empty one, I realized now.

"You stay here and wait for the police," the deep-voiced man said as he slid Carlo into the ambulance.

A huddle of people on the sidewalk aired opinions, each one an expert.

"No, I'm going with you!" To hell with the police! I wasn't going to get caught up in the red tape of explanations.

"He's my husband!" Fear for his well-being erased divorce and anger.

"Your husband?" He gave me a quick wary look, as if by being a wife, I was suddenly suspect. "Too bad, but you've got to wait." He left no one to guard me, not because he thought I was innocent, but because his job was with the victim, not the perpetrator.

I remembered. "He's also allergic to licorice!" The ambulance door slammed.

I ran back to Carlo's apartment to get my purse and scribble a note for the police, telling them where to find me and to inform Commissario Perillo. I knocked on the window-pane and mouthed a thank you to the wigged lady. She nodded. Then I skipped back down to the street and plunged across the Sant'Angelo Bridge, whizzing by Senegalese vendors offering fake Chanel bags, a sight now as permanent a part of Rome as the smiling stone angels of the bridge.

The *Pronto Soccorso*, the emergency room of the Hospital of the Holy Spirit, was crowded with cries and coughing. Beds crammed the corridor as I ran without direction, searching for the admittance desk, for the burly ambulance attendant. An old man looked up, his bleary eyes lighting up as I passed him, mistaking me for a relative or a doctor perhaps. His arm lay limp against his thigh. A woman hovering over a bed waved a towel at me and pleaded for rubbing alcohol. "She's burning up!" A nurse briskly took over, cooing to the child. A doctor rushed by. I grabbed his arm. "Admittance!" He pointed to a room with a closed glass door.

"Carlo Linetti," I told a blond woman squeezed in by a litter of files. Blue smoke curled behind her typewriter. "They just brought him in. Head wound. I'm his wife."

"Serious injury?" She was filling in a form with a fountain pen.

"I don't know. He's unconscious."

She kept on writing, her head bent so that I had a full view of her black roots. "Name's not familiar. The bad cases they take right up to the OR or radiology. I'll get the file later, if someone remembers. It's pure Kafka in here." She sighed, and reached for her cigarette. "Try downstairs at information."

"I already have!"

She didn't look up once.

I stopped a volunteer nun balancing a full bedpan. She sent me to radiology on the third floor. Carlo was not there.

"Where's the operating room?" I asked the desk attendant, a chinless man with lusterless eyes.

"What's the point of telling you? It's off-limits. If he's hit his head, sooner or later he'll come through here." He gestured toward a brown sofa underneath an arched window. "You can see a wedge of the cupola. It's a good place to wait."

The sight of St. Peter's, however small, was supposed to console me. A woman dressed all in black sat on one end of the sofa, her head dropped over her bosom, fast asleep.

Withered white knees peeked above her rolled black stockings.

"I'm going to scream," I whispered, my mouth so dry I could hardly get the words out.

The desk attendant reached out for my hand. "Let me get you a glass of water."

"I don't want water, I want my husband!"

He took pity on me and started making calls, endlessly repeating "Carlo Linetti" in a punctured voice, like a penitent reciting the rosary. At the fifth call, he tapped the desk.

"Dottor Cardinale's got him. He's being examined, then they're bringing him down here." He wrinkled his nose in a smile. "Could only have worked here, someone with that name, with the Vatican at two paces."

I went out into the hallway and called Mirella and asked for my mother, who had already left for the restaurant. I told Mirella Carlo had fallen and hurt himself. She gasped and offered to run over.

"No, please." I wanted my mother with her sensible, cool way of handling emergencies. Mirella would hug and caress, making me cry. That would not help Carlo. It would not find a killer. Besides, if Carlo had been attacked, I didn't want Mirella to know. Maybe I was trying to protect her, maybe the thought of those restaurant drawings made me suspicious. I don't know.

I called Babington. It was ten minutes past one. My mother had not yet arrived. I left a message. A worker walked up the hospital stairs, his newspaper hat held in a rough, tanned hand. Tears welled in his eyes. I bent my head as he passed me, not wanting to intrude, and left a message with the restaurant.

Back in radiology the bare-knees woman still slept. On her lap she held two oranges and a bar of chocolate. She, at least, was prepared for the wait.

"There are two risks to your husband's concussion," Dottor Cardinale said thirty-seven minutes later, as he pulled a discreetly striped cuff from under his white coat. Behind him, Saint Peter's dome pushed into view.

"Will he die?"

"It's highly unlikely, but he could have a blood clot on the brain which a CAT scan will determine." He smiled, showing off how handsome he was, as if his good looks should interest me more than Carlo's health. He reeked of what I took at first to be disinfectant. "Of course the absence of a blood clot at the present moment does not rule out a subsequent blood clot development." Dottor Cardinale stepped closer, and I realized his smell was aftershave.

"He was attacked." I had seen Carlo only briefly as they wheeled him in. The back of his head had been shaved. His face, cleaned of blood, was the color of mold, except for one reddened cheek. He looked like a corpse, and I had clenched my fists to keep from crying out.

"Yes," Dottor Cardinale said, "someone hit him hard in the stomach and the face, producing a severe nosebleed. He then fainted and hit his head against something very sharp."

The killer had waited for the mail, probably slipped behind the open door after the mailman left. Carlo had interrupted him.

"He went back upstairs," I said. "He was trying to reach the phone." The sight of blood always made him sick. "What's the second risk?"

"The possibility of diffuse axonal injury." Dottor Cardinale flashed teeth at me.

"What's axonal mean?" I had the desire to make Dottor Cardinale's nose bleed all over his Missoni tie.

"If he has injured a hundred nerves in a critical area, he might wind up with a cognitive problem. Speech impairment, memory loss. This is, of course, only a possibility. We will know more when he comes out of his coma. Who hit him?"

"That is for me to find out," Perillo said, his Timberlands squeaking on the travertine floor. "When can he talk?" He graced me with a nod and introduced himself to the doctor. A finger rubbed frowning eyebrows.

The doctor glanced at the wall clock, annoyance crossing his face. "I must go back downstairs."

Perillo followed him. The sleeping woman jerked her head up, aiming a half-opened eye at those noisy shoes. "Wait for me," Perillo called out to me with a twist of his head.

"That's what they all say," the woman grumbled. "I've grown old waiting."

I left.

I should have stayed to answer Perillo's questions, stayed to watch over Carlo. I should have, but I couldn't.

When hit by momentous events, I run away. This time I only went as far as the Lungotevere, the wide road that flanks the Tiber. The air was thick with exhaust fumes, the noise deafening as cars and buses honked in a useless protest against the lunchtime snarl of traffic. Italians think their cars are an extension of their sexual organs, an instrument they cannot do without no matter how many subway lines are opened or how bad the traffic gets.

The sidewalks were thick with nuns, gathered in Rome for Easter Week. A time of great sorrow and rejoicing, my mother had taught me. I paced, waiting for her.

Ten minutes later she came walking across the wide Victor Emmanuel bridge, clutching her bag, while gypsy girls not yet in their teens gaggled around her. One girl tried to grab her hand to read her fortune. Mamma's expression was grim.

A *vigile*, wearing a skirt short enough to stop traffic, shooed the gypsies away. Satisfied, she tucked mounds of black hair under a skewed white cap.

My mother marched me right back to the hospital. "To do your duty," she said in a tone that could not be denied.

Perillo leaned against a wall of Carlo's room, reading *La Repubblica*. Carlo was still unconscious behind a blue curtain, his mouth open, an IV attached to his hand. Tubes in his nose fed him oxygen. Relatives of the other four patients crowded the room.

I gaped at Carlo, willing him to open his eyes, wishing his mouth would move to say, "Ciao, Minetta, what brings you here?" in that happy surprised way he had when I used to wake him up on Sunday mornings, his coffee in my hand.

"It's good to talk to him," Perillo said. "They hear even in a coma."

My mother gave him a doubtful glance. "Your kind of talk is best done outside." She sat down rigid in the only empty chair.

We walked the corridor with friends, relatives, everyone with the tired, defeated air of a long vigil. Perillo had the same look. I answered his questions, told him my theory of the attack.

"The mailman confirmed the delivery of a package," Perillo said. "Carlo was waiting outside the building, along with half of Germany waiting to be fed next door."

"Did anyone see the attacker?"

"The mailman didn't. The tourists have left for Pompei. The neighbors are being questioned. What is interesting is that the mailman's package was twenty-two by thirty centimeters approximately. In inches that's eight by twelve, more or less. That was Leonardo's preferred manuscript size. I have been doing my homework. Except for the Leicester Codex which is—"

"Commissario, why wasn't Carlo being watched?"

"It is my fault this happened, but *il dottore* has asked me to tell you they found no evidence of a blood clot." He made no attempt to hide his Sicilian accent. Something had made him give up. "Dottor Cardinale is optimistic. Signor Linetti might wake up any minute, any hour. Any day. Let's hope in God." His Timberlands squeaked.

"I was counting on the police. You said you were going to intercept the mail."

"I asked that it be done. I asked for surveillance, but I have no control now. I have been taken off the case." He tapped short, square fingers against his full, plum-red mouth. He didn't look pleased.

"Because you haven't solved it yet?"

He lifted shoulders. Took a few steps and lifted eyebrows for extra emphasis. "It is in the hands of my boss and the art squad. The possibility of a lost Leonardo—"

"They're not doing a very good job!"

"I thank you for writing my name on that note. Otherwise I would not have been advised. I shall make a report of our conversation and pass it on. Signor Linetti's window-watching neighbor was a godsend in this case. Her report of your reaction on finding your husband—"

"Ex."

"—clears you of any suspicion."

I laughed. "You suspected me?"

"I did not, but others might. I will try to exercise what little influence I have left to see that you and your mother are not disturbed."

He held out his hand. I shook it.

"I took the liberty of informing Signor Linetti's mother."

"Thank you. I should have thought of that myself."

"Perhaps before you go back to the United States, we might have another *sorbetto* at Giolitti's?" His eyes were sad.

I nodded. Giolitti was the furthest thing from my mind.

"I will call. And do talk to your hus—to your ex. Good things that will want to make him wake up."

I didn't get a chance. Carlo's mother, sheathed in mink, descended in clouds of perfume with Carlo's girlfriend, Lea, timidly behind her.

Signora Linetti—I had, in six years of marriage, never been asked to call her by her first name—rushed to kiss her son, her gloved hands clasping his cheeks. "*Tesoro mio,* what have they done to you?" She let out a cry. "Your beautiful hair! They shaved so much off!"

My mother looked astounded. I was used to it. Carlo's mother is typical of many Italian mothers who think a son is a gift from God. *"Bello mio, bello di mamma"* gets uttered at a mamma's first sighting of her baby's penis. She croons to it while changing baby's diapers, changing bathing suits, toweling it dry after a bath, watching it grow, warily relinquishing that sacred organ only to a wife.

In the States, Signora Linetti might have been charged with child abuse. Carlo grew up thinking his groin held gold.

"I'm sorry, Signora Linetti, he was—" I started to say.

"You almost killed my son with your divorce," she whispered, turning her back to me. "Now you wish to kill him again."

My mother noisily stood up from her chair, lightning in her eyes.

Lea hugged me, tears streaming down her face. "Thank God you found him." I reassured her, told her what I knew.

Mamma gathered her coat and purse. "See you soon, Carlo." She squeezed his foot.

"Talk to him," she told Lea. "It helps him wake up." She plunged her arm in mine. At the door I turned around.

"*Arrivederci*, Signora Linetti. I am sorry."

Carlo's mother graced me with a blood-chilling stare. "Go back to America," she ordered. Lea held Carlo's hand.

Mamma marched me back across the river, her steps heavy with outrage. I felt stunned.

"Is it too late for Babington?" I asked. Her Panda was stuffed into a car-crowded sidewalk. It was now three o'clock.

"Babington will have to wait. You have had enough for one day!"

As she bent to open the car door, I burst into tears she hated seeing. I couldn't help myself.

Mamma offered me her handkerchief. "We'll talk tomorrow."

"No! I need to now." I wanted to stop feeling discarded.

19

*. . . a hundred brooding secrets lurk in this
inexpressive mask.*
—HENRY JAMES, ITALIAN HOURS

We sat in a gray and pink banquette in a corner of a caffe
called Biancaneve—Snow White. I tried nibbling at a
chicken sandwich. My mother quietly ate the bar's famous
ice cream, *la mela stregata,* the bewitched apple. In the
window behind her, Castel Sant'Angelo and its plague-ridding
angel were in full view. Mamma started off by talking
about Carlo, how she knew he would be fine

"He has something nice to wake up to. Lea will make a
good companion once he gets you out of his head. His fall
may have done the trick." She giggled, an incongruous
sound coming from my mother, but she was trying hard to
make light of things. I told her Perillo had been taken off
the case.

"Good, I'm sure his only claim to fame is his resemblance to Caravaggio's Bacchus."

"I find him sweet."

"You always had a penchant for strays. You will be careful now, won't you? Give up your questioning. I was wrong to get you involved."

"It had to be someone at dinner."

"What, *cara*?" She was distracted, looking out of the window, her eyes on a young driver checking his hair in the side mirror of his truck.

"Carlo's attacker had to be someone at Arthur Hensen's dinner."

"One of us?" The traffic light changed. The truck rumbled past. With her fingers my mother picked a piece of chocolate crust from her ice cream apple and slipped it on her tongue. Her expression was noncommittal.

"Carlo stupidly mentioned the package Tamar had sent him. How I thought it might be the Leonardo. That's why he was attacked. The package arrived. Perillo checked with the mailman. A box big enough for a drawing. No one else knew."

"I don't quite see Signor Hensen, much as I dislike him, getting into a fistfight. Certainly not Maffeo." Her eyelids fluttered. "Principe Maffeo," she corrected.

I passed on it. "Principe Maffeo didn't come to the dinner until later. And I don't mean one of us actually punched Carlo. Some kid did it for a quick fifty thousand lire."

Mamma frowned at the chocolate stain on her finger. "Mirella told Principe Maffeo while you were out on the terrace with Signor Hensen. Mirella might also have told someone at La Casa."

"There was no reason to. The students barely know Carlo. He told me the only time he'd been over there was for that documentary reception. She could have told Luca, though."

Mamma let out an impatient sigh. "It doesn't have to be

one of us. Please, Simona, stop. Let the art experts take care of it." She wiped her hands on a pink napkin. "If they're not too busy slipping envelopes into their pockets. An industrialist involved in the bribe scandal committed suicide yesterday. I read it in the paper this morning." She looked pleased, not by the man's suicide, but because she had brought the conversation on to safe ground, involving strangers. She knew I had brought her to this caffè with its fairy-tale name to discuss her.

"For the first time a woman has piloted the Concorde. Did you read about that?"

"I thought you wanted quick solutions," I said, a hollow forming in my stomach.

"I did, but it was a child's whim."

The barman brought coffee, a jockey-sized man with sharp, abrupt movements and a gold Rolex watch he flashed every chance he got. The hollow in my stomach spread. I could not feel my fingers and I didn't dare lift the coffee cup.

"Tell me, Mamma." Whatever she said, I knew I was going to hate it. I could tell by the intensity in her face. My mother was trying hard to keep that English stiff upper lip she so admired, but the skin underneath her chin quivered. Her eyes were full of anger.

"Tell me why you left Gigi."

"I have not left him. Please, Simona, let us worry about Carlo, nothing else."

I clutched her hand. "Come on, Mamma, you're brimming with whatever it is. Talk to me." I was already on the floor, how much further could I fall? "Maybe we can help each other. Why did you leave?"

She opened her mouth, shut it, opened it again. I let go of her hand, sat back, and waited. She stirred her coffee and finally spoke.

"I simply needed to walk away from my life. Not *my* life. I can't very well walk away from myself if I want to live. And I do want to. It is amazing to me how much I do want to live." She gave me a sudden smile that made me want to kiss her cheeks. "It is a passion I did not know I possessed. What I have created in these past two weeks is a pause in my shared life, a pause in which to reflect, to find myself. Not the wife or the mother." She leaned over and gave my hand a light tap. "That is why I did not want you here. I wanted to rediscover the simple, untethered Olga Vanin. I tried a hotel for a day, but that was too lonely. Mirella took me in. I have people around me, and yet they expect nothing of me. They don't interfere with my reflections."

"What do you need to reflect on? What has Gigi done?"

"Your father does not have another woman. I know that is what you think. You are so blinded by your own story, you see deception everywhere."

"I saw him with her!" I was stung by her words. "Sunday night at Rocca di Papa. And she answered the phone on Saturday and lied to me. She told me Gigi was in Spain."

"That's what he's having her tell everyone. Your father is quite angry with me for wanting my pause. Elena and Giorgio are friends, people I don't particularly like, to tell you the truth, but they are good friends of your father's. They stayed with him for the weekend, I think, trying to cheer him up. He doesn't like to be alone either." With a spoon, she dipped a sugar cube in her cup for a few seconds. She likes her coffee barely sweetened.

"There is no deception," she said after taking a sip. "If there has been in the past, your father was good enough to keep it from me. Now I think he is simply too old. Now I would welcome deception as a problem."

"No, you wouldn't! You never understood how awful it is. You wanted me to stay with Carlo."

"I didn't want you to run away. I thought you could find a solution together. I always thought there were solutions. If one is good enough, does one's duty, makes few claims, then all will be well. That is how my mother and the church brought me up. Maybe I was even angry that you had the courage to break that tradition. I was certainly angry that you were leaving me. Now I am filled with a resentment I am not proud of." She glanced out of the window. Clouds had covered the sun, and on the river side of the Lungotevere, a woman in a red tartan cap played the saxophone. Traffic flowed faster than the river.

"I am sixty-five years old and I have done what with my life? I gave up economics studies, I followed your father half across the world to places I mostly disliked, always the good diplomat's wife, giving dinners when I would rather have read a book, befriending people who added no meaning to my life. Your father expected good food, an ironed shirt, his head on his career, his heart with you. Not allowing me any more children. And you always wanted to be out, in the park, in other children's homes. Since kindergarten, I could never keep you just with me. I never seemed to be enough. And yet the two of you had to be enough for me." Outside, a mother stooped to wrap her baby in a blanket. A chain of Asian nuns, dressed in short-skirted gray uniforms, wound down the sidewalk. The saxophonist was gone. It had gotten colder. Passersby held their coat collars up.

Mamma turned back to look at me, her eyes warm. "You *were* enough. Forgive me, Simona. You always have been all important, except that now it's difficult."

I got up from my seat and sat next to her on the banquette. "You are still so young. Elegant and perfect and I'm always such a mess. You run me ragged with your stamina." My voice fell to a whisper. "Are you falling for the prince again? He told me about knowing you in Venice. Were you terribly in love with him?"

"Don't be silly, of course not." She turned crimson and tried to cover up by asking for another coffee. She had barely touched the one she had.

"Mamma, tell the truth."

"At eighteen I did think him handsome, but I never for a moment thought . . . I was just his vacation fancy. I was always aware that my origins were too humble for his family."

"Did Gigi come along right after that?"

"Two years later. I was living with an aunt in Rome and going to the university. But you know all that." She scrunched up her face. "You ask so many questions, my mouth is shriveling up answering them."

"Is that why you moved to Rome? To be near Principe Maffeo? Yes, that's why you did it!" In my enthusiasm I elbowed the table; the dirty coffee spoon fell into my lap. "You're stubborn, Olga Vanin, you wouldn't give up so easily. I bet you crossed his path every day, with a man on each arm, looking absolutely beautiful, making him cringe with regret."

She laughed. "The things you think of!"

I laughed, too, happy that I had dispelled the gloom.

"Well, he did declare himself here in Rome. He proposed, too, but then I had met your father, and well"—she pressed a finger above her upper lip—"Gigi seemed more suitable."

No mention of love.

"You'd have hated living in that palace. Think of the cobwebs!"

The waiter brought two more coffees. My mother firmly gave one back. "I ordered only one. You're right, Simona.

I'm pragmatic, like all Venetians, with a good eye for business. Do pick up that spoon from your lap. Here." She dipped the tip of her napkin in her water glass and offered it to me. "Your father was a much better deal than Maffeo. At least I did not have to contend with his mother." Her eyes went blank. "I'm sorry. I should not speak ill of the dead."

Her head bent down, and she frantically searched in her purse.

"What is it, Mamma? What are you looking for?"

She looked up, her eyes stunned. "My greatest fear is that you will be affected. I never wished this on you."

"Wished what on me?"

Her eyes filled with tears I had never seen.

"Breast cancer."

My heart burst. For a moment I saw my mother as the woman in the window across from Carlo's apartment. Gaunt with cancer, wigged and grayed by chemotherapy. "She knows about dying," the ambulance attendant had said.

I wanted to cry, scream, wail at the unfairness. Knowing that restraint is what she wished, I offered words, as medicine for her and myself. I held her hands and went down a list of her memorable deeds on my behalf. Whipping up two egg yolks with sugar every morning to make me grow, the beat of the spoon against the cup a riff of love; tying my hair with ribbons still warm from her iron; keeping her cool hand on my forehead until, despite the high fever, I fell asleep, reassured; standing up for my dating rights once we moved to a less restrictive America, surprising both my father and me; placing a bowl of gardenias on my night table when she guessed I had discovered love. I was finding images that would always keep my mother with me. A form of prayer.

"I love you, Mamma. You're going to get well, I promise."

My mother took back her handkerchief and patted her eyes dry. "I have every intention of getting well again. It's just—" She stopped, and suddenly her strength, the metal stays of the corset she had always worn, was gone. She was a slumped old woman with a narrowed future. My mother.

I cupped her cheek with my hand, returning a loved gesture from my childhood. "It's just what, Mamma?"

"With cancer, intentions aren't enough."

We took a walk, a *braccetto*—arms linked, shoulder brushing shoulder—down Via del Governo Vecchio, stopping to look at used clothing stores, at *rigattieri* whose old objects and furniture were not good enough to make the antique stores. We passed the medieval palazzetto that inspired Carlo and me to play Lotto every week in hopes of one day buying it. We circled behind university students and their motor scooters lined up outside Giovanni's to buy white pizza slathered with ricotta and chocolate. We kept hands in our pockets for warmth.

She told me of the lump she had found in her left breast a month before, only three months after her last mammogram. She'd gone ahead and had a biopsy, saying nothing to my father.

"I didn't want to worry him needlessly. I was convinced I was fine."

We walked across Piazza Pasquino with its "talking" statue, an almost shapeless ancient Roman torso on which love messages and political ironies are hung. Tuesday's message was *Carolina, nun me lascià. Son tuo. Roberto.* Don't leave me. I'm yours.

Another sign, taped to Pasquino's stomach, announced the fall of the Gods.

"They did not remove everything during the biopsy. I wanted to be told I had cancer first and not wake up to find the surprise of having only one breast. I will be operated on in ten days, on my breast and the lymph nodes under my arm. This morning my doctor outlined my choices. Your father is in Florence to consult with another specialist, an old school friend. He hopes to convince me not to have a mastectomy."

I shivered. Was a mastectomy really necessary, I asked. Was she deciding out of anger? Had she gotten second, third, fourth opinions?

I talked with her in her own tranquil tones, both of us sounding as though we were discussing what her dressmaker should do with a bolt of good English tweed. She believes that staying calm is a virtue that will redeem any situation. I was trying to sever any connection between her and cancer. Cancer, a word to ball up and toss in the Tiber, the Hudson River, the Mississippi. A word—no, a disease—I can say that now, looking back. A disease that had been recently dropped in my lap as a possibility. Small, and yet there, on all fours, ready.

Mamma? No, she was perfectly healthy. She was invincible.

We crossed the southern end of the elliptical Piazza Navona, in ancient Roman times conceived as a stadium, in the Renaissance often flooded for mock sea battles and ice skating in cold winters. The buildings flanking the piazza looked worn down despite the lineup of cyclamens and Easter lilies on the balconies. Dark stains ran down the yellow and ocher façades like permanent tears. Only a few had been newly restored. Children chased a soccer ball that landed in Bernini's *Four Rivers* fountain. A mutt jumped in to fetch it, laughter cheering him on. Teenagers gathered to listen to guitar playing in front of the church. Everyone seemed to be holding hands, linking arms, hugging—men with men, women with women, not because of any particular sexual orientation, but just because they enjoyed the physicality of each other. I leaned closer into my mother. This time she did not pull away.

Despite the cold, some tourists sat outside expensive cafés on the sidelines to film the scene with their eyes. The season hadn't fully begun and only a few caricaturists and painters huddled, waiting to sell their talent. A three-year-old watched her green Mickey Mouse balloon scale its way to a cloud.

"Her first lesson in loss," my mother said, resuming our walk. "Tamara's death has helped me, sad as that may be. When I feel most sorry for myself I think of that poor girl, her whole life before her, gripping at love. Desperately, dumbly, but at least fighting. She had more of a right to live than I have." She looked up at the gray church dome of Sant'Andrea della Valle floating ahead of us. "Where is God in this?"

"Mamma, you're not dying!"

"Perhaps not. I will get over this fear. I will fight, but right now I want my resentment, my anger. I feel I have a right to it. I'm not fit company to be with."

I tugged at her arm. "Oh, yes, you are. Always you are."

She hugged me on Via degli Sediari, the street of chair makers, holding me tight in a public show of affection I would never have imagined.

"I worry about you," she said, covering up her emotion by straightening her coat, running a rapid hand through her short hair. "What terrible legacy am I leaving you?"

"I'll be fine, Mamma." I swore then that I would never

mention my cystic breasts to her. "Only five percent of all breast cancers are inherited."

"Five percent too much." She slipped on gloves. It was getting colder. She raised the coat collar of my coat, took my hand, and led me on.

The street lamps had not been turned on yet. The sky was darkening. It seemed to me as if I were seeing my surroundings through the selenite that still covers the early church windows of the city. It's a magical moment of light, soft and unreal, that smudges the hardness of things.

We crossed her favorite Piazza Sant'Eustachio, passed the Pantheon, walked all the way to the small Piazza Sant'Ignazio. The street lamps popped on for us, enhancing the piazza's stagelike setting.

We kept on walking, as if by doing so we would scatter the bad news like ashes on cobblestones. It lightened our weight.

The ashes are now in my mind, markings along the route of my life.

20

La donna ne sa più del diavolo.
Woman knows more than the devil.

—ROMAN PROVERB

"Luca's been arrested!" Mirella said, holding her front door half-open, not letting us in. Fear bloated her eyes. "Some horrible magistrate gave the order to bring Luca to Regina Coeli. He stood there while I cried my eyes out, begging him to reconsider, he stood there and told me he knew Luca was guilty from the very beginning, even before they found the satchel, and now they know about Saturday morning." Gorbi hung his head between her ankles.

"Luca left Nonna with the Tarelli sisters to take measurements at the Olympic Village supermarket. He tried to explain about his university project, but they wouldn't listen. Retrogressive fascists, that's what they are. What Luca called them."

"That must have helped," Mamma said drily, pushing the door open. She took Mirella's arm and folded it over

217

her own, gently steering her away. "Have you called a lawyer?"

"I cannot find Artoor. I called Paolo from the dog park. Nikki's owner. He's a lawyer. He helps all the dog owners."

"You fool!" Nonna stood on the kitchen threshold, an open bottle of brandy in her hand. My mother took out her palm-sized leather agenda, neatly filled with a lifetime of friends, and walked to the phone. She held on to Mirella, as if she were a baby my mother couldn't put down.

I was too wiped out to think anything.

"Try Artoor again!"

"An American is useless with the Italian justice system. Vietnam is nothing in comparison."

"Drink this." Nonna handed Mirella the bottle. "There isn't a clean glass in the place. Not even in the bathroom!" Nonna Monti was dressed in a navy wool suit, the material worn to a sheen. She had put on jewelry, powdered her face, had even a trace of lipstick on disappearing lips. She had obviously put in an appearance at police headquarters.

"Why wasn't I told about the satchel?" she asked. "Am I or am I not a part of this family?"

My mother talked in polite tones to someone on the phone. She stopped to ask Paolo's last name.

"Bietti," Mirella told her. "The police came to the school after what happened to Carlo. Linda told them"—she swung the brandy bottle—"Linda told them she saw Luca on the Sant'Angelo Bridge, right at the time Carlo was hurt. He admitted that, but won't tell them why he was there. Oh God." She leaned her head against my mother's shoulder. "I'm sorry, Olga. I forgot about you, did you tell Simona?" Mirella loosened her grip.

"Yes, I know now." I caught the bottle. My mother listened to the phone.

"I am not dying!" Nonna grabbed the bottle from me and inhaled the fumes. "I run this house, I will not be pushed aside!"

"We were worried about your heart," I said. "That's why we didn't tell you."

Nonna's milky eyes raked my face. She looked like a blind fury. "Worry about your own heart. Mine is set in concrete."

It turned out that Paolo Bietti was a fine lawyer with some criminal experience according to the lawyer my mother had just called. She told Mirella to wash her face, and cream her lips, sent me to the sink to wash glasses while she cut thin slices of bread and mashed butter and anchovies together with a wooden spoon.

"I want my Luca back!" Nonna yelled, hitting her cane against the walls of the corridor.

When Mamma was done, she ushered all of us into the living room where we sipped our doses of brandy and ate olives and anchovy-butter canapés. I feigned hunger to please her. Tomorrow I would tell my mother about the no-fat diet American doctors recommend for cancer patients. Tonight let her worry about Luca. Gorbi got a peeled orange.

"We need our strength," she said simply. "There is no other action we can take." Nonna Monti tried to find answers from her tarot cards. Mirella ranged the room, tapping papers together with buttery fingers, shifting sheets of music, rearranging knickknacks, as if a neater apartment would bring Luca back.

I called Santo Spirito. Signora Linetti had moved Carlo to a private room. He was still in a coma. I tried my father's hotel in Florence. I wanted to say "I love you," and apologize. Luca was less important than my family. Gigi was not at his hotel. I left a message.

"Did Luca have a package on him?" I asked Mirella as she clipped sheets of student essays with bobby pins. "Did Linda say he was carrying something when she saw him?"

"What are you asking that for? That's what the police asked. He carried nothing! Don't you believe him?"

"Of course I do." I said it automatically, not at all sure I did. I wasn't proud of myself.

Mirella hugged me, her hands like claws on my back. "Linda thinks, she thinks I'm going to flunk her now. Stupid girl, she's a straight A student. How can I flunk her?" She shook her mass of gray hair. It smelled of pomegranate and anchovies.

"Let's get out of here," I whispered. I loved this woman, I had to help her. "A long walk with Gorbi."

Mirella clapped a hand to her chest. "A negroni at Lo Zodiaco on Monte Mario!" She tried for a smile, but her lips wobbled.

The dog careened out of the room to the front door. I could see his tail thumping dust, his mouth nibbling the end of his leash.

My mother nodded approval. "I'll stand by the phone, but I'm sure nothing will be resolved before tomorrow. Drink ten negroni if you have to. Simona will bring you home safe and sound." The place was only five minutes away by car.

Mirella grabbed her coat. At the door Gorbi's tail thumped louder. "Lo Zodiaco brings luck."

"Luck has nothing to do with it!" Nonna snapped a card on the dining table. "Stupidity. That's where the donkey stumbles. On his brainless head!"

———

"Lovers come here," Mirella said, a tall red drink in front of her, Gorbi at her feet. "Lovers bring good luck." We were sitting on top of Monte Mario, which houses the observatory and the sprawling Hilton. At our feet was floodlit Rome, the Tiber a bracelet of lights tossed among ageless monuments.

"Have you come here with Arthur Hensen?"

"No. Artoor likes fancier places." Lo Zodiaco is a hard to find café tucked high on the hill. In the summer one can sit in the terraced garden, smooching under the cover of trees and throwing an occasional glance at the spectacular view. It was too cold to sit outside, but we had a window table. Part of the luck, Mirella had said.

"I come here with Gorbi and watch all these young people with faces so ripe with love I get the urge to squeeze them open and spread some of their love on myself."

"They've got raging hormones." I fiddled with a glass half-full of peach juice.

"Oh, no! Boccaccio, Petrarca with his Laura, Dante with Beatrice. Byron, Keats." She quoted in English, " 'My heart aches and a drowsy numbness pains me. 'Tis not through envy of thy happy lot, but being too happy in thine happiness.'" She took a long drink of her negroni, a powerful cocktail of Campari, sweet vermouth, and gin. "Luca is even more romantic." She closed her eyes. "He believes there can be no hypocrisy in love. A fool. Nonna is right, we are all fools in our family."

"I know about the heroin you found in Tamar's drawer. You kicked her out."

Mirella pitched forward, her chin almost level with the table. "Drugs!" she whispered. "Drugs in my house. They petrify me. I have watched Luca, held my breath every time he has come home late, looked into his eyes to see if his pupils have dilated. When Luca was twelve, I had taken him to the market at Ponte Milvio, I found him staring at a boy, not much older than he was, crouched behind a car, a tourniquet on his arm, the syringe stuck in his vein. The boy was grinning at my Luca, telling him how great heroin was. Better than sex.

"I pushed Luca away and screamed at the boy to stop, that he was ruining his life, but that boy just plunged his thumb down on that syringe. For months Luca peered behind every parked car he passed."

"You're afraid Luca does drugs."

I heard the sharp intake of her breath, watched as doubt crossed her eyes. "No." She lifted herself up and looked down at her glass. "For one thing, he can't afford it."

I didn't need to remind her that people steal and kill for it.

"He told me he doesn't and I believe him." I knew I wasn't going to remove her doubts. Those were something she needed to work out with Luca, if he ever got out of the Queen of the Heavens jail.

"I also believe Carlo and Lea, who say Tamar had given up drugs. If both Luca and Tamar were drug-free, what's heroin doing in your apartment?"

"Nonna shooting up?" She laughed and drank at the same time, spilling red liquid on her white sweater. Gorbi stretched up to lick.

"Not quite. Maybe the heroin and the syringe were planted to get rid of Tamar?"

Mirella looked surprised. "I was the one who invited her. Why would I want her gone?"

"I wasn't thinking of you. Nonna disliked Tamar intensely."

"I asked her permission before inviting Tamar. She declared everyone was taking advantage of her, but she said yes. She likes having new people around."

"Maybe Nonna changed her mind."

"She knew all she had to do was say so. My family has always come first. Tamar put that heroin in her drawer. No one else!"

I edged to safer ground by asking about the lost Leonardo theory. Did Mirella think it was valid?

"Tamar planted the seed at the documentary party. She stopped the *onorevole* from the Cultural Ministry at the door. 'How many briefcases of money would you pay for a Leonardo drawing?' Of course he wanted to know what Leonardo. Principe Maffeo tried to gloss over it, but I could tell he was furious. Artoor, too. She was rude. She embarrassed all of us." Mirella dropped peanuts into Gorbi's mouth. "Tamar seemed so intensely convinced.

"We've all seen it happen. A woman stops in the middle of the street to look up at the sky. Every other passerby stops. She points. 'Look at that bird!' Now everyone is convinced the bird is there. If they'll only look hard enough, the bird will appear."

"In this case we at least have a bird feather," I said. "There's that one line in the account book. 'Thirty-two scudi to Messer Leonardo.'"

"Tamar started a dream. That is always dangerous. But then it could be true. An unknown Caravaggio was just found in a Jesuit school in Ireland. Attics have belched up many masterpieces." Mirella swung her head, her cheeks almost as red as her drink. "Well, if not masterpieces, at least good, valuable paintings. Should we call? What if Luca is home?"

"Mamma knows where we are."

"Police headquarters was full of lawyers. Some of the richest men in Rome are in jail tonight. You'd never know that by looking at this view. Rome is rotting from the inside out, and my Luca is innocent."

"We'll find the real killer."

"Will you?" She looked scared by that prospect. Was she thinking of Arthur? I finally told her about Deborah Hensen's unpleasant phone call.

Mirella shook her head. "She wants to destroy her father and anyone her father loves. Wait! How did she know about the drawing?"

"Arthur didn't tell her. The fax made that clear."

"What fax?"

It was still in my pocket. I showed it to her. Now she would know La Casa was closing down.

Mirella barely read it. "Nonna! Crazy family. No wonder Artoor doesn't want to get closer to me. I will give it back and apologize." She slipped it in her purse. "If only I could meet Deborah, she would see I am harmless."

"She's not! She got the board to close La Casa!"

Mirella flipped Gorbi's ear back. "I know. The principe told me last week. Artoor denies it."

"How did Principe Maffeo know last week?"

Mirella shrugged. "In May I will have no salary." She smiled sadly. "Nonna has no more money. Luca will have to help this time." She stopped speaking for a moment, taking in the view of nighttime Rome. The city looked calm, eternal. "It's all rotting."

I felt helpless.

She looked back at me, tilting her head so that her shoulder pushed up her hair and gave her a funny, lopsided look. A cracked doll, I thought.

"Who is giving Deborah information?" I asked. "Do you have any idea?"

Mirella frowned. "You don't think Carlo—"

"No!"

"I'm sorry, but his work isn't going well, maybe . . . "

"Mink-draped mamma will always bail him out."

"Well, I'm not Deborah's spy, although God knows I could use the money."

"You bought Tamar's drawings from Osteria dell'Antiquario."

"I could not let them fill with grease. She had too much talent for that." Mirella looked annoyed, not guilty.

"Did you examine them?"

"Why? What are you thinking? You think I'm hiding the Leonardo!"

"No." I no longer suspected her. I was hoping. "Wednesday night Tamar gave the restaurant a last drawing, a wonderful self-portrait, the owner said. Did you look at it? Could it be—"

Mirella squeezed my hand. "You! It's your portrait. Tamar must have drawn more than one. This one is lovely. It's at the framer's." Her lips broadened into her warm, welcoming smile. "I was going to surprise you with it."

I was the fool.

"Tamar was bartering with someone." It was one in the morning, seven P.M. New York time. I was having my nightly Greenhouse fix. This time I had asked him to call me back. I'd let the phone ring for only half a second. I told him about Mamma's cancer, how I felt the world had folded in and trapped me inside, unable to help my mother, unable to fully understand the horror she was going through. I warned him about my own cystic breasts, as if I were suddenly contagious.

Greenhouse listened. Then he quietly told me I was enthusiastic, adventuresome, passionate, strong.

"What strong?" I blew my nose so hard my eyes almost popped out.

"You're just too messy to find yourself." Like my

mother, Greenhouse likes to be neat. "And I really go for your cooking and that body you drag around, cystic breasts and all."

His teasing made me laugh.

He told me how his son Willy really cared for me but could not bring himself to say it yet, afraid somehow it would take away from the love he had for his mother.

"You have made a difference, Sim."

"Sure, you've both gained a few pounds."

"I love you." He repeated it many times. While I had an expensive cry, Greenhouse, a man who does not easily display his feelings, bolstered me with love. I could not help but think of Mirella, alone with her dog, squeezing love from couples' glances. I felt blessed.

Now we had moved on to homicide. He was humoring me for the moment. We both knew I was relishing the distraction.

"Tamar offers someone, Arthur Hensen probably, the Leonardo in exchange for, I don't know . . . an adoption. Lots of money."

"Why Hensen?"

"My mother overheard a conversation Tamar had with him. I'm not saying Arthur killed her. Someone else could have found out she had the Leonardo and gotten to her before she sold it to Hensen. Principe Maffeo for one. Last week he found out the school was closing down, which means no more rent money as of June, and yet he hires masons to restore his palazzo. Where is the money coming from? Maybe he knew Tamar had found the Leonardo and it was just a matter of time before he would get hold of it."

"Maybe he sold some paintings or furniture or pints of untainted blood. Listen, Sim, I've just told you I love the daylights out of you and I would like for you to stay in this world so I can go on loving you. So your parents can go on loving you. One student has been killed, one ex-husband is in a coma. I would like to ask you to let the Italian justice system take over."

"Ha! What justice system? They have the right to hold a suspect in detention for forty-eight hours without having to bring charges and there is no bail for homicide suspects. To quote Mirella, 'the place is rotting.'"

"Be with your mom. And your ex, if you want." The last was added with reluctance.

"Carlo's got two women already taking care of him."

"Does that bother you?"

I didn't like the question. "How do you feel about your ex-wife's boyfriend?"

"Relieved. She's no longer my responsibility."

I remembered how I had felt leaving the hospital room with Carlo's mother glaring at me and beautiful Lea holding Carlo's hand. I didn't like it one bit. Why? I loved this man across the ocean, not Carlo.

"I don't know how I feel."

"Maybe you two need to talk," Greenhouse offered, his voice sad. "When he wakes up."

"Yeah."

"And one thing about your murderer. Who in his right mind would hide the stolen satchel up on that terrace where it was sure to be found?"

I couldn't sleep. I felt achy and my throat was raw. Long gargles of salty warm water, that was my mother's remedy. I tiptoed to the kitchen. The light was on and Mamma was standing by the table, her hair combed, her bathrobe belt knotted in a perfect bow, pouring olive oil into green bottles.

"Good," she said, not looking up. "You can hold up the funnel. It pours faster that way."

My sore throat would have to wait. "You always do this at two in the morning?"

"My best work is done when I can't sleep. Your father's not under my feet at night. A retired husband is not an easy burden. I thought it would be nice if you picked him up at the station."

"A surprise?"

"No, I told him you were here. He was pleased."

So was I, to finally see him. "What does his doctor friend say about your cancer?" She wiped the full bottle, corked it with a sharp slap of her hand. I dripped oil from the funnel onto the table, wondering if she would ever answer me. My throat hurt.

Mamma dabbed a drop with her finger, then tasted it. "This is not virgin olive oil! Oreste should be ashamed of himself." She guided my wrist to an empty bottle.

"I find myself obsessed with Tamara's killer," she said. "I dreamed that I lanced him with a knitting needle, of all things. I watched him die, then shrivel into nothing before my eyes, like a vampire with a stake in his heart in one of those awful movies you enjoyed so much as a child." She started pouring again, yellow ribbons folding and pooling in a silvered funnel in my hand.

"The terrible part was my joy," she said. "I must have shouted my happiness, it sounded so loud in my heart."

"It's called imaging. You're fighting your cancer. A doctor told me a story of a seven-year-old boy with bone cancer. To give him a sense of control the doctor gave him a video game and told him to zap the bad cells with it." Mamma rested the demijohn on the table, to listen.

"The boy loved that game so much that his mom got very upset when he refused to play it anymore. She tried to egg him on, thinking he was giving up, getting depressed. He finally told her he didn't need it anymore. He'd zapped them all. And sure enough, when they checked, his cancer was in remission."

Mamma made an impatient sound with her mouth and started pouring again. We were now on the third and last bottle. "I know, it's probably apocryphal, but I think it's a wonderful story. So keep wielding your knitting needle."

"I do want the killer found. All my life I have clung to the belief that there is an order to life and I refuse to relent now, just because I have this cancer. Tamara"—she shook her head—"Tamar deserves to have her murderer found and punished. I suppose that is why I wanted you to find him. We'd be sharing a fight."

"Nonna said you were distracting me from the truth."

"Perhaps." She wiped her hands, her expression impassive. The demijohn was empty. Olive oil, someone had delivered it. My head felt like wet cotton wool. One squeeze of a thought and it would ball up to the size of a pea. I vaguely remembered a voice. Saturday.

My mother handed me the dish towel. "But promise me you'll leave the matter to the police now."

I leaned across the table and kissed her tall, lovely forehead, my lips tasting a veil of cream. "You sound exactly like Greenhouse."

She dropped down on a chair, her face suddenly eager. "Tell me more about him," she said for the first time. "Are you really in love?"

I asked a question back. "Who delivered oil on Saturday?"

"The demijohns up on the terrace? Why, Oreste's son, Aldo." She slapped her chest, eyes wide. "You think Aldo switched oil on us?"

I told her about Greenhouse and my love for him.

21

What is there in Rome for me to see that others have not seen before me? . . . What can I discover?
—MARK TWAIN, THE INNOCENTS ABROAD

Nonna was right. The next morning, Wednesday, I woke up with Gorbi warming my feet and a cold stuffing my head.

The triumvirate of mothers had gone to the Queen of Heavens to try and see Luca. I rolled off the sofabed. Gorbi wagged his tail and resettled on the warm spot I vacated. One nostril picked up the smell of the biscotti my mother had baked while I slept. Luca loved biscotti.

I called Principe Maffeo. Aldo had just quit his job and was on his way home, he told me. The head mason was happy. "Aldo is a litle slow." He coughed lightly. "Why did you wish to speak to him?" He coughed again. Was he nervous?

"My mother is not happy with the oil Aldo delivered." A notion suddenly punched its way through my cold.

"Mamma also needs a favor. Deborah Hensen called and left a message for Mirella but Mamma got the number wrong. Six-one-two-seven-eight-three—," I had copied Deborah's telephone number from the fax, "—six-two-five-one."

"Six-two-four-one."

"*Grazie.*" I hung up before he caught on that he'd given himself away.

I showered quickly while Gorbi poised his head on the toilet seat and caught some last sleep. Principe Maffeo was Deborah's informant, I was sure of it. He knew her telephone number by heart. That meant they communicated often. That was how he knew La Casa was going to be closed before Arthur Hensen did. That's how Deborah knew about the search for the Leonardo drawing. It might also explain why, after first accepting Hensen's offer to buy the palazzo, the prince had changed his mind. Deborah, anxious to thwart her father's plans, might have offered money. Enough money to pay for a team of masons to begin small restorations.

I got dressed in my all-purpose gray skirt and put on a GAP sweatshirt, the combination making me look like a cement block ready to be dropped into the Tiber. I grabbed Mirella's car keys from the corridor table as Gorbi leaped to catch his leash.

The first stop was the hospital. If Aldo had taken the bus home to Magliano Sabino, I had plenty of time. I double-parked behind Castel St. Angelo, paid one of the hundreds of men who make their untaxed living by claiming sidewalks as their own and charging for parking, assured him Gorbi did not bite, and went to Carlo's new private room. Before entering I wrapped my mouth and nose with a scarf, bandito style.

"He's coming out of it," Bob said after giving me a hug

at the door. Bob is a white-haired, craggy-voiced American editor who came to Rome with Joe Mankiewicz to work on the famous Taylor-Burton *Cleopatra* and never left. He is a full-time editor and one of Carlo's few male friends.

I stood at the door, afraid to go any farther. I didn't want to give Carlo my cold. All I could see of him was a small, pink face, his curls matted down over his forehead. Two tubes in his nose provided oxygen. The windowsill was covered with flowers. On the floor a fruit basket the size of a market stand bore the tag, *La tua mamma*.

"What are the doctors saying?" Carlo seemed years away from me.

"What doctors?" Bob laughed, wrinkling blue eyes the color of a Tiepolo sky. "Have you ever seen a doctor in an Italian hospital? I only see nurses and nuns. Lea told me. She just went off to work. Carlo's been mumbling, kicking the sheets. He'll be fine." Bob leaned against the doorjamb, a big, broad man who liked his homemade vodka and his own great cooking. "So how are you doing?"

"I've got a cold." I kept looking at Carlo, hoping he'd move, speak. My mother's illness was more than I could bear. I had no room left to worry about Carlo. And yet I had to. I had gotten him into the hospital with my big mouth. And he had, after all, been my husband. The connection was still there, no matter how often I said "ex."

"Shame about Tamar," Bob said.

"You knew her?"

"Carlo brought her over to the recording studio. I helped her edit that tape on the documentary party."

"How much did you edit?"

"Here and there. I wanted to rearrange scenes, make the party a bit more fun, crazier. Fast cuts of the dancers. Tamar nixed it. She said she wanted it to look like home movies. Just as boring. Which it was."

"You ran dupes for her?"

"Yeah. For Carlo, the Hensen guy. The school. Three in all, I think."

"Where's the unedited original?"

"She took it."

Carlo lifted his arm. The IV stand rocked.

Bob ran in to steady it. "Stop waving, Carlo. You're not the pope."

"Ciao," I said, the scarf over my mouth getting wet with my breath. "How are you feeling?"

Carlo turned, his eyes opening slowly. "Minetta." He smiled. He raised his hands. Bob clutched the IV stand. "Are you going to hold me up?" Carlo passed out again.

Oreste was in his courtyard, selling a gutted hog to *la macellaia*, the local butcher. A breeze cooled the sun and blew wafts of manure up one unclogged nostril. The sky had been wiped clean of clouds. I sucked on a lozenge, my eyes barely open.

"When did this hog die?" The butcher wiped her hands on a bloodied apron and eyed the carcass. "With Mussolini?"

Oreste laughed. "Five o'clock this morning. Ask my wife if you don't believe me."

"Sure, as if she isn't used to covering up your lies."

Oreste noticed Gorbi first. He was at one end of the courtyard, barking at the chickens fluttering in a coop of wire held up by wooden planks and sheets of corrugated tin. Behind the coop, the land swooped down into a white-flowering almond orchard.

"Shut your mouth!" Oreste yelled. "You'll put them off their eggs." He picked up a stick and threw it with a strong lash of his arm down the orchard, barely missing the string of colorful underwear that swayed between two trees. Gorbi took off.

"Glad you reminded me," the butcher said, hauling the pig over the front seat of an old Fiat 500. A huddled ginger cat with one chewed-off ear watched from the hood, looking like a relic from the Punic Wars. "How many eggs you got for me?"

Noticing me, Oreste removed his hat. "Signora Monti needs something?"

"I'm looking for Aldo."

"He's at work!" Oreste scowled. "He's got himself a good job finally. With Principe Maffeo."

The butcher smirked. "The higher the class, the stingier they get. But at least he's got a job."

I debated whether to tell Oreste his son had just lost the job. I decided not to, at least not in front of an audience. "Did you slaughter a hog yesterday, too?" That had been Aldo's excuse not to show up at Palazzo Brandeschi.

Oreste rubbed cracked hands over his lips. His skin had the color and texture of seasoned oak bark. "No, just this one so far this week."

"Having any job is more than I can say for my son," the butcher said. She was hefty and short with clipped brown hair that stood up on her head and made me think of hedgehogs. "He doesn't want to work meat. Blood makes him puke, he says. Mortar burns his hands. Wood gives him splinters. All he's good for is mooching. Thank the Virgin Mary I got me six daughters."

Oreste grinned, displaying a set of bleach-bright caps. "What about thanking your husband? Or was it the Holy Ghost?" Oreste limped over to the coop and unlatched it, reaching down for a basket. "Get all the eggs you want so long as you pay for 'em."

The butcher hurried over on muddied boots, hooked

the basket in her arm, and stepped on a flooring of mud, dung, and straw. Above her, corn and cherry tomatoes hung down to dry. White hens hurried over to her boots, expecting corn.

"What is it you want with Aldo?" Oreste had dropped his scowl and now whipped out a bottle from a cinderblock-enclosed space that held vats of wine and dozens of tomato-filled bottles. He offered me a glass of white, cloudy wine that tasted of sweet grapes. "It's the last of the October harvest. The saying is 'new oil, old wine,' but this *vinello* is good young."

Oreste waited for me to drink, for me to answer him, patience thick on his rocky face. Over his left shoulder, the town of Calvi hugged a hill like a cat's tail.

"Aldo delivered oil on Saturday," I said. "My mother thinks it isn't virgin oil."

"Mistakes can happen," Oreste said smoothly. If Aldo had switched oil without his knowledge, he wasn't letting on. "Did you bring it back?"

"I didn't think to."

"How many demijohns was it that Aldo gave you?"

"Don't you know?" I had seen two on the terrace.

Oreste settled his hat back on his head. "I am seventy-five years old. I cracked heads in the Resistance to free this country of the Nazis. I took three bullets." He slapped his limping leg. "I have worked eighteen hours a day most of my life. I forget how many demijohns I give the Monti family. If they paid for them I might have a record, but as they don't, it just doesn't sit in my head for long." He drank his wine. Gorbi dropped Oreste's stick at his feet and waited.

"Hey," the butcher yelled. "I want some of that *vinello* too, just for putting up with you and your war stories." She latched the coop gate. "Eighteen eggs. I'll pay for everything at the end of the month and tell your wife I'll drop the veal shanks on my way home tonight." She swung a full basket in the open window of her car and walked to the cinderblock hut. Above the door, a rough-skinned lemon drooped from its tree, as bright as a light bulb. "I'll get myself a glass."

"A small one." Oreste's eyes stayed on me. Inside the hut, the butcher laughed.

"I'm sorry," I said. "I meant nothing by that."

He accepted my apology with a nod, although I suspect he knew I had tried to trap him. He uncorked the bottle. The butcher did not come out.

"The glasses are in the sink!" Oreste called out.

She still didn't come. Oreste moved slowly, his limp more pronounced, as if the air had suddenly dampened.

"What's this?" The butcher stood in the doorway of the hut, holding a framed painting, its back facing me. "What's this doing behind the sink? It'll get ruined."

"My wife doesn't like it."

"Since when? It's her prized possession."

My heart jumped. For a split second I thought I'd found the lost Leonardo. Then the butcher turned the picture around. I only caught a glimpse of it before Oreste disappeared with it back into the hut. It was an oil painting of a man done in the Renaissance style. Crimson sleeves, a black vest, a black cap and frizzy hair. A handsome face. I don't need much time to spot handsome. Familiar, too.

"Mirella painted that," I said with an accusing tone.

"Mirella Monti, yes." The butcher walked back to her car, her glass of wine apparently forgotten. "It's Aldo. Dead on except for the hair. Aldo's is short and curly. He's as good-looking as a god." She dropped into the driver's seat and started the motor. The ginger cat slid off the hood, Gorbi in pursuit. "I warned my daughters to stay away from him. Any man with a dimple in his chin is a liar. Isn't that right, Oreste?"

He stood now in front of the lemon tree, hat lowered over half his face, the cleft in his own chin clearly visible. He held a demijohn of oil by both handles.

"Cleft in the chin, fork in the tongue!" The butcher laughed and drove off with the dead pig propped up next to her.

Oreste loaded the demijohn into Mirella's car, parked on the street. *"Puro olio vergine,"* he told me. Gorbi, turned into a mud cake, jumped in after it with a mortified look and a scratch on his nose. Ginger was perched on a branch above us, diligently licking her muddied paw.

I insisted on paying for the oil. Oreste insisted on refusing. "Let me know how many more demijohns I owe the Montis."

"Only one," I said. "I remember now." His sharp brown eyes told me he didn't believe me.

"If you don't want that portrait anymore, I'll buy it from you." I hated to see Mirella's work treated as if it were garbage.

Oreste sucked air, as if something had lodged itself between his capped teeth. "Aldo talks back to his mother, she takes the painting down. She forgives him, she puts the painting back up over the TV. That way she can look at both." He sucked again. "I don't get mixed up in it. We mean no disrespect. The Monti family is close to my heart."

"May I ask why?"

"They are good people. Not many of those around anymore."

"So good you supply them with expensive virgin olive oil. That's very good."

"We go back a long ways." With that he walked back into his courtyard with a low whistle. The ginger cat leaped down from her branch and went in after him.

"Never seen her," the butcher said as she wrapped a half dozen wild boar sausages in pink paper. My father loved them. "Donatella, you seen this girl?" the butcher asked. A young woman, cleaning Oreste's eggs with a damp towel, turned her long neck to peer at Tamar's three pictures, then slowly shook her head. She had the butcher's wide mouth.

Bianca—the butcher's name was stitched on the white coat she'd put on—handed back the photo strip. "Donatella would know. She eyes every girl who comes within a fifteen-kilometer radius of this town. Doesn't like any competition."

Donatella went back to cleaning eggs. Her neck turned red.

The butcher shop faced the main road, a perfect spot to catch anyone coming into town. Floor-to-ceiling white tile that sparkled brighter than Oreste's caps, a large, sloped glass case displaying the curly weave of tripe, a purple spleen, breaded veal cutlets, lamb kidneys wrapped in a caul of fat with a laurel leaf slipped in, ready for the grill, and thin steaks of *vitellone* cut from the flanks of half-grown steers, the Italian farmer too impatient for a return on his investment to let the animal grow into marbled beef. On top of the counter a gold crinkle-wrapped Easter egg would have made a mamma tyrannosaur proud. Two thousand lire would buy a raffle ticket, the egg the prize.

"Don't believe all that war stuff Oreste fed you." Bianca balled up some ground meat for Gorbi, who was standing up in the backseat of the car across the street, tongue flat against the windowpane. "I can tell you true war stories." She pressed a cleaver to her chest.

I leaned against the sloping glass below the counter and

got ready to listen, one eye out on the road. I was still hoping Aldo would show up. Once I saw him, divine inspiration would provide me with all sorts of pertinent questions, such as where were you on Saturday before you delivered the oil that wasn't virgin?

"The Nazis shot Resistance fighters up at the town square." Bianca said. "In front of everyone. The three Rossi boys and Ernesto Sensi, my father."

"Mamma, you'll make yourself cry." Donatella didn't bother to turn around.

Bianca wiped an arm across her face. "Oreste was no Resistance fighter!"

I wanted to hug her, but the counter was in the way and I did not feel brash enough to walk around. I held out my hand instead.

Bianca shook her shorn head. "I'm dirty."

Her daughter looked embarrassed and turned on the radio, mouthing the lyrics of an Italian pop song I didn't recognize.

"I get a certain satisfaction out of butchering," Bianca said. Her cheeks were red with broken veins, her eyes small and bleary. "And as for the great hero, Oreste, that bullet hole in his leg is no war wound. When the Germans swooped down after the Armistice, he deserted the army and holed up in Signora Monti's attic waiting for the Americans to show up. That's how he got shot, standing by one of her windows."

"A German sniper shot Oreste! No wonder Nonna stays away from windows."

Bianca laughed. Her daughter was singing out loud now.

I paid for my sausages and Gorbi's meat. "How did he get away from the sniper?" I added another two thousand for a raffle ticket. My mother would like that egg. "The Germans must have come after him."

"*Basta* with this radio!" Bianca snapped it shut. "Go get your brother, Donatella. Don't just stand here. Get him."

Donatella whipped around. "I was cleaning the eggs!"

"He's at the piazza bar for sure."

Donatella tossed her apron on a chair and ran off.

"What sniper?" Bianca whispered. "Her husband. He was fighting in the underground. He came home and spied on them. She and Oreste were"—Bianca twined two fingers together—"you know. He shot Oreste in the leg to warn him off. Signora Monti brought Oreste up here and paid farmers to take him in. Oreste was lucky. By then the Germans had already retreated." She started cleaning the remaining dirty eggs.

"Now Oreste pays her back by feeding her." I was swayed by the romance in the story.

"Surprises me," Bianca said. "That man's tight. He lets me pay at the end of the month because he knows I can take my business elsewhere, and I would, because I don't like liars, especially lying about the war. But his wife's a good friend. No, if Oreste's giving the Montis anything it's because he's looking out for himself."

"Nonna saved his life!"

A scooter's pierced muffler grated down the road. Bianca shot an angry glance at the door. "I don't believe any good of a liar."

Donatella ran in and took her place behind the counter. She had no need to make announcements. The sound got deafening. I turned around to see a *bullo*, a mean-faced ruffian I sure wouldn't want to have mothered. Perhaps deep inside of him there was a lost soul that needed loving, but it wasn't in sight that morning.

Bianca's son grinned at me, leaning back on his scooter, legs thrust out. His wrists, jutting out of a dirty denim jacket, worked the handles to produce the loudest noise possible. Long, thick black hair flowed to his shoulders. The memory of hair whizzing past me, of Tamar's pensive face, clutched at my stomach. Was he the one? If he was, how to prove it?

"Are you a friend of Aldo's?" I asked, reaching the sidewalk, pink parcel of meat tucked under my arm.

"*Vieni qui*, Ernesto!" Bianca called from inside.

Ernesto ran fingers down his scalp, eyes on his rearview mirror. "Aldo thinks he shits gold 'cause he works for a prince."

"Ernesto! Get me a side of beef from the freezer."

Satisfied with his looks, he aimed eyes at my chest. "You gonna let my mom sell those tits?"

"Get in here or I'm going to cut your ass off that scooter with a cleaver!"

Something flew past me.

Ernesto ducked.

A chicken neck, head attached, landed in the middle of the road. Gorbi, inside the car, started jumping back and forth on the seats, barking. I thanked Bianca quickly and slipped out before she started throwing entrails.

I drove up to the piazza. At the bar, I ordered a hot milk for my throat and asked about Aldo.

"In Rome. Working," the barman told me behind a pile of boxed Easter dove cakes. Above him, wrapped chocolate eggs hung across the room like garish Christmas lights. Old men held glasses of red wine in their hands, their complexions colored to match. They played cards or stood looking out of the glass doors on an almost empty piazza with white and yellow banners still flying to commemorate the Pope's visit two months earlier. No women were in sight. It was lunchtime. I had to go back to Rome. Mirella might need the car. My mother might need me. I needed her.

I blew my nose, and for two seconds I smelled a whiff of garlic simmering in oil. I pictured cans of tomatoes being opened, carefully poured into the sizzling pan so as not to spill anything. My mother, her crisp apron tied neatly around her, mashing up the tomatoes with the back of her wooden spoon. Ernesto's remark had made me flush with anger, not because of its lewdness. He released the thought of Mamma's cancer that I had hidden in a dark pocket of my head.

I had one more thing I wanted to look into before rushing home. It was a hunch that had come to me with Bianca's doubts about Oreste. At least that's what I told myself then. Looking back, I think perhaps I was simply putting off going back to Rome. I felt helpless, with a fear I would lose my mother that made me feel selfish. I wished I could change places with her, but then knew I didn't really. I tried to picture myself in her drama, but couldn't or wouldn't. I was too scared. I tried to reassure myself by thinking that no one can really step into a drama unless it's your own. It was her life. Her breast.

"Where's the town hall?"

It was a two-minute walk.

"I need to see the title records for Matilde Monti's property on the state road to Calvi. I'm thinking of buying the farm." I smiled and wondered if my chin was developing a cleft.

The woman smiled back and stopped typing on a machine that had seen the depression. Behind her, a poster announced a competitive exam for twenty-two civil servant spots in the registrar's office in Rome. Thousands would apply.

She handed me a form to fill out.

"I don't know the lot number."

The woman lugged out the land map, dropped it on top of the filing cabinet, and beckoned me over. I didn't understand the map. "I'm looking for the Monti farm."

She nodded and pointed a finger in the upper left-hand corner. "Block 865, lot 32."

"Thanks." Ten hectares. Approximately twenty-five acres zoned for agricultural purposes.

"What's land worth around here?"

The woman twisted her mouth. "My cousin sold eight hectares for 400 million. The house was in good shape."

250 thousand dollars. A good asset, not a great one.

The woman dropped a thick book of title records next to the map. I searched for Block 865, lot 32. Nonna's husband's family had owned the land since 1909.

Then I saw the last entry. My jaw slackened. I wasn't ready for my hunch to be right.

Something in my expression must have made the woman look at the page. "I guess you're trying to buy from the wrong person."

Oreste Pagani was the owner. Had been for the last five years.

22

---

*I then devoutly believed that a Roman was
a cunning composition of perfect honor,
bravery, and virtue.*

—SOPHIA HAWTHORNE,
NOTES ON ENGLAND AND ITALY

"He proposed!" Nonna clacked her teeth in triumph.

"Arthur?" I dropped my meat package on the kitchen
table next to a spread of tarot cards and dirty dishes.

"Not five minutes ago."

Mirella looked stunned.

"Congratulations." I stroked her hair, picked up a
bobby pin nestled in her collarbone. Gorbi spun around
her, yelping, as if he'd been without her for years.

Nonna eased herself back in the chair. "Holy heaven,
where's that dog been?"

"A little mud. Mamma? Luca?"

"Your mother has rushed off to Rocca." Behind Nonna
was the painted view of the farm she no longer owned.
"Luca is coming home tomorrow."

Mirella raised her arms. "Nonna, we don't know that." She dropped her arms.

"You don't, I do." Nonna gave me a wink and a lopsided smile, waving the ace of pentacles at me. "This card came up this morning. Twice! Victory!" She threw it down again into the pack. "Besides, Signor Hensen has friends in high places."

"That doesn't work anymore," Mirella said. "Nothing works now. Everyone's being arrested. The guilty, the innocent. Bribes, scandal, corruption. Luca got caught in the mire. Not his fault, just in the wrong place at the wrong time."

"Did Luca say what he was doing on the Sant' Angelo Bridge?"

"Taking a walk!" Mirella's face flushed with anger. "Is it a crime now? And where were *you*? Lea called from the hospital. Carlo keeps asking for you."

"I'll go now." I grabbed my coat. I really needed to go to bed and sleep some of my cold off, but I welcomed the excuse to leave again. "Did you say yes, Mirella?"

"To Arthur's proposal?" She pushed back her hair with both hands. Her eyes had darkened. The green band looked almost black. "I don't know yet. I don't want it to be out of pity. Luca is in jail still. I don't know what to do. Yes, I would like to say yes."

For a moment she held her head tight, as if she were afraid it would spin out of her reach. "I will say yes when Luca comes home."

"Tomorrow," Nonna said, laying out the tarot cards one more time, just to make sure.

Why did Arthur propose now?

Lea shot up when I walked in. "Carlo's asleep," she whispered. I held a handkerchief over my face, still afraid to give him a cold. The IV stand had gone, so had the tubes in his nose. Relief sagged my muscles. We walked out in the corridor. Lea looked exhausted but happy. She had tied back her thick blond hair with a shoelace. She was wearing jeans, a blue crew-neck sweater that heightened the color of her eyes, and a gray tweed jacket I had bought Carlo on a trip to London.

"He's fine now," Lea said. "The doctor is going to release him tomorrow."

"Does he remember what happened?"

"A policeman came by to interrogate him. I wasn't allowed to sit in, but Carlo told me afterward. He came down to wait for you. The mailman walked by and handed him some letters and a package. A box large enough for a sweater. He didn't open it right away. He walked out with the mailman, looking for you. There were lots of tourists trying to get into the restaurant next door. The sidewalk was very crowded. He was distracted. When he went back in, his assailant was waiting for him."

"Did Carlo see who hit him?"

"The man was wearing a black scarf over his face. He punched Carlo in the stomach and the face. All Carlo remembers is trying to get back upstairs." Lea smiled. "He's ready to scale Mount Everest after that climb. He knows he wanted to get to the phone but isn't sure who he wanted to call." Her face radiated warmth and beauty.

"His mother wants to take him away to the country for a month," Lea said. "I hope she doesn't."

"Mamma Linetti is tough competition, but she seems to accept you more than she ever did me."

Lea's eyes turned serious. "You're the tough competition."

"Me? Carlo doesn't love me anymore. He just doesn't like losing. Have you ever played Monopoly with him? One time he dumped all the hotels down the toilet because I was winning." Then he'd gone out and bought cherries to replace them. That way, if he lost he could eat all the hotels. When cherries weren't in season, we didn't play.

"You just left. You never explained." An intense expression covered her face. She believed her future with Carlo was at stake.

"If he wants explanations he should have a heart-to-heart with his penis. I'm a convenient excuse, Lea. Man grieving over lost wife can't possibly commit to anyone else." I stopped and stared at the blankness of the corridor wall. Wasn't I doing the same with Greenhouse, refusing to move in with him?

"He's not calculating," Lea said. "He's immature. Neither of you talked afterward. The raw anger is gone now. Talk to him."

Greenhouse had said the same thing.

I raised my hand in a futile effort to resist her. "A lot is happening right now and I'm not one of your drug addicts who needs trea—"

She clutched my hand. "I don't want to preach and you may think this is none of my business—"

"No, it's just tha—"

"—but it is my business. I love Carlo. I know his faults. I know mine. He loves me, he says, but he hasn't let go of you. He needs closure. Don't you need it, too? Carlo tells me you have a man who loves you in America. Do you love him back, without restraints?" Her eyes dredged my face, her hand still tight over mine. "Have you rid yourself of Carlo?"

"I'm getting there."

"Go in." She pushed me toward the room. "Carlo asked for you. When he wakes up, talk, let go." Her beautiful face was calm now. "We'll all be happier."

"What if we can't let go?"

"Then I'll know to leave." She walked away.

I stood on the threshold of Carlo's room. He was sleeping on his side now, his back to me. Flowers still lined the windowsill. The gift basket was unopened—yellow cellophane enveloping fruit nesting on slivers of shiny paper. The window was a flash of sun.

I stood there, hesitating. Divorce has no rituals to help ease the separation. There is no gathering of friends and colleagues to weep with you, no coffin as tangible proof that there is no turning back, that you are now on your own. You are given humiliating papers to sign; you divide inventory, sometimes even children. Society does not unanimously sanction your grief.

I glanced at my watch. I had two hours before I needed to leave for the station to pick up my father. I gazed at the back of Carlo's head, shaved clean. Bruised, yellow with iodine, black stitches showing clearly.

Why not? I asked myself. Sun rested on the wooden chair at the foot of his bed. I sat on it. Why not invent our own ritual?

Carlo and I had met at one of Daisy's quarterly dividend parties. Daisy, my good friend, a trust-fund baby who wore cowboy boots and wanted to act. She poured champagne and introduced us on a vast flowering terrace overlooking the Roman forum. The music was Brazilian. Not a bad backdrop. After that party, Carlo set himself on me with a persistence that eventually won me over. I'd find him at the corner bar in the morning, or in the recording studio where I worked. If I went shopping, he'd suddenly pop up on the same street. Each time he pretended he was there by accident.

I was taken. He was romantic, he was sweet, he seemed to breathe only the air I gave him. I thought that was true love.

Once we married, he went back to Daisy.

I met Greenhouse over a corpse. Maybe that was a safer start.

Carlo woke up and as he lay in his hospital bed and I sat in the sunny chair, we shared fruit and remembered highlights of our marriage. A trip to Paris. Another one to London. Our dinners on a cramped terrace overlooking the Tiber. We avoided bed stories.

We remembered bad moments. His refusal to have children. His mother insisting we spend Sundays with her. His need to control the air I breathed. My wanting him to be more responsible about his career. His mother giving us an apartment, then insisting we use every bit of claustrophobic furniture she had put in it. My getting so involved in my work—dubbing films—I'd forget to call to say I'd be late. My filling up the apartment with friends when he wanted me to himself.

We risked dropping into anger again, but, biting into a dry hothouse pear, I thought of Lea's serene face and I shifted the conversation.

"That tweed jacket looks great on Lea."

"You don't mind?"

"No." I laughed.

"I feel guilty loving her."

"Why?"

"I should still love you. You're the one I married."

"We're divorced now."

He looked wistful. "I lost all my hotels?"

"Cherries are coming into season again. Tamar stayed with you Friday night, didn't she?"

Carlo nodded barely, his eyes shifting to the window.

"She must have mentioned she had sent you something."

He looked back at me. "No. She was scared of exams, she said. I didn't believe her but I didn't pursue it."

"Why did you lie about it?"

"You already thought I was sleeping with her. And I didn't want Lea to know."

Now that I didn't care, I could see it written on his face, a trust-me expression that looked sticky to the touch.

"I told you I loved you the other night," Carlo said. "I wanted it to be true." He blinked and turned away. The sun lowered light on his face. "I'm sorry, Simona." He was sincere. I could tell that too, now.

"Thank you." I moved my chair so that my body shadowed him. He turned back, his eyes hidden by thick, ridiculously long eyelashes. It was the first thing I'd noticed about him. Eyelashes I envied. "I'm sorry, too."

His adultery had made me feel valueless, I explained. Discounted. I could only run away from that black space he had turned me into. With New York as a clean backdrop, I was able to see I still had all the pieces of me. Now I was putting them back together.

I leaned over and kissed him softly on the lips. He tasted of oranges. "You have to admit we've both got *un culo d'oro*." A golden ass is the utmost of luck.

"Yeah?" He looked hopeful.

"We get to try again." I picked up the last tangerine. "I may also have just given you my cold."

"I can take it."

Was I being romantic? Yes. Had I totally forgiven him? No. I am not that generous a person. But it made no sense to hold on. Kissing him, I let my sense of betrayal float as free as a balloon.

I offered Carlo half the fruit. He smiled like a child who, forgiven for breaking a window with his ball, is eager to go out and play again.

"Keep Lea close," I said. "She will probably forgive you any infidelity. She has professional patience."

"I'm not going to be unfaithful ever again." His mouth was full of tangerine.

"Of course not." I looked outside the window. The new leaves of the sycamore seemed bigger, greener. No doubt thanks to Monday night's rain and now the sun. Perhaps to a sense of release.

Carlo and I had finished. The gift basket was almost empty. We'd eaten four oranges. Two pears. Three tangerines. We closed up a marriage. We left the nuts, seeds someone else could grow.

"I'm looking for the VCR?" I asked a small-boned, dark-haired woman who was struggling with a large painting. "I'm a friend of Mirella Monti's. Here, let me give you a hand." I dropped my bag—Carlo's tape was in my pocket—and helped her find the hook on the school wall. Carlo had given me keys to his apartment and told me to screen the tape at the school. His VCR had been broken for over a month.

"Thanks," she said in pure American as she narrowed her eyes and stared at the painting—a stunning blue and orange canvas with two white, massive horses that reminded me of Paolo Uccello.

"You painted that? It's good."

"Thanks. Yes, it's my work. I have three more to hang before tomorrow." She bobbed her head as she spoke. She was wearing orange leggings and a brown oversized sweater. On her feet were burnt-butter ankle boots that must have cost her a painting or two.

"I'm showing for ten days here at La Casa. It's a great space. I teach here, too." Her eyes panned a room so blindingly white it looked like it had been hit by a blizzard. It was the first of boxlike interconnecting rooms created by plasterboard panels dotted with thumbtack holes. The boards were empty except for her two horses.

"My colors stand out well against white, although the eyes take a beating. What do you think? Will I make it?" Her voice was low and thick.

"Make what?"

She laughed, showing wonderfully straight, white American teeth. She was attractive, somewhere in her forties, with high, cutting cheekbones and deep-set grainy brown eyes. "My fifteen minutes. You wanted the VCR? Sorry. I'm Susan. Not Susie, not Sue. Plain Susan."

"I'm Simona."

"The VCR is in the back, by the john. *If* it's still there. The last one was swiped two days after we bought it. What movie you got?"

"A tape of the documentary party."

"Never saw it. You've heard about that stu"—she shook thin, graceful hands, the kind that belong on portrait laps—"of course, you're a friend of Mirella's."

She led me down a white corridor toward a door with the American flag painted on it. "That's the john, if you need it. The relief center the students call it. That's why the flag. I just put in toilet paper. It disappears around here. Next door—here, you need two keys to get in." She opened up. "The school's officially closed as of today for Easter vacation." She turned a chipped porcelain switch. Fluorescent lights flicked on.

The room was really a large storage closet filled with two bookcases holding vertical rows of canvases, pictures of the past three graduating classes, and metal file cabinets. One cabinet was crowned by a wicker rocking chair. Turpentine fumes pricked my eyes. Or maybe it was just my cold. By now I couldn't smell anything. I wanted her to leave.

Susan turned on the VCR, the TV. "Sorry. I've got to get back." She laughed at the door. "At the party I wore a handwoven patchwork skirt. You can't miss me. I weave in my spare time." She left.

I brought down the rocking chair, keeping my coat on because I was cold, inserted the tape, pushed PLAY and sat down. What had brought me here was Carlo's parting comment.

"I just remembered something," he'd said as a nurse dipped blue arms toward the door as if she wanted to float me downstream. "I shook the package after the mailman left. It rattled."

23

Je porterebbe l'acqua co' l'orecchie.
He'd bring her water with his ears.
—ROMAN SAYING

Susan spotted it. She had come back to see "just how fat that skirt makes me look."

I was on my second run-through. The first time I'd gotten lost trying to spot my parents among the dancing crowd, watching Carlo weave in and out, laughing, his face glistening with excitement. The principe looked pained. He had allowed the documentary to be presented upstairs in his grand ballroom, Susan told me. The students had come up with the idea of serving popcorn.

"His feet crunched popcorn for weeks. Serves him right. He wouldn't let us come up and clean."

The party was held downstairs at the school. The white rooms had been filled with the students' take on Italian masterpieces. The *Mona Lisa* had turned into a punk, with black leather bra, purple hair, and one ringed nostril. Michelangelo's *David* was winking at his elephantine erection.

Botticelli's *Venus* now wore Calvin Klein underpants. The man from the Cultural Ministry, a mustached corpse in blue pinstripes, forced a smile at the irreverence. Susan came into the picture, with her loud patchwork skirt that barely covered her groin and a red satin tank top. The man shook his head and headed for the flag door, Susan, Principe Maffeo, and the camera following. When he reached the door, he turned toward the storage room. Arthur Hensen unlocked the door, using both keys.

"I asked the *onorevole* to dance," Susan said, her voice gurgling. "That's what drove him away. They all call themselves honorables, which is the last thing they are, if you believe the papers. The music was great. U2. I was already hot on the idea of the Cultural Ministry backing a show of mine. I came on too strong or my boobs weren't big enough. Something. Hey!" She pointed to the screen. "Stop the tape!"

I pushed the red button on the remote control. The *onorevole* was coming out of the room we were in, his coat already on, a briefcase under his arm. He held up a hand against the camera.

"The VCR. That creep took the VCR. I told you our VCR got stolen two days after we bought it? There, see his briefcase! See how fat it is. The VCR would fit right in." She started bobbing her whole body as if she were still dancing to U2. "God, I'd love to get that honorable snot-head!"

"Maybe his briefcase was full of papers?"

"Rewind to where he comes in. Tamar shot that, right? Before we all went upstairs to see the documentary?"

"There's not much to see."

"The arrival of the king, it looked like. Art Hensen must have peed gold he was so excited. I tried to get Art to back a show of mine, but he hates horses. Stop there! Play that."

Tamar had taped only a few seconds of Arthur Hensen, his arm raised.

"He's pointing here, to this room. Everyone else dropped their coats in the administration office, even Art. But when it comes to the honorable, Art insisted he have his private cloakroom."

Carlo draped the *onorevole*'s coat over his arm, like a perfect butler.

"Ratty coat. You'd think he'd wear Armani. Versace. Fendi." Susan's lovely hands fluttered in front of her. She had picked up Italian habits. "Same thing with his briefcase. I noticed that right away. Cheap. The kind those little accountants use. Cardboardy. And empty. See?" She pointed a tapered, paint-stained finger.

For a second, maybe two, I could see Carlo take the briefcase, flat, flopping. Definitely empty. Then Carlo tucked it under the coat and the tape jumped to a student's rendition of Michelangelo's *God and Adam*, fingers almost touching. In God's hand, a wrapped condom.

Susan gave me a knowing look. "The next morning the VCR is gone. I'm telling you the man's coat was flea market. And he even looked like he hadn't eaten in weeks."

"Maybe." I stood up while the tape rewound and blew my nose. I had to get to the railroad station to pick up my father.

Stazione Termini was a party of Somalians. Bare-headed men in European clothes clustered with women in green, orange, yellow, red scarves and pleated headdresses, bolts of bright cloth wrapped around long-boned bodies.

Italy has become the America of many immigrants. Africans, Albanians, Russians, Yugoslavs. It is sometimes the first stop of a longer trip. But then the sun works its magic, the food is good, the rules of survival are loose. Here it is easy to be illegal and still find work. The Italians at first were not harsh. Now racism and xenophobia are setting in. And yet, on the late afternoon of the Wednesday before Easter, as I picked my way to my father's train track, the Somalians smiled, laughed, chatted, the station a glass-covered party place.

I heard the opening bars of *Eine Kleine Nacht Musik* before seeing him on the crowded platform. He stopped whistling to hug me tight. He has always been generous with shows of affection. I cried, blaming my cold. When we finally separated, I saw that he had shrunk since I'd last seen him, over a year ago. His eyes looked faded. Love clenched my heart. How could I have thought those terrible things of him?

"How did you find her?" he asked as we walked to the car double-parked blocks away. He insisted on carrying his overnight case and a large gift-wrapped package.

"Remarkably strong." I held on to the pocket flap of his coat.

"That's nothing new." He sounded resentful. "I only wish . . ." He did not finish the thought, but I knew what he was thinking. If only she would include me. It was something I had felt all my life.

As I unlocked the car, Gigi insisted on paying *"l'omino,"*—the little man—who had watched my car. He always insists on paying, even when I have invited him out to lunch or dinner. I have stopped getting mad at him. The role of provider defines him. He would not let me drive.

"Mamma loves you, Gigi, but she didn't want to worry about you or me right now. This once she wants to be the center of her own attention."

We were passing Cinecittà, the movie studio complex

that Fellini had made famous the world over. Beyond were the Alban Hills. The sun had gone and left an iris-blue sky. I was taking him home to Rocca di Papa. I hoped my mother was waiting for us.

"She's not trying to hurt you, Gigi." I blew my nose.

"Yes, I'm sure." He dropped a hand on my knee, repeating the gesture of countless trips, except the knee had always been my mother's.

"Except it feels"—he took back his hand and leaned over the steering wheel to see better—"strange, painful. Forty-two years of marriage. That's a long time."

Shifting down into second gear, he spoke of his Florence trip. He'd been to Angelino's for liver crostini and *finocchiona*, a thick salami crusted with fennel seeds. Three times he had indulged in tortelloni the size of stingrays, wet with butter and sage. The Uffizi defeated him with its kilometers of students waiting to get in.

"Easter Week. Impossible." I did not ask him what his doctor friend had said about my mother's cancer. He would tell me in his own time.

"I did get into Palazzo Pitti and the Rafaellos lifted my heart, but the Masaccio in the Cappella Brancacci—" He whipped a hand in the air, nearly colliding into a braking bus. It has always been clear who gave me my operatic genes.

"Soaring art. The shame of the expelled Adam, Eve's anguish . . . " He swerved to avoid a cyclist. "On Via Tornabuoni I bought your mother a linen tablecloth. You know how she likes those."

I apologized. "I thought you had fallen in love."

"I did a long time ago. With your mother."

"No one else?"

He frowned, letting go of the clutch. The motor died with a jolt. We were uphill.

Gigi started the car again, his foot dancing between brake and clutch so as not to send us sliding back to Rome.

"Marriages can be good, Simona." We were on our way.

"'Can be' doesn't sound very reassuring."

"At your age, I can't feed you fairy tales." We had never spoken about love. He was embarrassed.

So was I. For being childish.

I shifted the conversation to Hensen's hope to create gift shops in Italian museums.

"Yes, Guido Tagliacozzo told me. You remember Guido, university friend? His wife used to bring you candied violets."

"I hate those!"

"He's made a good career for himself by being nonpartisan. Takes great talent to do that. He's at the Treasury. Mirella's friend got the green light.

"The Ministry approved?"

"Last month."

Last month a representative of the Cultural Ministry had walked into a party with an empty briefcase and had walked out with a full one. I was willing to bet he wasn't watching videotapes with the contents.

"Good idea, I told Guido," my father said. "The Americans know how to run things and they are basically honest. The Ministry needs the revenue badly. All these restorations."

"Why doesn't anyone know anything about it?"

"In this French Revolution climate?" He honked impatiently at a stalled car. We were in the main piazza in Frascati. In the dusk, Villa Aldobrandini held on to its stately glory. In the rearview mirror I could see that Rome had turned on its lights. The city looked contained and remote compared to the Liberace-like cloak of twinkles I had seen from the plane leaving New York. Only a pale glow, a low-hanging cupola enclosing a city trying to survive.

"Best to keep it quiet," my father said, cutting a scooter off and getting the finger for it. "Quiet until heads settle in their baskets."

"Mamma doesn't even know about it. Gigi, be careful!" He was driving in spurts. He was nervous. We were getting close to home. Would she be there?

"Guido just told me last week. It wasn't important given . . . "

This time I was the one to reach for his knee.

"Did you ever take a bribe?" I asked.

"I've been tempted. The 'envelope' system is so pervasive, it makes you feel stupid if you don't."

"What stopped you?"

"Simona." His tone was a mixture of reproach and surprise. I was the one being stupid, he meant.

"Si. Certo. Mamma."

"Olga believes it is respect that engenders love. She would never have forgiven me."

Olga, Mamma, wasn't home. But she had left flowers in every room. Easter lilies in a Deruta ceramic vase on the old pine dining table surrounded by tall ladder-back chairs with straw seats and a white wall shiny with copper pudding molds. Blue and yellow irises in the living room with its comfortable blue cotton sofa and brown leather armchairs. A glass bowl of daisies and cornflowers in the terracotta and wood kitchen with new beams and a waist-high fireplace where Mamma liked to grill polenta and steak.

"She's left her signature," I said. My father bent down to unlace his shoes. I slipped off mine, both of us following one of my mother's rules. We were both trying to hide our disappointment.

"As if flowers can replace her," Gigi said, straightening up, shoes in hand like beggars' cups. "She does not think I have loved her enough. And yet, without her . . . " He turned away, shame on his face. Walking up the stairs in his gray and yellow argyle socks, my father made no sound.

I called Mirella's. Mamma was there.

"Eight-thirty at Hosteria dell'Archeologia on Via Appia. You'd be meeting us halfway. I think that's fair." I was angry and determined to bring us together again. *"Siamo una famiglia!"* We're a family.

She accepted. She even thanked me, as if my anger had somehow helped her.

I yelled up to Gigi that we were going out to dinner with his wife. My treat. I heard him laugh, then turn on the shower.

I made another phone call, this time to Fono Roma, the recording studio where Bob had edited Tamar's tape. I was lucky. Bob was in the *sala mix*, the room where all the sound tracks—voice, sound effects, music—get "mixed" on to one thirty-five millimeter magnetic tape. He'd just finished a reel and had "two minutes" to talk.

"What's up? Carlo okay?" His low voice crackled over the phone.

"Fine. His head's a rock." I asked him about Tamar's tape, did he remember what he had cut?

"Barely remember last week's film."

I reminded him of the school bathroom with the American flag door.

"Sure. Made me think of Jasper Johns." He answered a few questions, then got called back in to finish his mix.

I went up to the guest room, a soft yellow space that

looked out on the roses in the garden and a wedge of valley below. It was lined with bookcases filled with my old schoolbooks, paperbacks of every kind, and art books that Gigi kept buying for which there was no room downstairs.

I slipped out a book, stretched out on one of the twin beds and started looking at art from the Palazzo Pitti.

24

. . . all the doings of old Rome,
swarming around her rife with scandals,
crimes, joys, struggles, triumphs, . . .
    —WILLIAM WETMORE STORY, POEMS

My parents pecked at each other's flushed cheeks. I talked too much, going on about how exhilarating it was to eat on the Appian Way, where even the pebbles dripped history, how I remembered coming to this restaurant for my First Communion luncheon. Nothing had changed since then, my mother added. Same Pompeian red walls covered with unshined copper pots, old prints and photographs of the Appian Way and its eating places dating back to the 1890s. On the ceiling, the ubiquitous wooden beams, at the far end of the main room, a fireplace ready to be lighted. I remembered the frightening catacomb where the owner stored his wine and "bad little girls." Outside, in the courtyard, a four-hundred-year-old wisteria made a vast roof with its leaves.

"You let me sit at the head of the table and I had this long white dress with stick-up dots—"

"Dotted swiss," my mother corrected, smoothing the skirt of her brown tweed suit before sitting down. Gigi held her chair out.

"Weeell, whatever that material was." I dropped down on the chair between them. "I felt glorious and beautiful that day." Why hadn't I let them sit together? Why was I acting like the eight-year-old I was on my First Communion, competing for affection?

"I thought you two were breaking up," I told them after my father relayed our dinner choices to the owner. My mother pressed her lips together. Gigi brushed his chin with the palm of his hand.

"It was a terrible feeling. And I want to say this before I drink any wine or eat too much and get sentimental. You, Mamma, asked me to help figure out who killed Tamar. Maybe you were distracting me. Maybe you really want to know who killed her—"

"I do."

"—and I've tried, halfheartedly, but I've tried and what I've come up with will hurt you, but it's made me understand how lucky I am and how selfish I've been. Tamar got killed because she wanted to create a parent she didn't have. I have two wonderful ones and I've shunned you. I don't know how I could have done that and I'm sorry. I love you both."

My mother nodded and rearranged the napkin on her lap. Gigi squeezed my knee and asked the owner to bring a bottle of our favorite—Pinot Grigio Santa Margherita.

"Your mother and I could never separate," he said, looking at her, his eyes filled with hope rather than conviction. "And now I want to say that I have loved your mother and respected her since the day I met her, forty-four years ago. I do not like being shunned by my daughter, although I think it is fairly natural. I have long ago given up my star role in your life, although I didn't like doing it one bit. When you brought Carlo home, my first instinct was to give him a resounding punch in the nose."

I laughed. "You should have."

A waiter poured wine. My father's eyes darted from my mother to his wineglass, anxious to say his piece. The waiter left.

"I do not, however, want to give up my wife. I understand your need for your own time, Olga, but what you are going through, with this . . . this sickness."

"Cancer, Gigi," my mother said. "Don't skirt the reality."

"Cancer." He whispered the word, his eyes filling with tears. "Don't shut us out, Olga. We suffer, too."

I clutched both their knees.

My mother sipped her wine, rearranged her napkin once again. Gigi blew his nose. I willed myself not to cry. If I did, my mother might just walk out. As she waited for my father to regain control of his emotions, I realized that it was his and my pain that she was running from. She was ashamed of her cancer, of its intense ability to make her family suffer. I realized also that the harshness she had given out at times had nothing to do with me. It was turned against herself.

"I've called the office in New York," I said. "They're giving me a month's leave." My voice was firm. I planned to call the office tomorrow. If they didn't agree, I'd quit.

"No." Mamma leaned back to let the waiter slip a plate of pink carpaccio in front of her.

I got fresh artichoke salad with slivers of parmesan on top. "I need new clothes. We can go shopping before the operation. I've got fifteen percent at Monique's Boutique!" I waved the card Monica had given me.

Mamma broke a bread stick and eyed my lap. "You could use a new gray skirt."

"And a blue one." I had won.

Gigi ate clams with oil, garlic, and parsley and made a big to-do about the shells. A snapshot of him popped in front of my eyes, a small yellowing picture with white scalloped edges glued to the black page of an album. Gigi at the beach, five years old, making a house of seashells. His tanned cheeks are streaked with tears. He can't remember why he cried.

"How will it hurt us?" Mamma asked.

"My cooking is not as good as yours."

She flicked her eyes with impatience. "What have you discovered about Tamar's death?"

"I don't think she was killed for a lost Leonardo." I explained what I had seen on Tamar's tape.

"That's not much to go on," Gigi said. His chin was oily from sucking clams.

"I called Bob at Fono Roma. He edited and transferred the tape. He remembers that Tamar had him edit out a shot of Arthur Hensen, alone, going down the corridor toward the john, except instead of going into the john, he went into the storage room. He had the keys. And no one else had left their coats in there. Only the Cultural Ministry *onorevole*. When the man left, instead of an empty briefcase, he carried a full one. One of the teachers who saw the tape with me thinks he stole the missing VCR. I say it was full of Arthur Hensen's money."

Gigi nodded. "Ah, the museums-of-Italy deal. No wonder it went through."

"It went through?" My mother tapped her chin to indicate that he had to clean his, which he did.

"They are keeping it quiet until the worst of the corruption scandals are over."

"Good! The worst will never be over." The waiter brought my mother *saltimbocca alla romana*, jump-in-the-mouth veal scallopine with ham and sage. "Then Tamar was blackmailing Arthur Hensen!"

"That's right," I said as the waiter boned my paper-thin Mediterranean sole with the backs of two spoons. "Arthur didn't want to get into trouble with the Italian authorities and lose his museum deal. He also didn't want his daughter to find out and kick him off the board of HGI."

"Therefore he had Tamar killed!" My mother nearly dropped her knife.

After a few deft flicks of his wrists, the waiter presented me with three moist, white fillets. I dropped a forkful in my mouth, avoiding my mother's eyes. The sole was as sweet and salty as sea air.

"Hmm." My father looked at his roasted baby lamb and potatoes, a typical Easter dish. "The SEC would be extremely interested. The Foreign Corrupt Practices Act made into law during Carter's idealistic administration forbids employees of a publicly traded company to offer payment to any foreign official for purposes of influencing any act or decision, et cetera, et cetera. I'm told by certain friends that it's put a damper on quite a few deals."

"Don't call them friends," my mother said. "And it hasn't stopped anyone. The American government is the biggest briber of them all, handing out money to keep the likes of Andreotti and his DemoChristians in power when they're more corrupt than the Socialists, and I don't know why you're having lamb now, Gigi. You know I always make it Easter Sunday!"

"I wasn't sure I'd be invited this time."

"Of course you are." She feigned annoyance, but her eyes betrayed her. She was happy to be with us.

Gigi winked at me, a trophy winner's beam on his face. "What did Tamar want from Signor Hensen in exchange for her bits of tape?"

"I get the feeling she didn't know what she had at first. Why wait a month to blackmail someone? She probably

found out about Hensen's bad relationship with his
daughter while she was painting a fresco in Hensen's bathroom. Tamar overhears a telephone conversation in the
library or picks up a fax like Nonna did. Maybe the fax men-
tions the museum deal that Deborah's dead set against. Tamar
remembers the *onorevole*'s thin, then fat, briefcase and realizes
she is in a position to ask for an exchange of favors."

"Money." Of his lamb dish, Gigi was only eating the
roasted potatoes. My stuffed nose wouldn't let me smell
the rosemary.

"No, adoption, I think. She wanted a family."

My mother frowned. "How can you adopt your own
blackmailer?"

"She thought she could get away with it. Two days
before she died, she told her friend Linda that she was
about to change her name. On Friday you overheard her
talking to Hensen about the party, offering to show him
something."

"Show him what?" Gigi asked.

"The master tape. Unedited. With the shot of Hensen
unlocking the storeroom where the briefcase was kept."

"Carlo was asking about the master at the dinner," my
mother said.

"That's what started me thinking. Why hadn't Tamar
given Arthur the master? He'd paid her for it."

Gigi looked doubtful. "That shot isn't very hard evidence."

"It would be enough to get Deborah Hensen to start a
full investigation. She's got a lot of hate and a lot of
money. Besides, she already has a paid informer in Rome."

Mama lowered her fork slowly. "Maffeo."

My father squirmed.

I nodded. "That's how he knew the school was closing a
week before Arthur Hensen did. That's why Deborah

Hensen knew about a lost Leonardo. When I asked him for her telephone number, he knew it off the top of his head."

There was relief on my mother's face, as if the news confirmed her choice of husband. "I wondered where he had found the money for restorations, and why he didn't stop them when he knew the school would close. He was being paid all along. Signorina Hensen probably gave him a nice sum to compensate for losing rent revenue."

"I think that might be why he didn't want Tamar sniffing around the palazzo. She would have found out and probably ratted on him."

"Whereas Luca is a trusting boy, with romantic ideologies. Maffeo was safe with him."

"Mamma, he's not a boy! And you know what else I think?"

Mamma wiped her lips. "I'm sure you'll tell us."

"I think Tamar had left the master tape in the prince's library. Then, when she realized she had blackmail material, she had to steal Luca's keys to get it back. Why else go back there? The library had already been scoured for the drawing. Wednesday night she gets the tape. Thursday she mails it to Carlo. Friday she calls Arthur."

"You're not making much sense, dear," my mother said. "If she mails the master to Carlo, what is she going to show Signor Hensen?"

"Thursday morning Tamar went back to Fono Roma and got Bob to run another dupe. This time of the master. Arthur was going to see a dupe of the master. Sending the original to Carlo was Tamar's insurance."

Gigi laughed. "Insurance for what? Chaos?"

"She used the Vatican post office."

"That one works!"

Mamma refused fruit or dessert, suddenly seeming eager to leave. Her face was tired.

My father had coffee. I excused myself to go to the bathroom. Instead, I paid the bill, feeling gloriously in charge. When Gigi found out, he lowered eyelids in a mocking gesture of mourning.

"Another role I relinquish." He was smiling.

When we got up to leave, Mamma said, "Simona, you drive your father back to Rocca."

Gigi's face sagged as he held up her Burberry.

She slipped her arms in, and as he wrapped the raincoat over her, she held his hands. "I'll follow in Mirella's car."

"Nope. You go with Gigi. I'll take the car back. Mirella probably needs it in the morning."

Gigi pointed to the art book I had slipped under my arm. "You taking that with you?"

"Don't worry, I'll bring it back."

My mother tugged at the belt of her raincoat. "Your room is waiting for you."

"I know." Tonight I wanted them to be alone together. Gigi looked pleased.

Her face was red. "Is it hot in here?" She tried to pass off her embarrassment as a hot flash.

I hugged her. "It's broiling in here."

She looked at me and my father. "It doesn't hurt me about Principe Maffeo. I want you to know that."

Let her sleep well with my father in their house full of flowers, I told myself. The hurt could wait another day.

25

Chi appicca foco e nun conosce er
vento, o s'arruvina o cerca spavento.
*Who lights a fire without knowing the wind,
is looking to be ruined or scared.*

—ROMAN PROVERB

"He descended from a family of wool weavers, prominent
in Florentine history as far back as the thirteenth century."
My father's art book lay open on Mirella's bed. "A man
who loved art, but didn't like to pay too much for it,
according to Vasari." Gorbi sniffed at the page. Nonna was
in bed in the next room.

"He commissioned Michelangelo's tondo of the Holy
Family to celebrate his marriage to fifteen-year-old
Maddalena Giovanni Strozzi."

Mirella closed her eyes and sank back, hair and pillows a
frame of clouds around her puckered face. "You've done
your research."

"I wasn't even looking!" Anger was building up—at her.
At my own stupidity. "I was curious about that painting

273

you had copied. One of the Renaissance greats, I knew that much. Then I found it, on page thirteen of the *Masters of Color*. You copied a Raphael. I didn't see the painting long enough to know how good a job you did, but I'm sure to Oreste and his family, it's the best. A portrait of Aldo with his cleft chin, a black cap on his head, flowing red sleeves, a black vest." I pointed to the painting, which took up the entire page of the book. The portrait was one of Raphael's most famous. I should have remembered, but I have always been a lazy student.

"You painted Aldo's portrait to look like Raphael's and Michelangelo's frugal art patron. Agnolo Doni. 'Doni' as in the *Doni Tondo* by Michelangelo. 'Doni' as in Tamar's last word."

Mirella raised her hands. Her arms were bare. "I worked hard on that portrait. I wanted every detail to be right. Aldo looks like Doni, the chin, the mouth . . . " Her hands fell over her face.

I took my feet off the bed, half-expecting Mirella to kick me out of her room. "What I remember most clearly about the minutes before Tamar died was her expression. She wasn't shocked. Surprised. Scared. No, she was thinking. I found the same expression in Melzi's portrait of Caterina."

"Both murdered women," Mirella whispered.

"I don't know what Melzi had in mind, but Tamar was trying to figure out where she had seen the face of the scooter driver. She might have seen Aldo at the school, but she didn't know his name. What she did spot, being an art student, was the resemblance to Raphael's Doni."

"I was proud of my portrait. I didn't mention Aldo's name, but I had shown it to her. She didn't like it. She wanted me to stop copying, to paint my own ideas. She had so much talent, she didn't understand that I wasn't good enough. And now she's dead and I'm still alive."

"Aldo wasn't the one to kill her. He couldn't have done that while driving the scooter."

Mirella opened her hands to expose one staring eye. "He was driving?" Gorbi licked her wrist.

"Up at Magliano Sabino, the butcher told me Aldo has short, curly hair. I remember seeing lots of black hair flying from the man in the backseat. When the police unearthed your wigs, I thought the killer might have worn a wig, but then I met Ernesto. He knows Aldo, he has shoulder-length black hair. He's also a butcher's son, he knows how to wield a knife. A knife plunged between the ribs from a hovering scooter demands expertise."

Mirella sat up. "Aldo needed a partner. He'd never mugged anyone before. Ernesto is supposedly an expert. I pray it wasn't Aldo who killed her. I want to believe he agreed to help only because it was a simple theft, one of the hundreds we have daily. I've seen him grow up." Her eyes looked transparent, breakable. "Oreste brought him up well. He's not bright, but he's good. Obedient."

"In fact, he was obeying someone's orders."

Mirella reached for a Pall Mall and lit it. "Every second since you told me in the dog park . . . you remember telling me? We were relaxing, talking. Paolo had just left with his dog. And then you told me what Tamar had said just before she died—every second after that has been like a blade-sharp pendulum striking my heart. Doni is such a famous name!" She coughed as the smoke hit her lungs. I had never seen her smoke before.

"That policeman, Bacchus, he'd been to the Uffizi, maybe he'd been to Palazzo Pitti, seen an art magazine. I got so scared my art students would see Aldo and link him to the Doni portrait that I forced him to quit his job."

"I thought Oreste had done that."

"No, me!" She pounded her chest. "Aldo likes heroin. I

threatened to tell his father. He worships his father, tells everyone what a hero he was in the war." She coughed again. "I told Oreste to destroy the painting. Why didn't he?" Small bursts of smoke hit my face. Gorbi sniffed and slunk off the bed.

I did not tell her that the art squad was now on the case, agents who, on hearing the word *doni,* would first think of Raphael's portrait.

"My mother must have made the connection." It had suddenly hit me that Mamma must have known all along. I wasn't protecting her from anything.

"She did. I know she did." Tears filled Mirella's eyes. Maybe from the smoke. "She said nothing. I can count on her."

Mirella turned to me. A furrowed, tense, needy, unhappy face. A face I loved.

"Mamma asked me to find Tamar's killer," I said.

"She said that to distract you from finding out about her cancer."

"No. Tonight I asked her if she wanted me to find the killer. She said, 'I do.' Present tense. I think she wants justice. Except she can't be the one to point the finger. She's too loyal for that. I'll be off soon, back to New York. She thinks it's easier for me. Mamma has always presumed a lot about me."

"I want justice, too. Tamar was not meant to die. Can you believe me?"

I covered Mirella's bare shoulders with the blanket.

"Yes, I do. But I don't think keeping your mouth shut is going to bring justice."

"They'll never find proof."

"They'll arrest Aldo sooner or later."

"Aldo won't talk. His father forbids him to talk. Aldo is retarded. He's obedient!"

"What about Ernesto?"

Mirella clutched the blanket. "He knows nothing. Aldo just told him he wanted to snatch Tamar's satchel, that she had a lot of money."

"Think of Luca!"

"They're releasing him tomorrow. There's no proof!"

"Luca knew about Aldo, knew he was going to try to get the tape from Carlo. That's why Linda saw him on the Sant'Angelo Bridge. He was watching for the mailman and Aldo, wasn't he?"

"There were so many tourists." Mirella ran hands across her hair, her face. She tugged at her nightgown. Shivered. Covered herself up. "Luca didn't want to get too close. He was afraid Aldo would see him and run off before he had a chance to steal the tape. Luca was going to destroy it! He hates Arthur. He wanted to destroy the tape. Arthur would then forget about his marriage proposal."

Mirella started shaking. I leaned over and hugged her.

"All my life"—she talked to my shoulder—"I've lived with my family. For my family. I don't love Arthur, but I do want a man in my bed. And I want a man who will help with money." She smelled of smoke, not of the pomegranate perfume I loved.

"Luca is never going to amount to much, you know," she said. "It's my fault and Nonna's. He was our only man. We gave him too much love."

Pull back. Let him try on his own, I wanted to tell her. It was the wrong moment.

"Nonna ran out of money years ago," Mirella said. "My school is closing. We don't even have the farm anymore. Nonna insisted she would only sell to Oreste. He couldn't pay for all of it in one lump, so he doles out money monthly, adding food to keep us happy. In a year it'll be paid for." Her hands were tight on my arms.

"Nonna is still in love with him. They stayed lovers even after my father came home from the war. Papà must have suffered terribly, he wrote such beautiful love letters. The day of my father's funeral, Nonna threw them away. I found them in the kitchen garbage, wet with coffee grounds. I've never forgiven her that, but she's my mother. I will always love her. Oreste came to the funeral. I was pregnant with Luca and I marched right up the aisle of the church, my stomach leading the way, and told Oreste he had no right to be there. Nonna said nothing. Oreste didn't leave."

Gorbi broke us apart, snaking his body between us until he lay across Mirella's lap, a triumphant look on his face. She kissed the dog. "I'm sixty-four years old. I should be wise, fearless. But I'm not. I'm tired and I don't know what to do."

I offered Perillo's inane advice: *la notte porta consiglio*.

The night brings counsel.

The night brought Nonna's death. She had heard our conversation, of course. I had planned it that way, expecting her to march in and interrupt. Confess. Instead she died.

When I woke up, the doctor had already examined her and written "heart attack" on the death certificate. I called my parents. My mother whispered "Thank God" when I told her.

Mirella wouldn't let me see Nonna until she had laid her out, hands folded over a rosary she would not have used in life. Luca helped her. He had come home at dawn while I was deep in a dreamless sleep.

Nonna's profile was sharp, hard, her nose a knife edge, almost transparent against the white morning light from the window. The lobes of her ears were bare, obscene in their nakedness. It was the single detail that crystallized her death. Her coral earrings sat in an ashtray on the bedside table.

Next to the ashtray were her tarot cards. I found the ace of pentacles and slipped it under her crossed hands, right side up: success, bliss. Reversed, it signified the evil side of riches.

Doctors are kind in Italy. They will, to permit a Catholic burial, fudge suicides, if they can. One of them, the doctor, Luca, or Mirella, had hidden the evidence, but not well enough. Gorbi brought it to me, as proud of this trophy as he had been of the bloody knife.

A plastic bag.

I'm sure Nonna left a confession. She would, after all, want to make sure her family was safe. Mirella, I am equally sure, has hidden, but not destroyed, the letter in case Luca should ever be implicated. But also knowing her, she has probably lost it among the thousands of papers and books she has in her apartment. I don't think she'll ever need it.

"I understand Nonna's heart," Mamma said after the funeral on Easter Monday, *Pasquetta,* a day that is usually reserved to picnicking in the country, eating salami and hard-boiled eggs. "She worried out of love. She was willing to steal out of love. She had nothing else to offer her daughter and her grandson. After last summer's heart attack, she knew she didn't have much time left."

Mamma had suspected Nonna was behind Tamar's death because of the Leonardo. Nonna had planted the idea that Tamar had found the drawing. My mother, pragmatic, down to earth, did not believe the story. She knew

Principe Maffeo had scoured the palazzo clean. There was no drawing to be found. And yet Nonna insisted. Why?

To put us off the track.

What had made me suspect Nonna was the syringe and the heroin in Tamar's drawer, planted the day after my mother overheard Tamar's mysterious phone call to Arthur. I was sure that Nonna had overheard the entire blackmailing conversation. Only Nonna, with Aldo's help, would have put the heroin in Tamar's drawer. Luca was too loyal, Mirella too fearful of drugs. Nonna had found a way to get rid of Tamar. With Tamar somewhere else, the family would not be implicated in the purse snatching.

Nonna changed her appointment with the Tarelli sisters to Saturday to give Luca an alibi. She made Luca drive her up to the farm that afternoon, anxious to get the tape from Aldo. Aldo didn't show up, but she didn't worry. She would see him Sunday. Nonna planned Sunday's lunch in order to tell Arthur in person that he had to marry Mirella if he wanted the tape.

When I had accompanied Nonna up to the farmhouse bedroom, she'd been happy. Aldo hadn't appeared, but she was confident. She had taken care of her family. In her mind, that absolved her of Tamar's death.

Arthur, on Sunday, invited all of us to dinner at his apartment the next night. "I have an announcement to make," he had told my mother.

Monday night he made no announcement because Nonna still didn't have the tape. No tape, no marriage. Nonna kept getting up from the table to go to the bathroom, probably trying to reach Aldo. Arthur's marriage proposal arrived Tuesday afternoon, *after* Aldo had attacked Carlo and finally delivered the tape.

Aldo had panicked when his friend Ernesto stabbed Tamar, and he had gone back to Nonna's apartment with inexpensive oil he had bought from a store. He wanted an excuse to see Nonna, to show her the empty satchel, maybe to make sure she believed him. Except that Nonna was up at Magliano Sabino with Luca. And a police inspector was in the living room. All he could think to do was to hide the satchel behind the wisteria.

Aldo panicked again when Perillo showed up at Principe Maffeo's palazzo. He thought one of the La Casa students might have seen him pick up the knife in the classroom where Luca had left it the night before. He accused Luca of taking it, not knowing the knife came from Nonna's kitchen.

On Good Friday, the day after Nonna died, Mirella went to visit Aldo at the Queen of Heavens jail. "Luca's got a bad smell under his nose, he doesn't treat me nice," Aldo told her, then started crying.

My mother thinks Oreste made Aldo give himself up when Nonna died. Aldo is, as Mirella said, an obedient boy. He sticks to the story he told Ernesto. He thought Tamar had money. No one put him up to it. In fact, Mirella said, he seems proud that he's put one over on the police. Aldo had meant to snatch Tamar's satchel near the school, but he had trouble with the scooter and she slipped away by taking the bus. He didn't find the right moment until she was in front of Nonna's building. Aldo swears he did not want Tamar killed—the knife was only meant to cut the straps of the satchel—but he refuses to say who his partner was.

Ernesto has been taken care of by person or persons unknown. Shot in the head, like his namesake, Bianca's father. In a forest of chestnuts up on the Sabine Hills. This time it wasn't the Nazis.

Probably Oreste, but I'm only guessing. I wondered why Nonna didn't pick Oreste to help her, but Mamma says Oreste is too old to go snatching bags from motorscooters by himself. Too bad she didn't tell him. He would have understood that Aldo was not bright enough to act alone, and if someone else had to get involved, the risks were too high for his son.

The picture I am painting is mostly conjecture, which seems fitting in a country that lives by innuendo and vagueness. I also wonder about the sloppy police job—why Perillo was taken off the case. You always have to wonder when the reputation of a government ministry *onorevole* is at stake.

"Nonna did not mean to kill Tamar," my mother said as we walked out of the small church on the Lungotevere after the funeral. I remember looking up at the clear sky and seeing the first starlings of the season, a good-luck omen for Mamma.

"She must have asked Aldo simply to snatch the satchel." Mamma linked arms with my father. "Nonna would think it a simple thing. A twist of the wrist, that's how she handled all hardships"—Mamma flicked a gloved hand—"voilà, the ace of pentacles."

My father nodded. "She expected Oreste's son to do the same!"

As they walked, I hung back to enjoy my picture, the one I had taken to America. Their clothes were different, but the essentials were the same.

Mamma walks with Gigi, her purse swinging from one arm, the other tucked in his care. He stands as straight as he can, to minimize the fact that she is taller. He wears his pants a little too high on his waist, a tweed jacket hides his sinking chest. He is getting old, but he looks proud to walk by her side. She looks, as always, somewhat stern, but satisfied, even pleased. Their arms stay linked, and although I am now too old to lean on them, I will always love them.

epilogue

———— ❧ ————

I may justly say with the hook-nosed fellow
of Rome, "I came, saw, and overcame."
—WILLIAM SHAKESPEARE, HENRY IV

Even though only one breast was affected, my mother insisted on a double mastectomy. The specialists, my father's Florentine friend included, assured her that a partial mastectomy of her left breast was sufficient, but she said she didn't want chemotherapy and she didn't want to worry about a recurrence. She also refused reconstructive surgery, claiming she was tired of carrying her breasts around, tired of being defined by them. I can only think that she was terrified.

HH&H, the advertising firm where I work, has been understanding. They let me stay the month. Four days before I had to leave, we got the results by phone. Her lymph nodes are clean. The cancer hasn't spread. She's going to be okay.

My mother nodded her satisfaction. My father cried. My first thought was to run to the garden to bury the frightening wig my mother had bought. She wouldn't let me. "Let's not defy fate." I ended up in the kitchen, concocting a celebratory low-fat pasta. I saved my tears for the plane.

Mamma is back at home in Rocca, exercising her arm by kneading dough, taking care of the roses that are now in full bloom. She's also started a new blanket. During my weekly phone call, my mother sounds hurried, worried about me. She does not mention Carlo anymore. I lecture her on diet. She answers, "Everything in moderation." Yesterday she asked me to send her the recipe for *"Pasta Allegria."* The wheel is turning, and now I am the one to offer love through food. It makes me feel close to Mamma as I never have before.

I have made a note in my calendar not to forget her name day, July 11. Saint Olga.

My father tries to sound cheerful, but the shock of mamma's cancer still has him wobbling. I know she will see him through.

Mirella has found another job. In September she will start teaching at the Overseas School of Rome. My mother visits her often, and in her last letter complained that by the time she left, her beige linen suit was covered with long, dark, dog hairs. It seems Paolo, the lawyer, brings his dog, Nikki, over a lot.

Luca is studying for his next exam. His work for Principe Maffeo is over, but he drops in often. He refuses to believe the prince was Deborah Hensen's informer. The prince has given up on finding the Leonardo.

Arthur Hensen has sold his Trastevere apartment and gone back to Minneapolis. With the bribe scandals besieging Italy, all government contracts have been suspended until further "examination." He has probably destroyed the incriminating tape Nonna gave him. What he doesn't know is that Aldo had a dupe made, which Nonna was going to hand over after both the prenuptial agreement and the wedding vows had been signed.

Mirella wants no part of Arthur anymore. My mother has elected herself guardian of that dupe, just in case Arthur wants to come back to "denigrate" Italy's artistic heritage.

The day before leaving, I did have that sorbet with Perillo over at Giolitti's. I recognized his mother right away, the woman who had witnessed Tamar's death and called an ambulance, the woman with the Fendi purse the thieves had not taken, the woman with the Sicilian accent and her son's puffy cheeks. That's why he had seemed familiar to me.

We talked about New York. She wants another trip. This time she wants to see the Grand Canyon. I gave them my business card and told them they should look me up. This time Perillo did not ask me why I did not order the fantastic ice cream. But as we shook hands outside the café, he said, "I think it worked out best for the old lady, don't you?" He tapped the notebook in his breast pocket. "*La mamma italiana*, she can also be the most ruthless."

As I said, you have to wonder when the reputation of an *onorevole* is involved.

At work I'm preparing for a new print ad campaign with my boss. This time we're selling Wow Chow dog food. I have so far interviewed 133 dogs of all shapes and sizes. If Gorbi were here, he'd get the part in a second.

Willy and Greenhouse gave me a rousing welcome. Greenhouse picked me up at the airport and took me back to his place. I found Willy busy setting the table, with my postcard of the Pietà propped against the saltshaker. While I sat in a chair telling them the end of the story, Willy cooked chicken burgers. Greenhouse made the salad.

Outside, sirens wailed, a radio pulsated. Part of me felt as if I had never left New York. For the first time, Willy and I both stayed the night.

I have thought a lot about Nonna. At times I feel guilty I did not confront her directly. Maybe she wouldn't have killed herself. Then Tamar's sketch of me stares back, each stroke beautifully executed. I get angry. Talent or not, Tamar deserved to live.

I am too sentimental to remember only the bad of Nonna. I push memory back, to her birthday party, Nonna throning over the room, telling her story, complaining about the cheap champagne, about Pia Tarelli's voice, at ninety still lusting for life.

I go further back, to Nonna nudging my elbow to get out of Rome. To cross the ocean.

I have done just that. I will always be grateful to her for the help. I now realize that I have two homes. Sometimes I'm sure it will continue to confuse me. Mostly I feel lucky.

My mother's birthday present to me was the crocheted blanket she'd finished the day Tamar died. It's beautiful and warm, but it's the wrong size for a double bed. Greenhouse wants a June roommate, which means now. I have opted for October. For one thing, that's when my lease is up.

And now, to quote Mark Twain, "The surest way to stop writing about Rome is to stop."

Pasta Allegria

(Serves four as a main course)

4 small, firm zucchini
1 large Japanese eggplant (Long and slim, the color is
    light purple. It is sweeter than the Italian eggplant
    found here.)
2 large yellow bell peppers
2 pounds ripe plum tomatoes
Salt and pepper
2 cloves garlic, minced
10 large leaves fresh basil
2 tablespoons extra-virgin olive oil
Kosher salt for pasta water
1 pound short tubular pasta (penne or rigatoni)

TO BE PREPARED
FOUR TO SIX HOURS BEFORE SERVING:

Remove grill from broiler and cover with aluminum
foil. Turn on broiler. Slice zucchini in ⅛" horizontal strips.
Repeat procedure for eggplant. Cut peppers, remove seeds
and white cores, and slice into 1" strips. Halve the tomatoes.

Lay out zucchini on foil-covered grill, season with salt
and pepper, and grill on top rung of broiler for 4 minutes
on each side. When done, remove to a large serving bowl.

Repeat procedure for eggplant and peppers (peppers may take longer depending on thickness). The vegetables should turn golden brown, with a few burned edges. Broil tomatoes, cut side up, for 10 to 12 minutes. Mix the cooked vegetables together, and cut them into smaller pieces inside the bowl. Add minced garlic and hand-shredded basil leaves. Check for seasoning and correct if necessary. Add olive oil. Let the vegetables macerate in the bowl at room temperature for 4 to 6 hours. (If it is a hot day, you may put in refrigerator, but remove at least an hour before serving.)

Bring a large pot of salted water to a boil. Add pasta. Cook until al dente (10 to 12 minutes depending on quality of pasta). Drain, and add to vegetable bowl. Mix well and serve.

Eat and be merry!

Author's Note

An aristocratic family by the name of Brandeschi does not exist, to my knowledge. Palazzo Brandeschi is fictitious. Rome and the surrounding countryside are real.

Rome has changed since Simona went back to New York. In the Sistine Chapel, Michelangelo's restored Last Judgment has been unveiled. Simona's mother's favorite, the Carafa Chapel in S. Maria sopra Minerva, has been restored to its original splendor. Mirella can once more point out to her students the Egyptian granite bathtubs that serve as fountains in Piazza Farnese. Other churches and monuments are being cleaned behind their shrouds. The museums stay open late now, although only the Vatican, always a clever marketer, has organized a real museum shop. National elections have brought new, bright-faced politicians to the fore, all of whom swear that they are honest.

The beauty of the Eternal City remains the same.

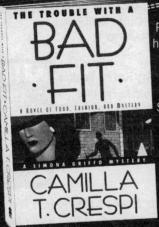

The Trouble with Thin Ice
by Camilla T. Crespi

A bride-to-be, is arrested for a very cold-blooded murder—the week of her wedding. Simona Griffo, a friend who likes to meddle in such matters, starts asking questions. As she puts the pieces together, however, she unwittingly pushes herself onto thin ice.

Hearing Faces by Dotty Sohl

Janet Campbell's neighbor has been brutally killed, and there's no apparent motive in sight. Yet Janet refuses to live in fear. When a second murder strikes the apartment complex , Janet's life turns upside-down. Seeking answers she discovers greedy alliances, deadly secrets, and a vicious killer much too close to home.